Titles by Liana Cincotti

Don't Be In Love
Picking Daisies on Sundays

DON'T BE IN LOVE

Liana Cincotti

For the ones who deserve to be loved but haven't. Just hold on.
It'll come.

1

Don't Be Infatuated by a British Accent — Adelaide

I hated remaining sedentary. Sitting in a lecture hall in Boston, staring out a window at falling leaves and then soon enough, dreaded snow, sounded whimsical and did indeed set an academic scene similar to *Dead Poets Society* (minus the dead part). But it wasn't England.

Don't get me wrong, if you wanted to live somewhere where the seasons turned as they did in London, and exist in an area that had that old, vintage feeling of Cambridge, then Cambridge, Massachusetts (a Boston suburb) was the place to go to college. But when you lived in the area your whole life, it started to feel old. And not in the Shakespearean way.

Hence why I practically tripped up the stairs in the business building on my way to my Global Marketing exam in April. A window-sized cork board with a neon pink flyer made me pause. In big bold letters with an image of Big Ben behind it, it read:

STUDY ABROAD OPPORTUNITY: EXPLORE LONDON AND RECEIVE CREDIT.

I met with my advisor the next day and applied. One month later, they either made a mistake or really enjoyed my essay on London's fashion, because *I was accepted.*

Senior Year. *In London.*

I screamed with excitement until my throat burned. Almost even sent my roommate into cardiac arrest—the poor thing was already a computer science major, she had enough to be on edge about.

June came and I was boarding a cramped flight to London Heathrow to study marketing at one of the most prestigious colleges in the world: Townsen University. My back was as stiff as a board, the airplane chicken was cold, and I regretted not packing my sixth black skirt. But none of it really mattered because I was going to *London.*

The London from *The Holiday* and *Harry Potter.* The home of tea and scones. An epicenter for fashion week twice a year.

Fast-forward to now—the end of August—where I was wishing I could go back to the day I landed in Heathrow in June, taking a black cab to my *flat,* to do it all over again. It kickstarted a summer with my two new roommates, Sabrina and Mia, exploring the city, staying up late eating British sweets, and divulging every secret.

Mia, a journalism major from Washington who hated to be out of bed before 10 a.m. and gave every emotion away with her eyes, walked beside me with an arm looped around my elbow. She was a woman on a mission, directing us toward a club that may or may not be the site of our future death.

"It's safe! One of the Townsen students posted about it!" she defended herself but still tightened her grip on her purse. "I'm not turning this opportunity down—*invite-only*—do you hear me?"

"I'm pretty sure cults are invite-only too." I narrowed my eyes. If Sabrina was here right now, she would've agreed. Fortunately for Sabrina, both her dads had forced her into attending another networking event tonight.

One of her dads was the owner of several luxury hotel chains across the UK and Europe, so he was always at glamorous parties.

Her upbringing was no different than most of the students at Townsen.

About ninety-five percent of the students came from rich families who were either known in Hollywood, a political party, or were just incredibly wealthy for investing in something like tech or zippers.

Which put in me the other five percent: the students who came from households with no money and relied on scholarships.

"We're here, we're here, stop mentioning cults," Mia shushed me, tugging me into a pub. She ran for the bar before the door could close. I watched as she leaned over the barstools, grabbed the bartender's attention—frightened him a bit—to whisper something to him. She reared back after a moment and came running back to pull me in a new direction with no explanation.

"I'm going to take a guess and assume he granted your wish," I questioned.

"The invitation worked!" she sang. "He said we just go through this door down the hall and down the stairs—"

"And into the creepy dungeon?"

She opened said door. It was like opening Pandora's box. If the box was filled with music and clinking glassware.

Mia turned and gave me a *I was right and you were wrong* look.

I rolled my eyes. "Let's just get on with this," I said, giving her a slight push. I was on a mission to get home early to mentally prepare for the first day of classes on Monday.

She ran down the staircase, forcing me to chase after her before—*oof.* "Mia, my head," I complained, rubbing my forehead after running straight into the back of her skull.

I looked up to find her staring in awe at what appeared to be a jazz bar.

A band of older gentlemen played music on a short stage for the audience of young dancers twirling in mini dresses. Women wearing stiletto heels held onto men with gelled-back hair and button-downs. While others sat at petite wooden tables decorated by antique lamps made of yellow stained glass, emitting a low light in the dusk room.

A plethora of people spanning a range of ages held glasses of liquor like purses. They wore sapphires on their pinkies, and relaxed smiles on their faces. The bar stretched behind us to the left, covering the entire back wall. Mirrors acted like portraits hanging above the alcohol.

"Maybe we can find Sabrina a new guy here," Mia commented, eyeing down men.

"Don't waste your time," I sighed. "She has no interest in finding someone new."

"She doesn't even know him." She threw her arms up. "That's like me being in love with the man that reads the weather on the TV back home."

"But *you are* in love with the man who reads the weather."

"But I don't talk about him as if he put the sun in the sky! She'll talk about him but then clam up when we ask for a photo or if they've ever spoken. We don't even know his last name. He could be fake for all I know."

"She has a crush. It'll wear out." *Hopefully.*

Concern for my new friend had become an annoying neighbor, reappearing every time she mentioned this guy. But I wasn't going to push her away with my whole philosophy on love.

Liana Cincotti

Especially not when her entire being was as delicate as a hydrangea. I loved her for it. But I also wanted to wrap her in cellophane as I explained that thinking about men was the equivalent to watching paint dry. Useless and it'd always end up disappointing in the end.

My eye for picking paint wasn't great.

Mia groaned. "*Dorian.* Honestly, how hot could this guy possibly be?"

She worried for Sabrina too, but sometimes that was bypassed by her impatience to listen to people that weren't *doers*. Brina wasn't looking to do anything about her crush on Dorian. She was a *hoper*. Someone that *hoped* for the rom-com moment where she dropped her books in the hallway, and he was there to swoop them up. Next thing you knew, they were married, straddled with kids, with a vacation home in Tuscany, and a wiener dog that only ate salmon-based food.

"I don't know," I sighed. I scanned the room for an empty table. As I came up empty, I searched faces, wondering if any of these people would be my classmates in two days.

The acceptance rate for Townsen was something like five percent. As someone from a college where students woke up at 7 a.m. to study for an 8 a.m. exam and still passed, I was nervous. None of these students would come from homes whose mother had to quit her medical career to stay home to parent while her husband took every construction job he was offered.

Academics and working would be my number one priority while I lived in London. This scholarship was the only way I could afford being here.

Mia said, "Let's go sit—"

"Excuse me." Her proposal was cut short by a *really* handsome guy. The kind of handsome that made you check the hinges on your jaw.

He stood several inches above me with a sly smile and a dimple on his left cheek. The color of his eyes and hair matched the color of black coffee, sitting neatly above his ears. His skin was a few shades lighter than his hair; a tan that complimented his dark brown eyes.

Then he opened his mouth, and this unfairly beautiful British accent came out.

2

The first rule I made with myself before coming to England was that I would stick to my morals and not get involved in anything romantic. *Nada.* It didn't matter if 1999 *Notting Hill* Hugh Grant approached me; I wouldn't succumb.

Was that difficult when a beautiful six foot British man approached you and said *excuse me* in his British accent? *Obviously.* But it was easier when I remembered the second rule: love didn't last. And what if he was looking for love? Of course, he'd never admit that. He'd probably start by asking if I wanted to dance, which would turn into a flirtatious conversation, which would lead to a date, and then a kiss.

I would just end up breaking his heart!

I was getting ahead of myself, yes. This Brit (bloke?) was probably just looking for a dance, not my hand in marriage. But avoiding these interactions altogether saved me time and complexities I didn't have space for in my to-do list.

"Do you want to dance?" he asked. Mia made some type of Poltergeist-choking noise from behind me.

I smiled awkwardly. "Actually, I was just about to sit with my friend …" I waited for him to fill in his name.

"Rye," he extended his hand.

I shook it. "Like the bread?"

"More like the town two hours south of here." He almost let a laugh slip.

"Oh. That's interesting. I'll have to look that up later. But I'm actually about to sit down with my friend." I began to turn but his hand slipped around my wrist.

"You can't," he said in a slight panic.

I blew out a breath. "To think I thought the guys in Boston were stubborn."

"I'm not some perv. Do I look like one?" he asked, slightly horrified.

"Depends." I made an effort to look at his hand on my wrist.

He dropped my arm instantly. "I have a bet going with my mate over there." He gestured to someone sitting at a table across the room. He looked just as tall, but other than that, he was the complete opposite of his companion. Darker eyes. Lighter skin. Silver hair the color of the first snow in New England. "He thinks you'd say no to a dance with me."

"Well, it looks like your friend won," I replied, I turned to grab Mia—

"So you're saying no?" he asked, touching my elbow. He smelled like fresh espresso and sandalwood, a piece of his dark hair dangled over his left brow.

"It's really not my thing."

"Can't dance?" he asked.

"Oh, I can dance," I argued.

"Doesn't seem like it," he contended.

"Are you trying to bait me into winning this bet?" I narrowed my eyes.

"Is it working?"

"Possibly."

"What if I bought you a drink after?" he asked.

"Well, you should've just started with that. And I want two drinks."

"Two drinks it is." He put his hand out for me to take, his sleeve retracting to expose a tattoo on the inside of his arm.

What was I doing?

It's called having fun, my subconscious argued.

Well, this was a horrendous attempt at trying to have fun. Fun wasn't supposed to have uncalloused hands, pretty eyes, and back muscles that were apparent through his shirt. Fun was supposed to be whimsical charms hanging off a new purse and the taste of a thick vanilla frappe on a movie night.

Too late now!

I followed him through a sea of people where the music flowed, and pairs danced. *What am I doing? What am I doing? What am I doing? What am I do—*

I was pulled into his chest, and we were dancing. Chest to chest, hips against hips, his hand on my back and mine in his palm. It pulled the air right out of my chest.

"Do you do this often?" I asked.

"Dance with beautiful women?"

"Make bets to coerce women into dancing with you?"

"I usually don't have to coerce women."

"You didn't answer the *bet* part of the question."

"What do you want to know next—my home address?"

"I'm sure that's easy enough to find online, especially if you're seeing women this often," I explained.

"I'm not some womanizer. I don't even know your name, matter of fact." He narrowed his eyes. "You could be the threat here."

I stared at him back. "Adelaide. But I'm not telling you my last name."

"Alright, Adelaide With No Last Name, where are you from?"

"I think you know the answer to that."

"Yes, evidently the States, I'm not an idiot. I meant which one."

"Massachusetts."

"When do you fly back?" he asked curiously.

"I'm actually living in London right now," I admitted.

"Where are you staying?"

"Plan on breaking in and rummaging through my things to find out my last name?"

He rolled his eyes. "I live in London as well. Kensington." He waited for me to return the same response.

"Marylebone, is that close to Kensington?"

"I wouldn't recommend walking, but it's half the time via the Tube. Have you taken the Tube?"

"The public transportation? By myself? Definitely not." I'd only been here two and a half months, so I wasn't ashamed that I hadn't tried the Tube yet. Sabrina was the only British person I knew but even living in London without her parents was a new beast for her.

"It's easy. I don't know much about Massachusetts, but I know the Tube is better than the subway in New York. What are you doing after this?" he asked with a cunning look.

"Are you recommending we go for a ride on the Tube?" I laughed.

"Why not? You can't live in London and not know how to use the train system."

It felt spontaneous to say yes. To put myself out there.

I may have moved across the world to live in a foreign place, but I still wouldn't call myself *spontaneous*.

Though … I guess this wouldn't interfere with the rules. If anything were to happen it wouldn't go anywhere. And I'd get a knowledgeable lesson on how to use the Tube from a local.

"Alright, let's go," I said.

3

*Don't Be So Sure of the First Name
You're Given — Adelaide*

"Why am I even surprised?" Mia laughed, walking into the kitchen in her pajamas the next morning, spotting me at the kitchen table with a glass of water and *The New Yorker*. "You were out until almost two in the morning last night and are, somehow, still awake before everyone and look ready for a Pilates class with single moms." She rubbed the gook out of her eyes.

Not knowing whether that last comment was a compliment or not, I said, "We start classes tomorrow! I couldn't sleep."

She sat down across from me, taking a big sip of her coffee with both hands. "So no immediate mention of last night? Because I know going on the Tube was not the only thing that happened. I want to hear *every single detail.*" She leaned forward with curiosity.

Running to the Tube in my heels with Rye's coat on my shoulders felt like a scene from a movie. He paid for both of our rides with his Oyster card and showed me how to pay with my own card for the future. The he latched onto my hand, pulling me onto the departing train before its doors could close, and explained all the colorful lines that made up the routes on the roof of the Tube.

One minute we were racing up and down the empty train, and the next, I was bumping into him when it came to a full stop. I perfectly landed on him in the plastic seat. My face hovered above his, giving me the ability to explore the angles of his cheeks, and the flecks of gold and valleys of chestnut brown appearing in his eyes when only inches away from them. Before I realized it, I was kissing him and going to his—

"Every detail of what! What did you guys do last night?" Sabrina yelled from the hallway in her charming accent. Her voice grew as she walked into the kitchen, pulling her short hair into a pony, and ruffling her bangs. Champagne-colored pajamas made of silk hung from her frame. The opposite of Mia's gray sweatpants and a black Washington State University hoodie.

"Adelaide danced with the hottest man I'd ever laid my eyes on," Mia announced in glee.

"*That hot?*" Sabrina gasped in amusement. Her eyes were wide, genuinely curious.

"*That hot!*"

"Well, I want to hear every single detai—*oh my gosh!*" Sabrina began screaming in front of the coffee machine, clutching her phone, jumping up and down.

"*What!*" Mia and I shouted in unison, not knowing whether to be fearful or excited.

"*Look!*" She ran to the kitchen table, shoving her phone in our faces. "*Dorian Blackwood is back in London!* He was spotted in London last night at a jazz club! He must be returning to Townsen this semester!" she screamed, jumping with excitement so violently that her long blond bob fell out of its elastic.

My heart plummeted. All my pumping blood evacuated the premises and fled to my face. It stole the air right out of my lungs and wrapped it around my throat in suffocation.

The photo. That photo—of Dorian Blackwood—the man Sabrina hadn't stopped talking about since the day I met her.

I turned to Mia for confirmation, and I found the same look of horror in her dropped jaw.

That was a photo of Rye on her phone.

"*That's* Dorian Blackwood?" Mia looked up in question. I sat still, processing this nightmare. *Rye is Dorian Blackwood. I slept with Dorian Blackwood. As in the Dorian Blackwood they call the UK Bachelor. As in the man my newest best friend is in love with.*

"What's wrong?" Sabrina's excitement diminished, looking between me and Mia.

"Oh—oh! Nothing, nothing! I'm just stunned, he's cuter than I imagined," Mia spoke quickly, smiling up at her.

"*I know!* I can't believe we'll be attending university with him now! He's been abroad for the past year so it's as if he wasn't even a student. Maybe I'll get the chance to introduce myself." Her shoulders were high, and her smile reached the furthest depths of her cheeks. The way she squeezed her coffee mug and continued to talk in a high-pitched tone was enough to prove her feelings for Rye—*Dorian.* I had yet to see her smile this big before.

Oh my god. She couldn't know what happened last night. She could never know. She would be *heartbroken.* I already knew how she thought of herself; the way she rejected compliments and used self-deprecating humor. If she was gathering the confidence to talk to him, then I needed to be her support system, not her reason to give up.

The last thing she needed was to find out that her best friend slept with the guy she was in love with.

Sabrina *loved* him, and I couldn't be the one to ruin that.

I … I could simply avoid him at school. There was a minimal chance I'd ever see him! And there was an extremely high chance he had enough alcohol in his system last night to not even remember me.

I wouldn't ruin this for her. I wouldn't let him jeopardize this friendship.

It was only one night anyways.

4

Don't Make Deals with Rich Men — Adelaide

Approaching the university on Monday morning was mesmerizing. Towering above us was a castle of limestone wrapped in climbing ivy and vines, with archaic archways and roofs that met in triangular peaks reaching into the sky.

Townsen University sat on the edge of London, with the front courtyard of the school immersed in the city, and the back surrounded by acres of green grass, gardens, and courtyards.

Students in blazers, trousers, and tweed skirts waltzed up the front entrance of the school; a wide staircase that ascended towards a set of doors fit for a horse-drawn carriage.

Since this was Sabrina's second year at Townsen, she helped us navigate the rotating schedules and various entrances. She wore a dreaded look as she broke it down.

The poor thing was a biology major who hated Biology. It was the compromise she and her dads made when they let her transfer to Townsen last year; they'd pay the tuition and let her minor in interior design if she studied biology.

"The left and right hallways will bring you to professors' and administrators' offices, which also lead to the courtyards and gardens at the back of the building," she explained slowly. "Now let me see your schedules so we can get to class on time."

Even after she rifled through everything in great detail, twice, I was still confused. But she ushered us off to our classes anyway, dropping me at a large doorway that was supposedly my Social Media Marketing class.

Windows covered the left wall of the class, looking into one of the courtyards. While a podium and chalkboard stood at the front. The room smelt of fresh wood and ink. About half of the class was already seated. I took the first seat I saw right as the professor walked in.

"Good morning, students," she sang.

"Good morning, Professor Emmerson," everyone greeted.

Sylvie Emmerson. In real life. Not on my dingey computer screen.

The corporate mogul was in her late 50s sporting a tan pantsuit and passionate smile, with dark blond hair chopped short. Everyone who worked in marketing or wanted to, knew her. She worked for several luxury brands, building up their brand identity and loyalty for over three decades. After retiring, she began teaching at Townsen. I had dreamt of having her as a mentor ever since.

She spread out papers on the podium. "Welcome to—"

"Apologies, Sylvie!"

The entire class turned to the voice, some even gasping. At least all the women in the class had because it was—

"Dorian, it's *Professor Emmerson*," she corrected.

Holy shit. I held onto my chin to keep my jaw in place. *Please tell me my vision has taken a turn for the worst and that's not actually him?*

Maybe he wouldn't recognize me ... What were the chances

of him not recognizing me?

I just needed to sit still and be quiet, just like they did with dinosaurs in the movies.

"Yes, Professor Emmerson," he said smiling, nodding his head.

He brushed a hand through his hair, moving pieces out of his face like he was in a romance movie. Clad in black trousers and a rustled button-down (with a few buttons at the top undone). He didn't look as clean-cut as he had Saturday night, but this time he looked *rich*. It was in the lavish fabric of his clothes and how he carried himself in front of everyone in the class. Casual. Haughty.

The way every movement felt like a slow-motion moment.

Like when Hugh Grant entered *Bridget Jones's Diary*.

I could still feel the softness of that hair when it had brushed my forehead on the train and at his flat.

I cleared my throat. It went unnoticed. I could stand on my desk and start reciting the four Ps of marketing and go undetected. Everyone's eyes were glued to the notorious Dorian Blackwood who hadn't been spotted in London since the start of the year, according to *The Scandal Sheet*.

London Today, ModeSense, RBY, Celeb Chronicle, and every other news outlet I read from last night described Dorian Blackwood as the UK's most coveted bachelor, despite the fact that he was only in his early twenties.

Rising to the limelight for his "physical attributes," dating life, and oh—extremely famous parents: actress, Anna Blackwood, and film director, Finn Blackwood.

The parent part was buried under numerous headlines of who he was (allegedly) dating. Models, singers, daughters of iconic 90s actors, daughters of iconic 90s models.

Apparently, the men in England were as bad as the ones in America. Wonderful.

"Now take a seat so I can finally start class," Professor Emmerson said.

Dorian finally moved away from the entryway. I turned my head down immediately.

His stare moved across the room deciding which empty seat to fill. Quickly scanning the desks, his gaze almost skipped me, *almost.* His eyebrows slightly rose, followed by the tilt of his head, walking toward the empty desk in front of me, and taking a seat.

There goes the dinosaur tactic.

"It's you," he whispered. His face bloomed with surprise. It made his lips look even fuller, making it difficult to remember that this wasn't the person I met the other night, but the person I read about online.

My spine stiffened. I hadn't planned for this.

"Sit down, Mr. Blackwood," Professor Emmerson ordered.

I'd need a plan. Because apparently, I was going to have to fix this. No more hoping to go unnoticed when he was in the same class as me for *an entire semester.*

As excited as I was for this class, it was impossible to pay attention now. I wrote down the words coming out of Professor Emmerson's mouth about the semester-long project, but I didn't register any of it. The back of Dorian's head kept pulling me back to Saturday night when we ran along the Thames River, moonlight flickering off the top of his head as if to create a constant halo.

I needed to get as far away from him as possible.

Maybe it was possible that he could be a gentleman about this situation and never speak a word about the other night. But I wasn't taking any chances.

The moment the class hour was up, I followed him out of the room. Time for crisis management.

His long legs were difficult to keep up with. But I did my best to rush without looking like a maniac to catch up. Then the hall flooded with students as a nearby room emptied out.

I lost him.

Ugh. I brushed a hair out of my face and continued down the corridor. I squeezed through the groups of students, whose fancy tweed and wool brushed my shoulders. I'd have to leave the Dorian-situation alone until I could talk it over with Mia. She'd help me formulate a plan.

Pulling my phone from my bag, I began typing a message in our group chat, until a hand latched onto my arm and yanked me into an empty classroom.

"What happened the other night?" Rye—*Dorian* asked, closing the door behind me.

"Excuse me?" I asked, pulling my arm from his grasp.

"The other night: the club, the dancing, the Tube, my flat. You left while I was sleeping." He waited for my reaction or some realization.

Maybe I could convince him that he had the wrong person. He's probably dated enough women to mix them up.

"I'm sorry, you have the wrong person," I apologized. I turned and grabbed the doorknob. But he was speaking again.

"I may've drank but I wasn't *that* pissed, Jesus. You wore that same skirt. And I remember because I took—"

"Fine, fine, you caught me. I may've lied about not remembering you, but you lied about your name."

His eyebrows scrunched together. "I didn't lie about my

name—it's a nickname. They don't have those back in the States?" *Smartass tone.*

"Who gives someone they're meeting for the first time a nickname?" I questioned.

"A person with privacy problems." He crossed his arms. "Who pretends not to recognize someone they slept with?"

"Someone who obviously thinks it was a mistake."

His brow ticked upward with surprise. "I could've sworn I wasn't the only one who had a good time."

"Piss-drunk though, remember?" I shrugged my shoulders. "Now, I'd prefer if you never spoke to me again. Or acted like we'd never met. Yes, that would be better. So it was nice meeting you, but no." Opening the door—

He placed a hand above mine, shutting it. "Woah, what? Why not?" he asked.

Looking up at him, all that filled me was an abundance of agitation. I huffed, "It's complicated."

"I can be very persuasive."

How could someone be handsome enough that I wanted to lean into their cologne-like coffee scent, while also being equally maddening? I wanted to push him off the London Bridge and let the problem float away.

"Are you always like this?" I asked.

"An amusing conversationalist?"

I narrowed my gaze. "Do you know what people say about you? They call you the 'UK Bachelor.' 'The Man That Doesn't Repeat.' One article even called you a drunk pig."

"I don't remember it being a crime to drink."

"Maybe not, but it's an unappealing look."

"Unappealing to whom?" he argued. "Couldn't have been

you."

"Maybe I was just looking for a good night!" I admitted.

"Says the woman who didn't want to dance."

"What do you want me to say, Rye—" I shut my mouth.

His eyes darted over my face. "I want you to say that you remember Saturday night the way I did."

"Not all of us are great at understanding when a woman is no longer interested, and that's okay," I reassured him, patting his chest.

"You're really not going to say why we can't know each other?" he asked.

"Did my previous responses not answer that question already?" My hand waited on the doorknob.

"What do I have to do to get you to go on a date with me?" he asked with purpose, finally removing his hand from the door, and stuffing it into his pocket.

"*A date?* Are you insane?" I gawked.

"That's not the usual response I get."

"What do I have to do for you to leave me alone?" I asked with a lack of patience. I could feel my cheeks turning burning with frustration.

A moment of silence passed. God, I didn't think he was actually going to take a moment to consider my question. What could this man possibly want from me? Wasn't being rich enough?

He opened his mouth. "I'll make a deal with you: I'll keep our night quiet if you help me pass this class."

"The class just started …"

"I've taken it before, so as you can imagine, it didn't go well."

"I work almost every day after class. So you'd have to come to me."

"That's fine." He waited for me to say yes.

I considered his offer, trying to calculate how this plan could go wrong. It took only two seconds to compile the list of things that could go awry. But the bottom line was that no one could know what happened between us.

Hence why I said, "Okay."

5

"I met someone," I said.

"Dorian, you meet someone every weekend," Jasmine said.

"You know what, I don't quite remember why I called—"

"Don't hang up! Don't hang up!"

I waited for her reason.

"I told Tristan I had an important phone call, so I'm hiding in the bathroom hoping he'll realize I'm busy and then just leave. If he hears that I've stopped talking, then he'll never go."

"Tristan? The guy Mum set you up with last month? You're *still* seeing him? I thought you said he smelled like spicy crisps?"

She groaned. "*I did.* I just feel bad."

"That he smells like crisps?" I readjusted the phone between my ear and shoulder as I tightened the easel against the canvas before sitting down. Everyone in the art studio—sitting in our large circle of easels facing one another—had already begun on their paintings since I was late "as usual" (according to Poppy, the owner).

"No, no, I'm talking about Mum. You know how she is with the whole 'I want you to fall in love like I did' crap. I can't tell her no now," she complained.

"Yes, you can."

"Oh yeah, like how you tell Mum no all the time."

"That's different," I argued, picking up a pencil and beginning to sketch a silhouette.

"Is it though?"

"One, I live in the same country as her. Two, me not caring about university compared to you not wanting to date some guy are completely different situations." I put the pencil down. "Aren't you supposed to be helpful? Older sister and all?"

"I was referring to Victoria when it came to saying no, but alright, I see we're still avoiding that problem until she's London-bound. And by the way, *I am* being helpful."

"Well, it's a good thing you're not a therapist."

"That's why I make pottery for a living smartarse."

I responded to her with silence.

"Fine, I'll humor you. Who's this woman you've met?" she asked.

"I think I rather just hang up. Is the crisp boy gone yet?"

"No come on," she whined. "I want to know now."

I sighed, erasing the nose and restarting. "I met her this weekend. We went out, had a nice time, and then two days later, I find her in my class."

"That's a bit eerie."

"You'd think but I wanted to see her again, so it felt like fate in a way? That was until she pretended like she'd never met me."

I pulled the phone away as her laugh rang through my ear. "That has to be the funniest shit I've ever heard. What did you do to her?" she shrieked.

"Nothing! I thought we had a good night! I tried asking her

out and she told me no."

"Oh, Dorian." She felt bad, but I could hear her holding back another laugh. "So now you're stuck in class with her all semester? That's embarrassing."

I scratched the back of my neck. "Actually, she's tutoring me as well."

"And why would she agree to that?"

"You ask a lot of questions for someone who wasn't interested ten seconds ago."

"How do you even know she's any good?"

"Because I looked her up. She's had a number of scholarships and internships in marketing that make a Harvard business student look like a failure. We met at her work yesterday to go over the semester project—you'd think she already took the class."

"What's her name?"

"Why?"

"I want to see a picture of her."

"Adelaide Adorno," I said hesitantly.

A pause and then, "She's really pretty."

"I know," I exhaled.

"This is a terrible idea," she tsked.

"James was a lot nicer about this when I told him. Supportive even."

"Well, that's James for ya." A door-like creak sounded behind her. "I think he left," she celebrated with a high-pitched whisper.

"Happy I could provide some help."

"Eternally grateful." A muffled noise passed over the speaker before she returned. "Alright, I'll talk to you later. I have to get back to this mug set."

"Send me a picture when you're done."

"Will do—oh, and Dorian."

"Yeah?"

Her voice switched to her Semi-Responsible Sister Tone. "Be careful. You only just met this girl. I just … I don't want it to end up like Victoria."

6

Don't Trust His Friends — Adelaide

The first two tutoring sessions were … fine. He didn't laugh in my face when I showed him my vibrant graphics that broke down a social media marketing plan—paid vs organic media, campaigns, social media SEO, branding—so I guess that was something.

All that mattered was that it wasn't going to interfere with my shifts at the bookstore. The job that Mia and I had Sabrina to thank for since she was close with the two women—Iris and Dotty—who owned the place. We'd only been working there for three weeks but I could live in the shelves if the offer was extended. My clothes would probably smell like dusty paper and the scented firewood plugin Iris insisted on keeping in at all times. But at least it meant more time with Iris and Dotty every day.

The older women lived together, trading jewelry and watching the same reality TV every night like exhausted college roommates. Iris's husband passed away ten years ago, and her two daughters and three grandchildren lived outside London. She moved in with Dotty after that, who had lived alone her entire adult life, never marrying. *Living the dream*, Dotty had said.

For bosses, they were laid back. Or at least Iris was because

Liana Cincotti

she was the only one who signed off on Dorian staying while I worked. She was alarmingly excited. Apparently, she kept up with the tabloids.

It was concerning.

Nonetheless, Dorian promised he'd do the work I assigned him from the semester project while I continued my shift at the bookstore. Whether or not he planned to keep that promise when Monday rolled around, I didn't know.

That was a tomorrow problem.

My main concern right now was trying to find where the Entertainment Media class was. I would've asked Mia to help me get there since we're both in the class, but every time we had a moment to talk this week, I was so focused on updating her about Dorian.

She was both horrified, and envious. *He's in your class, recognized you immediately, tried asking you on a date, and then blackmailed you into tutoring him? Why haven't I found any guys like that?*

Today's class together would be a nice distraction from the Dorian situation. If I could figure how to get there.

I should've taped the locations to the bottoms of my boots to make sure I wasn't late for class. But Townsen was set up like a hedge maze made of stone. And I didn't do closed spaces with zero direction.

All the buildings were connected through corridors and outdoor hallways that led to gardens and courtyards. Not a single building stood alone. It was confusing.

I pulled my phone from my bag to reread the class location. And … I was going in the completely wrong direction. Wonderful. I took an abrupt right into the next corridor and *shit*.

The fall backwards was long with my heeled loafers. Landing

on my tailbone, my bag and books hit the marble floor. *Ouch.*

"I am so sorry, that was completely my fault—" I stopped short, taking in the familiar person sitting across from me on the floor. He had a head of hair that was as white as snow.

In a soft British accent, he replied without looking up. "No, no, it's alright—" Lifting his head up, realization spread across his face. "I know you, don't I?" He pushed himself up from the ground.

"I, uh … " *Say something. Lie!*

He began collecting my books. "Adelaide, right?" There went that. "We met at the pub Saturday—or at least you and Dorian did," he laughed.

I stood, flattening out my sweater, and plucking the books out of his arms. "I think you have the wrong person—"

He clutched onto the book I was trying to take. "Hey, it's alright, Dorian filled me in," he explained, rather kindly too. As if it was *our* secret now. Phenomenal. Another problem.

"Did he now?" I asked flabbergasted. I made a deal with Dorian not to tell anyone about our night and here he was telling friends.

I rearranged the books in my arms and focused on getting out of here immediately. But as I scrambled for an excuse to go, my Entertainment Media textbook slipped out of my grasp. The *smack* against the floor was a good interruption for our conversation, but he bent down to pick it up.

"Two-thousand and one Beverly Spring collection." He gestured to my shoes, standing back up and handing over the book.

"How—how do you know that?" I stammered.

"My mother works for Beverly." He stated it as if it wasn't

single-handedly the coolest job ever.

Not *at* Beverly, but *for* Beverly.

He said it so nonchalantly that I considered for a moment whether we were talking about the same company.

The Beverly. The most iconic fashion house of all time. The one I dreamed about even when I wasn't sleeping. The one I've spent the past eight years achieving a perfect GPA for in hopes of joining their marketing team.

"My name's James, by the way," he remembered, giving me his hand.

I shook it. "Adelaide … But you already know that." He smiled shyly in response. It was so warm and kind. Something that could've melted ice. An odd contrast to the grimace his friend wore the two times I saw him this week.

"Don't worry by the way, I would never say anything about you and Dorian."

I wanted to throw my palm against my forehead. "Do you happen to know who else he told?"

His eyes widened. "There is no one else. He would never do that. We're practically attached at the hip, so I usually know too much. Which can be unfortunate at times," he pondered.

"Oh, alright," I exhaled, while also trying to piece together which parts would be unfortunate. "I'm sorry again for running into you. I'm still trying to figure out what makes this brown hallway different from that brown hallway." I blew a strand of hair out of my face.

"Which class are you trying to get to?" he asked.

"Entertainment Media in the Archer building."

"With Professor Dover?"

"Yes, that one! Have you had her before?"

"I'm in that class too," he said. "I guess you can just follow me this way then."

Walking side and side, we headed in the completely opposite direction that I had been going. The light coming in through the skylight above us flickered over our shoes as we walked through the outdoor pathway to the other building. I took my strides wide to keep up with his footsteps.

I attempted to listen to the words coming out of James's mouth about the history of the buildings, but I was more focused on memorizing this path and trying to figure out if he was trustworthy (all while ignoring how pretty his mouth happened to be).

Green flag #1: He seemed sweet.

Red flag #1: He was a friend of Dorian's.

Green flag #2: He appeared to be the complete opposite of Dorian, despite the similar height and dark eyes.

Red flag #2: He chose to spend time with Dorian.

Green flag #3: He had a really pretty smile. Maybe that was a beige flag since it intervened with the No Dating rule.

"Are you a senior?" he asked.

"Yes," I responded, trying not to let my thoughts paint themselves across my face. "I transferred here from Boston."

"Me too—well, I'm in my final year too," he rushed to clarify. "Not from Boston, clearly." He blushed. I suppressed a laugh. I didn't need to make his shade of crimson any worse.

He cleared his throat. "So why here?"

"Study abroad opportunity. I always wanted to live in London though." The romanticization of movies set here may have contributed heavily. "Tea, scones, rolling countryside hills, a reason to carry an umbrella every day." And there was nothing left for me back in Boston. "Townsen also has one of the best marketing programs in the world."

"So you gave up burgers and American holidays for stale scones and rain?" He was baffled.

I shrugged. "I don't care much for the holidays."

"Nonsense," he argued.

"Just days on a calendar," I pointed out.

"So, you're an American who hates holidays, likes the rain, is willing to travel for a scone, and … majors in marketing," he hummed as we entered a building with a plaque labeled ARCHER above, walnut walls welcoming us.

"Public relations," I clarified.

"Anywhere in London you're hoping to intern?"

"I'm not sure yet," I lied.

"I would ask more but we're here," he confessed, stopping in front of a large oak door. "Same hallway next Thursday?"

It wasn't as if I could say no. "Next Thursday it is."

7

Don't Stare At Him for Too Long — *Adelaide*

Walking into class, James and I diverged. I took the stairs to where Mia sat at the back of the auditorium-style classroom picking at a thread in her sweater. The rows of desks hugged the curve of the wall, holding about eighty students. Or at least it felt like eighty students because they all had their eyes on me as James and I snuck in at the last minute.

"Hello, hello," I whispered as the professor stood from her desk. I shrugged my bag off my shoulder and took a seat.

"Don't you *hello, hello* me, who was that?" Mia whispered in a volume loud enough that I hopped in my seat.

I smacked my hand over her mouth. *Who knows what else she was going to say if I didn't.*

"First off, you're not allowed to whisper anymore because that was not whispering. Second, that was James," I explained, removing my hand from her face, and wiping her lip gloss off my palm.

I twisted forward to write down the lecture topics—

"Why are you smiling like that?" I grumbled.

There was a mischievous grin on her face. She looked like an impersonator for the cat from *Alice in Wonderland*. "You know his name ..."

I continued writing down the bullet points displayed on the projector, trying to get them on paper quicker than the professor could read them off.

"And what do we know about James?" she asked.

"He's a friend of Dorian's and that's all we need to know."

Her mouth fell open. She took up the entirety of my left peripheral with her gaping mouth. It was like there was a galaxy in there. Unfiltered words just swimming around. "You're telling me that we're going to pretend that man doesn't exist?" She peered down at him.

Even with a packed lecture hall, I had no problem spotting James's head in the front row. But I was surprised to find him glancing back in my direction. He brought his hand up ... and waved. A delicate, shy smile inched its way into his cheeks. I casually waved back before he faced the projector again.

Mia's galaxy widened.

I pressed the pen back down. "Dorian can't be trusted, so neither can his friend," I explained.

"Guilty by association?" she questioned.

"Exactly."

"But he's really cute," she stressed.

"Good thing we're in a country filled with them."

"So, we can't invite him over for dinner?"

"Mia." I glared at her. She would be the one to let her pen "slip" on a piece of paper that just so happened to write our address and find its way into his pocket. "I will never tweeze your eyebrows again."

"*You wouldn't.*"

"*Would.*"

"Fine. I'll let you think about it."

There was no way in hell I was letting a co-conspirator of Dorian's into my apartment. I was already getting more involved with men in the past ten days attending this university than I had in the past three months I'd been here.

Not over my dead, rotting, decaying body.

"Where's your flat?" Dorian asked.

"Excuse me?" I flipped my head up from where I was hunched over pulling a stack of books from a box as I had Dorian start on research for his target market. He picked a company that sells anonymous antique paintings. As odd as it was, I didn't feel like having a conversation about it, so I didn't ask.

My nails scratched the bottom of the cardboard box as I tried to get a grip on the books. Our latest shipment was a set of clothbound classics, so they were twice as beautiful, and also twice as heavy. My back ached from carrying books. Carrying books around campus. Carrying books to and from the bookstore. Carrying them from campus back to the apartment.

I wasn't expecting to frolic around England while studying here. I knew academics came first. But gosh, I didn't realize I was signing up for early-on back problems *on top of* everything else that came with attending a university that enjoyed its low acceptance rate and seeing students drop out the first week in.

A shadow bled over the stack in my arms. Before I could look up, Dorian was lifting half of the books out of my hands.

"I was just wondering how far you have to walk from here every night," he clarified, standing up.

I stood with him, turning out of the backroom. He followed me towards the Classics aisle. Hoisting my books up, I slid them one-by-one into the correct spots on the shelf. Dorian stood on the opposite side of the bookcase, pushing books beside mine.

"Plan on leaving a series of mouse traps in my bedroom?" I asked, sliding a book in front of his face.

"Bear traps, actually. Mouse traps aren't nearly as effective."

"Get the idea from the gift I left on your stoop?"

"Is that what the trickle of blood running down my leg is from? I thought I tripped on one of the steak knives you carry around in your pockets."

"That'd be my set of fountain pens. Very sharp. Easy to mix up. Happens all the time."

A quick laugh came through the books. It sounded like a spoon tapping a teacup with one swift *ring*. Then he steered the conversation in the other direction. "You really shouldn't be walking home by yourself."

"Ah, a protector all of a sudden," I replied.

"Funny." I jumped back as his head popped up across from me. He slid a book beside the one I added. "I just can't stand to fail this class. Losing my tutor probably wouldn't do me any good."

"My walk home is perfectly safe."

"How far is the walk?"

"Not far."

"Do you get some high from arguing with people?"

"I do not argue with people," I argued—*stated*. I shoved a book through the shelf. An inch closer and I'd perfectly collide with his face.

"You know where I live. It's not like I'm going to do anything with this information."

I pursed my lips. "Twenty minute walk from here. Why?"

"It's already dark. I can walk you home."

I shoved a book in front of his face. "It's fine, I'm here past when we finish anyways."

"I can wait. I don't have anywhere to be." He slid the books out of his way. Now he was staring back at me. He *wanted* me to argue. Joke's on him. I was determined enough to keep my mouth shut.

Two hours later, with a scowl on my face, I was locking up the shop with Dorian at my back waiting for me.

The quaint bookstore was tucked away in an alleyway, hidden from the city-goers of London, making it difficult to find if you weren't a local, so I wasn't too worried about anyone seeing us. Even the tailor across the street went home already.

"Good to go?" he asked as the lock clicked.

"Is this really necessary?" The streetlamp flickered with impatience ahead. Only a week and a half into September and the temperatures from August were already cooling at night. The wind pushed at my hair as I took a step forward, retracing the route I'd been taking since July.

"Told you. I can't lose my tutor," he replied.

"Shouldn't tutors be disposable to you? Can't you just fetch another one?" I waved my hand.

His brow furrowed with amusement. "What makes you think that? Do I look like I have an inexhaustible amount of tutors locked up in my home?" Now it was my turn to raise my brow. "You googled me, didn't you?"

"I had to make sure you didn't have some type of criminal record."

Liana Cincotti

"Oh sure. Did that search come before or after you looked up if I was lying about my name?"

"Before," I mumbled.

He laughed. "At least you're honest. What else did you find? Handsome, young fellow that—"

"—has rich parents, lives in the most expensive flat in the Kensington and enjoys his reputation of getting drunk and collecting women like they're coins," I finished for him. When he didn't respond, I continued as we passed a bakery whose lights were turning off. "I'm honestly surprised you aren't driving around in some rare car."

"I don't drive," he replied.

"What do you mean you don't drive?"

"I don't have a license," he explained. "Many raised in London don't."

"Wait, *you* can't drive?"

"Oh, I can drive," he corrected me.

"But you don't have a license," I pointed out. I held onto the strap of my bag and hopped over a puddle from last night's rain, landing on the ball of my foot with a *tap*. I wobbled and he grabbed my elbow to steady me, the same way he did when we rode around on the train the night we met. My heart hiccupped unexpectedly.

It looked like the same thought passed him as he withdrew his hand.

"If I had to drive, I could." He narrowed his eyes.

"What if you were in a car with a murderer, forced to act on instinct?" I tested him as we passed our third telephone booth. I resisted the urge to stare at them every time. As dirty as they were, they still looked like cute trinkets in life size form.

"I'd open the driver's door, shove him out, and take over the wheel," he responded with a look that said *obviously*.

"That'd never work," I snorted.

There was a shimmer to his smile that I couldn't determine if it was from delight or the moonlight. "What would you do then?" he asked.

"I'd push you toward the murderer and hop out of the car."

"I'm so happy I decided to walk a woman home who's willing to sacrifice me," he commented as we took a turn. Marylebone's row of brick buildings sat quietly without the morning chaos I usually left it in. Cabs were still whizzing by, and apartment windows were still illuminated. But the bike racks were empty, and the shop windows read *Closed*. "Write something nice in my obituary while you're at, will you?"

"He had a lovely accent, terrible manners, and was always full of himself," I recited.

"You think I have a lovely accent?" he asked, only a small curve to the corner of his lips.

"Don't be fooled, everyone around here has a nice accent."

"Well, I think you have a lovely accent too," he commented, his eyes bright. Whimsical and boyish. A second later, he cleared his throat. "Have we not converted you?" He lifted my blue Boston Red Sox hat keychain from the strap of my bag. "Shouldn't you have some ridiculous phone box keychain on here?"

I smacked his hand away. "Those keychains aren't ridiculous," I huffed. There was a tiny red telephone booth hanging from my bedpost in my room as we spoke. The epitome of adorable. "They just don't match my ... collection," I pointed out. The blue and gray of the silk scarf, white pearls, and gold rings looped through the strap of my leather bag would clash with red.

His brows rose. "If you could even see it," he criticized, shooing the pile of charms around.

"Good thing they're mine and not yours." I smacked his hand away. "We're here."

I stopped in front of the black door of the apartment building. The tree that greeted me from below my balcony each morning curved above us. A branch was close to poking Dorian in the head. He looked up at building's dark red bricks and wrought iron railings.

"Is that your flatmate?" he asked.

My head snapped up, where Brina stood in front of the window—

"What are you—" I shoved him off the sidewalk and pulled him behind the tree, rustling the branches as we hid. Slowly, I peeked out from behind the trunk to look back up at the window. *Phew*. She was just brushing her hair.

If she had seen us, I … What would I have done? Act like Dorian and I happened to run into each other? Ignore him? Explain that he lost a contact and needed help home? (Convenient because we apparently had the same exact route home!)

Ahem.

I twisted, but my face came within inches of his. His eyes were lowered toward my mouth. A fast breath came from his lips. The same espresso scent on his clothes that peppered his room surrounded me. I could count his eyelashes from this vicinity. Long blots of ink that drained into dark eyes.

"Is there a reason we're hiding behind a tree or do my eyes just look better in this light?"

I immediately pulled my hands off his chest as if it was covered in cyanide, seeping into my skin.

A glare riddled my brow. "I'll see you Wednesday," I said, walking away.

"Wait." He grabbed my wrist, humor gone. "You're not going to tell me what that was about?"

Maybe I could trust him. Maybe it was possible that he'd keep the caveat to my secret about Sabrina. But the articles I read about him—*Dorian Blackwood Runs Through Women like They're Shoes*—the privileged lifestyle and gawking from all the girls in class were already glaring red flags smacking me in the head. And the fact that he was holding our night together over my head so that I'd tutor him was gnawing my skin down to the bone.

I was better off not trusting anyone.

"Goodnight, Dorian."

8

Don't Hide with the Enemy — Adelaide

Forty-eight hours ago, waves of anxiety had been rolling off my chest as I recovered from Sabrina almost seeing us from her window. Forty-eight hours and I still couldn't get rid of the smell of Dorian either. It was nauseating. Glued to the sweater I had been wearing, which now sat in my hamper begging to be cleansed. But the speed at which my heart was racing behind that tree was nowhere close to the pace it was beating at now.

"The paper will be worth fifty percent of your grade," Professor Hudson explained—and not to be dramatic but—ruining my life in the process. My pen almost snapped in my hand. His mouth was moving but that didn't matter, I already knew what the assignment was. One hundred pages on globalization and its effect on British industries.

One hundred pages.

Going out on Saturday nights just *poofed* out of thin air. Going out *any* night, actually. At this point, I was going to have to pencil in my meals.

Fifty percent. Fifty percent of my grade. A grade that needed to be an A in order for me to keep my scholarship and afford the tuition here.

Going back to Boston wasn't an option. I had already fallen in love with London.

The light of the London Eye, the sight of the double-decker buses, the cobblestone corners, the history, the *people*. The people were full of life. Dotty, Iris, Sabrina, and even Drew, the man at the Borough Market who entertained my need to pick out each individual ravioli from his display. The warmth of the art museums, the breeze of the Thames, the chatter of the trees in St. James Park, the hum of the audience in a theatre, the comfort of tea times.

The more I breathed them all in, the less I could handle losing them.

I couldn't go back home anymore. I didn't even have anything to go back to.

Professor Hudson continued talking as I opened my planner.

There wasn't a free day in any of the blocks for the month of September ... or October. Each square was filled with *Work* or a chunk of an assignment to do to stay on track.

Now I'd have to find somewhere to fill in this assignment. My head was already throbbing at the number of words I'd have to write today.

I looked around the room where students were either on their phones or shopping on their laptops. Not one person looked worried. Yet here I was getting hot, while my hands grew clammy, struggling to grip the pen.

This was worth it. It'd all be worth it. A perfect GPA meant free tuition and getting to stay in London. That much closer to finishing my degree, getting the perfect marketing job, being financially independent, and never having to go home again.

Liana Cincotti

"I'm here!" I shouted to Dotty as I entered the bookstore, using my hip to open the door.

The pile in my arms seemed to grow each time I arrived. "Can you take this?" I held my arm in the air, waving the to-go cups like a flag.

Mia dropped the box in her arms, letting it slam against the floor to run over. I lifted my knee up to catch them as she took the drinks from my hand.

"Good thing we aren't working in a China shop!" Dotty commented as she peeked into the open box Mia dropped.

Mia smiled innocently at her. "They're just the books on marketing, it's fine."

I shot her a look. "I'm going to start mistreating the books on journalism."

"I'd thank you, actually. My dad is already on my ass about coursework because I've yet to start anything." She shook her head before taking a sip of her coffee.

I bit down on my cheek to keep my jaw from dropping. She hadn't started *anything?*

I couldn't imagine my mother ever asking if I had done my work. She never even asked me about school. I was an entity that existed in our house. Another working individual. I tried to see the silver lining about being forced to learn the reality of life early (that it was only as good as you were willing to work) but it still hadn't made me numb enough in moments like this.

Watching Mia talk with her family on the phone every Monday night, and waving goodbye to Sabrina every time she went out with her dads was the other end of my double-edged sword. If they failed out of Townsen, there was someone to support them. If I failed ... well, I didn't think my aunt was looking to house me for another five years.

There weren't many opportunities to make friends on campus back home. Everyone was looking to party or drink or step on you to get the best grade. I chatted with girls in class, but I didn't have the energy to follow up on after-class plans.

Mia and Brina had become the friends I saw in sitcoms and rom-coms. The friends that remembered your birthday, offered you their favorite dresses for a date, and tucked you under their umbrellas when it began to rain. But watching them lean on their families for support and reminders of deadlines was ... difficult.

"How's the tea?" I asked Dotty.

She smacked her lips together. "Arnold made it, didn't he?" Her eyes brightened.

I nodded satisfyingly.

Was it incredibly awkward to request a barista? Yes. But did I know it would make Dotty smile and coerce her into going easy on me for having tutoring sessions during shifts? Of course.

"You're good." She pointed her little bony finger at me. "But you didn't need to get me tea with Arnold's special goat milk to convince me about letting the handsome fella in—that's Dorian Blackwood for heaven's sake!"

"He's already here?" I asked, my eyes widening. I assumed after how Monday night ended, he'd show up late. I was actually counting on him to not show up *at all* so I could focus on this new paper. Apparently, I was the only one who found us pressed against a tree together awkward.

"He's a charming thing too. But I still have a lot of questions as to why you're tutoring him and not dating him." Dotty disapproved, according to the woman who never married and didn't believe in monogamy. Hypocrite.

"Even if I was interested in dating someone as arrogant as him, I couldn't. Sabrina's in love with him." I waved my hand.

Her face fell. A melancholic look swept the corners of her lips.

Sabrina didn't work here, but she was a frequent-customer-turned-friend before getting me and Mia jobs here. Dotty and Iris treated her like a granddaughter.

"Exactly," I replied to the look on her face.

"Why don't you set her up then?" She leaned forward from behind the desk. Mia went over to sit beside her.

For a millisecond, I had considered connecting Dorian with Sabrina. But that was before he opened his mouth and I realized he was full of himself. She may have claimed to be in love with him, but she had no idea who he actually was. Maybe this semester would change that now that she could bump into his arrogant ass at any moment on campus.

I looked up at the ceiling and rolled my tongue over my teeth. "Well, the thing is we kind of … spent the night together." Dotty gasped. "I had no idea who he was!" I defended myself.

"What are you doing tutoring him then?" she asked, horrified.

"It's how I'm getting him to keep this whole thing a secret."

She nodded, collecting each piece of information to surely share with her book club. "You're going to get yourself into trouble with this," she considered, chewing on her lip.

"If you have any better ideas, I'd love to hear them."

Dotty and Mia looked at each other without responses.

"That's what I thought. Now I'm going to take care of the problem in the backroom until you two can come up with something better."

"Talk loudly so we can hear," Mia asked before I crossed

through the threshold of the backroom and shut the door.

There was a stack of boxes propping up his feet where he was … sleeping. You had to be kidding.

His long figure was extended on the couch, arms crossed behind his head. He had black trousers on, and a white T-shirt that rose above his lower stomach. I could see the tattoo that rested on his hip. My gaze glued to it, trapping me. I couldn't tear my eyes away. The ink followed the curve of the muscle in his torso, the way a quill guided above a line on paper. The last time I saw it, my thumb was pressed into it.

"Is it not rude to stare in America?"

I jolted at his voice. The tattoo was quickly covered up by his shirt as he sat up, rubbing his—now open—eyes.

"Because it's awfully creepy here, just so you know," he responded, his accent making him sound considerate despite the smart-ass tone.

"I'll keep that in mind next time I have someone taking a nap in my place of work. You could've at least started on what I assigned for today," I pointed out, throwing my jacket onto the couch.

"How was I supposed to know what was assigned?" His eyebrow quirked.

"Because I printed you out the rubric for the project and added a calendar to the back, breaking down what had to be completed by the end of each session."

"That's quite smart."

A pause passed over the conversation.

"So you lost the paper?" I deadpanned.

"Forgive me?"

"Do you take anything seriously?"

"Do you want to talk about why you were staring at me?"

"We're supposed to be working," I grumbled.

"Fine, let's get to work then." He stood up abruptly, forcing me to take a step backward to give myself space. Suddenly, I could see the flecks of gold in his brown eyes. "You look tall today," he thought aloud. It was odd. Spellbinding, almost.

I turned away, placing my things on the table. "New shoes," I commented haphazardly. Lots of talking. No studying.

I rifled through my papers, pulling out folded pieces from my textbook that I stuffed in each time class was up. The calendar I made was here somewhere. Maybe it'd be easier to find it if Dorian wasn't staring at me.

Without picking my head up, I glanced at his shoes. 2021 Beverly Autumn Collection. "Did James get you those?" I asked.

"Who?"

"Your friend, James."

"You know James? *My* James? Platinum hair, quiet personality?" Confusion wiped across his face.

I responded casually, "Yes, I met him a few weeks ago. I assumed he would've said something."

"No." He scratched the back of his neck. "Just surprised he wouldn't tell me. How do you know him?"

"We have class together. You know you could sit down and pick up where we left off while I look for this paper." I pointed to the chair across from me.

"Why didn't you say anything?" he asked curiously, still standing. "You could've mentioned it."

"Because this isn't social hour and—I give up, I'm printing a new paper," I exhaled with irritation. I slid the tower of textbooks to the side and pulled out my laptop to find the file.

"Do you fancy him?"

I slowly lifted my head up. "Are you kidding? Oh my gosh, you're not." I rubbed my temples and stood up straight. "I've spoken to James maybe three times. I don't even like that he knows about us." I waved my finger between us.

"James is practically a saint. I'm not sure he's ever lied in his life. A church confessional's nightmare, truly."

I didn't need Dorian to convince me otherwise. The last time James and I spoke, we had a fifteen-minute conversation about how scarves were his favorite piece of clothing. *Saint* was encrusted in the shape of his smile.

"If you're into him, I could always set you two up."

I pressed *print* on my laptop. "I'm not looking to date. I have better things to do than entertain boys."

"Oh come on, James is a nice boy." He took a step forward, now trying to plead his case.

Four steps to the printer and four steps back. I held the paper up to his face. "I. Do. Not. Date. Now sit down, time to get to work."

He grabbed the paper out of my hand and smacked it down on the table, a crease already forming on the page. "So you're not bringing a date to the Dinner then?"

"The Dinner?" I asked.

"The Annual Townsen Class Dinner that's in two weeks." he exclaimed, waiting for my reaction. But no, nothing. Was I supposed to be subscribed to some university newsletter?

He sighed. "The Annual Dinner takes place every autumn to celebrate the new year and new students, like you."

"And we just…eat dinner?"

"Eat, dance, network. Boring shit like that."

"If you find it boring, why go?"

"For James, he enjoys it." He shrugged.

"No one else?" I raised my eyebrows, thinking back on the collection of girls who stared at him twice a week in class.

"What makes you think there's someone else?"

"There's *always* someone else with guys like you."

"You mean incredibly charming and handsome guys that—"

"Sabrina, I didn't know you were coming!" Mia's voice pierced the room from the other side of the door.

Holy shit.

My head snapped to the wall in horror. Panic crawled up my throat and threatened to suffocate me as my heart nosedived. I searched around the room for a space and locked in on the couch.

"You need to hide *right now,*" I whispered like a psychopath, grabbing onto whichever part of Dorian was closest to me and pulled.

"What? Why wou—"

"Is Addy in the back?" I could hear Sabrina getting closer now.

Shit, shit, shit, shit.

"I need you to lie down behind the couch." I pointed to the floor.

He looked at me like I was a maniac. "No way am I—"

"Do you have to have a response to *everything?* Just get behind the—"

The knob of the door creaked, and I did what was best.

Shoved Dorian onto the floor.

But suddenly, his hand was on my wrist, and he was pulling me down with him.

9

"Addy?" Sabrina's voice couldn't have been louder than the pounding of my heart. The pounding of my heart which was beating against Dorian's ribcage …

I hated him. I hated him, I hated him, I hated him.

And I was completely lying on top of him. Chest against chest, torso against torso, hips against hips. My right knee was wedged between his legs, pressed against the hardwood floor. My cheek was smooshed against the cotton of his T-shirt. The buckle of his belt uncomfortably poked my stomach.

I slightly rose with each breath he took. I could even feel the pulse in his fingers, where he was holding onto my arms to keep me from slipping off of him.

May as well strap me to an operation table because even that'd be less excruciating.

"She must be in the bathroom," Mia spoke up.

"Oh bollocks. Well, I have to print these papers anyway. The printer at the flat stopped working and I didn't feel like going to campus," Sabrina explained.

"I'll give you a hand," Mia responded, much too

enthusiastically.

"What's wrong with you?" I whispered, pushing my hands into his chest to create some space. I wanted to look him in the face as he tried to give me his bullshit answer.

"Why don't you want her to see us?" he shot back, his brows furrowing. As if *he* had a reason to be questioning *me*. "Answer the question."

"Because she can't know that I know you. And she definitely can't know that I'm tutoring you or *why* I'm stuck tutoring you," I exhaled.

"Why?" His nose scrunched up.

"Because you're off limits."

"I'm off limits? How's that?"

I pressed my fingers to my eyes, having to tilt my face down to meet my hand. My forehead lightly grazed his chin. "My friend is interested in you. I obviously didn't realize who you were beforehand or else I would've never ... ya know."

Based on the crease in his forehead, that was not the response he was expecting.

"Do you get why I need you to leave me alone now?" I repeated. Maybe he'd gather some decency and let me off the hook with this tutoring thing.

There was a pause in our back and forth. He searched my face. Up close, I could only imagine how much he was finding. The earring that sagged in my right ear because I couldn't help but pull on my hoops as a kid. The dark strand of hair that always curled at my temple. Or the scar on my face from the time I tried to teach myself how to swim in my grandma's pool and hit my chin off the diving board.

"Come to the Dinner with me," he asked with determination.

"As your date?" I questioned, dumbfounded.

"Of course."

"No," I scoffed.

He frowned, the pressure on my arms loosening slightly.

"Did you not hear any of the words that just came out of my mouth?" I pointed out. My cheeks were getting hot. Strands of hair were blocking my peripheral vision, and my patience was thinning to a strand so thin I could floss my teeth with it.

He let go of my left arm to push a piece of hair back behind my ear. "Oh, I heard you. But all it sounds like is you're protecting your friend from getting hurt, which is inevitable sooner or later."

"What are you talking about?"

"I'm not interested in her, so there's no point to this."

"You don't even know her. She's very easy to love."

"I'm sure she is, but I'm not interested."

"You don't even know what she looks like, that's ridiculous." Why was I even arguing with him about this when I just said ten minutes ago, I'd never set them up?

"Come to the Dinner with me."

"God no. And before you open your mouth again, I don't have time for it anyway, I have too much work to get done along with dealing with you." I pushed my finger into his chest.

He was unaffected. Each notch my anger rose, his composure remained stagnant. "What's the point of going to Townsen and living in London if you're not going to experience it?"

"You don't get it."

"Adelaide!" Mia called. "You're good now, she left."

I scrambled to get up, pushing off his chest and brushing the dust off my knees. I couldn't believe neither of us realized the background noise of their voices had stopped.

He stood up after me, but I was already taking a seat at the table. "Don't talk to me unless you have a question about the project, or I'll delete your slideshow."

"Are you going to the Dinner Saturday night?" James asked.

"Not you too," I groaned.

"Have something against food and dancing?" he responded.

"Love food, despite the questionable cuisine they offer on campus, and I love a good dance. I just don't have time," I emphasized, feeling like a malfunctioning parrot who couldn't figure out how to say anything else.

The final two weeks of September, I had gathered a rhythm. I figured how to get to my classes without counting the number of hallways I turned down. On the days I wasn't tutoring Dorian, I was working at the bookstore or staying in the library until it closed at 11 p.m. to work on assignments. On the mornings I didn't have an 8 a.m., I went for a run or prepared my dinner for that night.

Class, work, homework. Class, homework, tutor, work. Run, class, homework, class, homework.

Somewhere in between there also included: pretending that Dorian wasn't quietly looking at me from behind his laptop during tutoring, and shooing Maureen's cat out of our apartment back to its home next door.

I shifted my bag on my shoulder as James and I approached Westminster Abbey, Big Ben coming into view. I wasn't sure how I still had air left after seeing this view so often. Each time the face of the clock adapted to the moon's glow, it genuinely pulled wisps of air from my diaphragm. It was so beautiful. A piece of art pulled straight from a postcard piercing the night sky.

Green leaves were beginning to collect on the sidewalks. They crunched and scraped against the cement as foot traffic moved through. The first days of October had no effect on the color yet. But the streets were littered with people in peacoats and long belted jackets.

"Adelaide, this is a Townsen tradition, you can't miss it. Clear your calendar, put your reads to the side, close your door so the neighbor's cat doesn't get it, and shelf the self-improvement podcasts for a night," he reasoned.

"You're starting to sound like Dorian. No wonder you two are friends," I commented with a chip in my mouth.

A smile pulled on his lips. "He's dramatic, we have a good time. Think about the networking," he nudged my arm.

I pursed my lips. "You're good. I'll think about it."

We sidestepped a woman in the middle of the sidewalk who bent down to pick up her dog. James grabbed my arm, pulling me to his side before a bicyclist could drive straight into me.

I exhaled in relief. "That was close." I felt my bag to make sure everything was still there.

"They don't have cycle lanes in your city?" he asked concerningly.

"Most of the time they're an after-thought," I winced. "I'll be staying on the sidewalk from now on." I looked down where his hand was still around my elbow. He followed my gaze, a strand of silver hair falling forward. It contrasted his dark brows and lashes but complemented his lighter skin. It wasn't cut neatly like Dorian's. It was grown out, reaching the middle of his neck, waves curling around his ears, almost like a fairy's.

He let go of my elbow, stuffing his hand into his pocket. "Fortunately, we're here so we don't need to worry about anymore cyclists. I'll grab the tickets. Want to find us a seat?"

I saluted him with a chip in my mouth and turned. The park beside Westminster Abbey was almost completely covered by felt blankets and crossed legs. Everyone faced the Abbey, where a large screen was propped up. I could've watched a movie on my laptop for our class assignment tonight, but it was hard to say no to James's outdoor film idea. Especially when I mentioned it to Mia. Who then mentioned it to Sabrina. Who I could see sitting at the back of the lawn on a pink gingham blanket.

"Over here!" Sabrina sat up on her knees, waving her hand.

"Sorry, excuse me, sorry, thank you, excuse me." I finally dropped onto the blanket without stepping on any legs or dogs.

"Where's James?" Mia asked, pushing up on the palm of her hand and swiveling her gaze.

"Hi, Mia! I had a lovely day, thanks for asking, what about you?" I said.

"He's still going to sit with us, right?" she asked.

I leaned backward to see Brina's reaction.

She's crazy, Sabrina mouthed.

I know, I mouthed back.

"He's coming! He's coming!" She smacked my arm.

I rubbed my arm. "You're *insane*," I whispered.

"*No*, I just want to be able to go home during Christmas break and tell each one of my cousins to suck it because I got a British boyfriend," she spoke with a frightening amount of determination.

Sabrina looked at me in fear.

I turned and threw my arm in the air to catch James's attention. He stepped over everyone's extended legs with much more grace than I had before sitting beside me.

"It's nice to meet you both." He leaned over me to extend his hand to Mia and then Sabrina.

They both responded with some iteration of *nice to meet you too*, paired with a gawking look from Brina and a wide smile from Mia.

Well then. "How much were the tickets? I can—" I reached for my wallet.

"It's fine, I dragged you all the way out here," he shook his head. "You haven't seen *Dirty Dancing* anyways."

"A crime in itself," Mia interjected.

"Exactly," he agreed. "Now you're stuck with this memory forever, knowing that we saw it together."

"Well thank you, I appreciate it." I bumped my shoulder against his.

Being around James was easy. Settling into his *hellos* and listening to his melodic voice was easy. We only talked once a week, but it was never not full of laughs.

I knew about the books he was in the middle of reading, how he made his tea, his plan to work in publishing after university, how Dorian had dared him to dye his hair platinum years ago and hadn't stopped since. I even knew the chips he brought to campus every day.

"Chip?" I angled the bag of elbow macaroni-shaped chips toward him.

"*Crisp*," he corrected me, putting his hand in the bag. "You're starting to sound like a tourist."

Brina leaned over Mia to grab a chip. "I've tried, she's hopeless," she added on.

"We're going to add that to the list of things you need to work on. Townsen traditions first." He took another chip. "You must be going Saturday." He looked to Brina, but her eyes were wide with confusion. "Unless you're new to Townsen too ..." He hesitated.

"No, I just tend to avoid social gatherings." She smiled awkwardly.

"Free food guys, come *on*," he said it like it pained him. "It's my favorite event, you're all coming then." He nudged my shoulder as if to threaten me, but it only made me laugh.

An echo of *Shhhs* ended our conversation. The gray screen at the front of the lawn sparked to life singing "Big Girls Don't Cry" as a car flew down the highway.

The sky's deep pink glow quickly shifted to a midnight blue. My head fell back. The one thing I missed that London couldn't offer was the stars. My mom used to look out the kitchen window after cooking dinner to point out the constellations in the sky. She had an easier time remembering the stars than the street names in town.

"*Addy.*"

I flicked my gaze to Sabrina. She gestured for me to lean over behind Mia.

"I didn't realize that the James in your class was James Breyer," she whispered with wide eyes.

I stared at her, waiting for what that was supposed to mean.

"James Breyer—Dorian Blackwood's friend!"

My heart lurched. Physically threw itself against my chest as if someone directed a confetti cannon at my eyes. Except this was the worst surprise ever.

"They're always seen together at pubs and events. Their families even holiday together," she explained. "They're practically brothers. It's well known that he's Dorian's closest friend. If James is going Saturday, Dorian might be too. We *have* to go."

"I don't know, I have a lot to get done. Why don't you and Mia go? I can even help you get ready beforehand. It'll be like I'm going with you! Getting ready is the best part anyway," I tried to argue my case. I could not be in the same room as Sabrina and Dorian, at the same time, *again*. That was like putting a candle in a ballroom with gunpowder and waiting to see who tipped the candle over first. No matter what, the night would end in some type of bonfire.

"You have to come; you never stop working. I missed out on so many of your and Mia's outings. This is the only time all three of us will be in university together. This could be our only chance," she pleaded.

There was an anxious puttering in my stomach. It was split in half, pulling me in two different directions. One was urging me to stand my ground and say no. To stay away from Dorian and get my work done.

The other was telling me to please my friend so that she wouldn't grow to resent me. It was rash. An irresponsible decision. But the idea of letting her down more than I already had made me sick. I didn't have anyone else.

So I said, "Alright."

10

Don't Get Competitive — Dorian

"Summer away make you rusty?" James asked as he hit the ball to my side of the court. "They do have tennis courts abroad."

The force of the ball hitting my racket went up my arm and down my torso as I hit it back to his side.

"Oh really?" I winked as I watched it sail past him satisfyingly. His racket slumped at his side.

"I stand corrected." He jogged to the fence where the courts divided us from the students practicing on the football fields.

We used to play tennis in secondary school and even during sixth form. We probably could've played on the university team, but James had no interest. He was more dedicated to a career in journalism, and it wouldn't be worth playing if he wasn't there. We had to fight for time to play between my trips abroad, his coursework, and now, the jacket-wearing weather the autumn would bring in the coming weeks.

He grabbed the ball and bounced it off the court before tossing it high and thwacking it to my side. The *whack* echoed through the acres, behind the academic buildings. I waited for the ball to bounce off the ground before I took a few quick steps backward to slice my racket under it and send it back him.

"I heard you met Adelaide," I mentioned in a brief breath.

"You did?" His gaze jumped from the ball to me, almost missing the ball. *Almost.*

Whack. Back to me.

"At least that's what the chip I planted in the back of your head that night you got pissed had recorded," I responded.

Thump. Back to him.

"Is that what that weird ringing noise is when I wash my hair?" He touched the back of his head for comedic effect.

I laughed. "Adelaide mentioned it in passing the other day."

"What'd she say?" he asked.

"Just that you guys have class together. She thought it was odd I didn't already know."

"Do you think it's odd?"

"I'm just surprised you hadn't mentioned it."

"I can start mentioning it, but it felt like I already knew her based on everything you've said about her. We did go to Westminster's outdoor movie last night for a class assignment though. Her roommates came too."

"How was that?" I grunted, rushing toward the net to sweep my racquet under the ball. I backed up as he rushed forward to do the same.

"Good," he exhaled.

"That's good," I nodded. "She's fun to be around, isn't she?"

The side of his mouth kicked up as he hit a forehand. "She is. She always makes me laugh. She's really pretty too."

Thwack. "She is," I exhaled. "And smart. She's really smart. The way she always comes up with these witty responses when we argue is concerningly invigorating."

"We don't really argue," he said, hitting another forehand.

The ball hit the court behind me. "Really?" I asked, letting it roll further back.

"Maybe it's just a testament to how comfortable she is around you," he offered, walking forward to the net. *If comfortable was a synonym for exasperated.* "How's that project going?"

"We only just started on it. For all I know I'll still fail out of the class."

"She wouldn't let you fail."

"You're probably right. She's too competitive for that," I said.

"Are you worried about it at all?"

"Being around Adelaide?"

"No, failing."

"No, I'll make it work. I'm not looking to graduate top of class or anything, I just need the degree to satisfy my mum. Once that's done, then I can focus on art."

"The Blackwood Gallery," he said, shaping out a sign with his hands.

I laughed, pulling the bottom of my shirt up to wipe my forehead. "And then James Breyer can write about all the young artists we're showcasing."

"Gotta get through the semester first."

11

*Don't Get Caught in the Rain, It's Much
Too Romantic — Adelaide*

Only five minutes into book club and Jane already spilled red wine
on the carpet, Evelyn provided points on why her book on the
creation of the British Flag should be the October read (*again*),
Lottie shared too much about her daughter's romantic life, and
Beatrice realized she'd been reading the wrong book.

"You said *Gonzo Girl!*" Beatrice argued, holding her copy of
Gonzo Girl up.

"No, you numpty, I said *Gone Girl!*" Dotty responded.

"I even put it on the e-invites," Iris reminded her.

Beatrice rolled her eyes and dropped the book into her bag.

"Not like we were going to talk about the book much
anyways." Cora pulled her shawl tight around her shoulders and
took a long sip of wine, eyes to the ceiling.

I pressed my lips together to keep from laughing. The few
customers that walked in and browsed the aisles gave the book
club a look. Some smiled. Some questioned the wine on the
carpet.

The first Friday of the month was easily one of my favorites.
Iris, Dotty, and their five friends, all in their 70s, drank wine, ate

Liana Cincotti

slices of cheese, and pretended to talk about a book for two hours.

I'd join the gossip circle if it weren't for the number of customers walking in and Dorian in the back working on his project.

The customers were an easy excuse to sit out here. My face was hot from him glancing at me so often.

"I should sit at the desk since Iris and Dotty are busy. Just come get me if you need help," I had said in a rush, pooling everything into my arms and leaving the backroom as he stared at me with confusion.

I needed to focus.

The research for International Business paper: halfway done.

Slide deck for the Consumer Behavior week six assignment: done.

Dress for tomorrow's dinner: done if it weren't for this damn seam.

This was the result of wearing my good dresses to the pubs with Mia. A broken zipper, a torn seam, and the smell of the pizza we'd get on our way back. I handled the broken zipper, scrubbed out the pizza smell, but I was losing my patience on the seam. The material was just so slipp—*ouch*. I yanked my thumb away from the needle, bringing it to my lips.

"Addy darling, what are you doing?" Jane asked. Tight curls of salt and pepper bounced as she leaned forward with intrigue.

I lifted my head. All seven women were watching me.

"Are you sewing a dress?" Cora questioned.

"Just fixing a hole." I smiled, holding the fabric up.

"She has the Townsen Dinner tomorrow," Iris explained.

"Oh, how fun!" Lottie smiled.

"Come sit with us," Jane waved me over.

"But the customers—"

Dotty shooed the words away. "I'll close the store then." She clapped as if to say *problem taken care of*, getting up to flip the door sign.

"No, you don't have to—"

"Bring the dress over, I'll take care of it," Evelyn ordered, putting her reading glasses on. "Don't argue with me, come here."

"Thank you," I responded in an apologetic manner, taking a seat in the plaid upholstered couch between her and Cora's ginger bob.

"Your mother didn't send you here with any other dresses?" Jane asked, her sequenced cardigan swaying forward as she reached for a slice of cheese on the centered coffee table.

My stomach twisted. *Your mother.* It was easier to say, "I guess she didn't think about it," than to explain that we hadn't spoken in over five years.

Iris and Dotty shared a meaningful glance. I didn't talk about my mother, or my father, but I wouldn't have been surprised if Mia or Sabrina filled them in enough.

"Addy actually lives with her aunt," Iris explained.

"Oh," Jane said, looking regretful. "Well, that's nice. What's your aunt like?"

Quiet. Stoic. Possessed by conversing in a monotone voice. "She's nice. She works at a bank. Lives by herself."

"Have you spoken to her recently?"

Not since I started college three years ago. "We're not very close," I shrugged with a closed lip smile.

Iris came to my rescue. "Addy's been doing so well in class that another student asked her for help with his project."

Definitely not a rescue.

Liana Cincotti

I threw my hand over my face, almost poking myself in the eye. Out of all the topics this woman could've picked, she went straight for the jugular. The result of telling gossip to your romance-obsessed boss.

"Oh my, that's quite a compliment!" Lottie's long face turned up in a smile, making her pearl earrings perk up.

"What's the project on?" Evelyn asked as she pulled the needle through the fabric.

"Putting together a social media marketing campaign for a company that's lacking online branding."

Beatrice raised her glass. "You lost me at social."

"Wait, did you say *he*?" Lottie crossed her legs and leaned forward. Her gaze swung from Iris to me.

Iris began to open her mouth.

Oh *shit*.

She turned to glance at the back door where I left Dorian. I sat up urgently to stop the stampede she was about to create toward the backroom. "He's just another student in my—"

The back door swung open on its own. All eyes shot to the creak of the wood.

"Hey, I had a question about—" Dorian stopped. His laptop open in his arms and his lips parted. His hair was ruffled, like he was twisting strands in thought before walking out. He shut the laptop abruptly. "Sorry, I didn't realize I was interrupting. I'll just—"

"No, no, no! Stay!" the older women protested and cooed.

I slowly shook my head. *No.*

What am I supposed to do? his wide eyes said.

I scowled as he succumbed, moving closer to our circle.

"Is this the student you're helping?" Beatrice asked. Everyone seemed to move forward in their seats. I pinched the bridge of my nose.

His brow arched in curiosity. *Talking about me, huh?*

I rolled my eyes. "Yes. This is Dorian."

"You didn't mention he was handsome," Cora whispered conspicuously.

He bit his lip, catching a laugh before it could escape.

"Are you two dating?" Lottie dug for more information.

"No!" I interjected.

"Leave the poor things alone," Dotty attempted to quiet them down.

"Why aren't you two dating?" Evelyn asked, knotting the end of the thread.

"Because we're not interested in each other like that," I blurted out.

He bit the inside of his cheek, crossing his arms. *Oh really?*

"That can't be possible," Evelyn shook the idea away. "Isn't she pretty?" she asked Dorian.

"She is very pretty." He nodded. His eyes met mine. It was so earnest that it was painful to absorb. Brown orbs swirling with a palette of golden watercolors that threatened to pull me in.

"And isn't she smart?"

"Incredibly smart." He nodded. I couldn't read his face. It was quiet but full of thought. A closed book full of wisdom written in foreign languages, disguised with a simple cover. Only, his face was never simple.

"Well, why don't you ask her out!" Evelyn argued.

I lost hold of his gaze. He turned to Evelyn. "I have. Unfortunately, *she's* uninterested in *me.*"

Oh.

He had rosy cheeks, the color of the strawberry jam I had added to my buttered scone that morning. I looked down at my lap and fiddled with my ring.

The women gasped as if he had told them he was cheated on by his sixth wife and was left without a home and prospects. Theatrical as usual.

"But she's willing to tutor me, so I'll take whatever she offers."

My spine was taut like the Union flags pulled across Regent Street. But my legs were a pool of useless muscles, muddled by unfamiliar emotions. The more he spoke, the more I questioned if this charming act was habitual … or if it was genuine.

"Alright, let's let them get on with their night. They have a party to get to tomorrow," Iris spoke up. "We have a book to discuss anyways. Well, except Beatrice."

The group—minus Beatrice—laughed.

"Here you are, darling." Evelyn handed me the dress, the seam repaired. "Have a fun time." She winked.

"I am so sorry about that," I groaned.

Never did I think I'd be apologizing to Dorian Blackwood, but here I was.

I shut the front door behind me, leaving us in the quiet of the street.

I sighed. "I probably should've mentioned the group of women that are intensely interested in everyone's personal lives. I completely forgot about book club until they were walking through the front door with a bottle of wine and a tray of cheese. I should've known the second Iris asked me if you were coming today."

He smiled as we passed under a streetlamp. No moon or stars tonight in the sky. Only gray clouds swirling around in the wind like cotton. "I'm happy I could supply the entertainment. Even if it means they'll look at me with pity each time I see them."

"They will not pity you." I shook my head.

"Oh really? Because the woman with the big earrings handed me her daughter's number." He held up a piece of crumpled paper.

I grabbed the paper from his hand to verify. "Lottie, you mischievous woman!" I shouted when I realized it was real, handing it back over. "I am *so* so sorry. That's so inappropriate."

He accepted it and threw it in a passing trash bin. "I'm flattered she thinks I'm good enough for her daughter." He laughed.

"I'll warn you the next time they come," I promised.

I opened my bag and pushed the dress in between my laptop and marketing textbook.

"Someone change their mind?" he asked, gesturing to the dress.

"What?"

"The Dinner tomorrow."

"Oh, that. Yeah, James had mentioned it. And then talked Mia and Sabrina into it. So looks like I'm going now." I brushed my hair out of my face. The wind was picking up. The trees on the sidewalks were battling, branches colliding.

He nodded understandingly. "If I knew James could've convinced you in the first place, I would've had him invite you."

"It's not like that. Sabrina was insistent on going the second she knew that *Dorian Blackwood's friend* was going," I explained, not that I needed to. But I didn't want him thinking there was something between me and James. I was serious about staying away from all things Dorian.

"Does that mean I'll get to see you?" He glanced over at me.

"From afar," I said pointedly.

"What if I happen to bump into you on the dancefloor?"

"*Dorian.*" I glared at him.

"I like it when you say my name with your cute accent. It sounds better your way." He smirked, and it was tumultuous. The boyishness charm in his cheeks was deafening. I wanted to capture it, box it up, and hang it on a keychain so I didn't have to face it again.

"Do you ever give up?"

"I don't know what—"

The rest of his sentence was cut off by a thunderous clap in the clouds. One raindrop ran down my forehead. As I wiped it away, ten raindrops replaced it. I looked up, and buckets of rain fell, painting car windows and the skin on my arms, pounding surfaces like a drum.

Our walk quickly became a run. "We're still ten blocks away and I didn't even bring my stupid umbrella!" I shouted over the sound of the rain hitting the street's pavement. I pushed my bag under my jacket. My laptop, my textbook, my *dress.*

"We're not that far!" he shouted, running beside me.

Then I felt his arm around my shoulder. "Don't touch me!"

"You're so stubborn, I'm trying to help!"

"And you're too persistent!"

Suddenly, some of the rain lessened. I looked over and found fabric blocking my left peripheral.

He was holding his jacket over my head as we ran. The rain was completely soaking his hair. Dark brown strands became black, matting themselves to his forehead.

My heart scaled my throat. I held onto the sides of his jacket to cut off the image and keep the wind from pushing it away.

"Some people like my persistence!" he argued.

"Is that what they tell you?" I yelled.

"To think I was going to ask you to dance tomorrow!"

"I told you we can't be seen together!"

"You're saying that, but do you really mean it?" he countered.

"You're the most unbearable person I've ever met!" He was *infuriating*.

The lights coming from the apartment windows lining the street were blurred. But I could still identify the leaning tree that lived outside my balcony.

As we reached the awning that stretched outside my apartment lobby, he pulled the jacket off from over my head and wrung it out. He clutched the material and squeezed, the muscles in his arms tensing. The white fabric of his T-shirt clung to each curve and sharp angle of his body. From the line of his shoulders to the dip between the muscles in his chest to his torso. It made the roman numeral tattoo on his chest poignant. Rising and fall, taking in air.

The last time I had seen that tattoo was the first time. He had been kissing my neck. Saying my name in that accent when—

"Is your dress okay?" he asked, worried, his jacket hung at his side now. He was looking at me. Waiting for me to respond. Rain running down his neck.

"What?"

"The dress, in your bag?" he wiped the moisture from his forehead.

"Oh. Oh my gosh." I swiped the leather of the bag, watching

the water jump off before slipping my hand inside. I exhaled. "I think it's okay. I'm sorry about your jacket. I can buy you a new one."

"I don't need a new jacket, Adelaide," he responded.

"I feel really bad," I apologized, patting down my hair that wasn't nearly as wet as his.

"I'm not worried about the jacket."

"How are you going to get home?" I asked. The rain was still coming down in full force.

"I can call someone. I'm not worried about it."

"You're sure?"

"Goodnight, Adelaide. I'll see you tomorrow. From afar."

From afar. That's what I asked for. So why did I feel like a hollowed out tree?

12

*Don't Stand Near Ponds, Especially During
Arguments* — *Adelaide*

It was raining, again. Usually, I'd be excited to have London greet me at night with a patter on my window like an imaginary Romeo.

I enjoyed watching everyone stop in the middle of their routes to collectively swing their umbrellas up over their heads and then continue on, like a snippet from a musical.

Birds bathed in the puddles. Trees became as vibrant as the ones in watercolor paintings. Even the Thames got a chance to join in on the city's noise.

But it was all ruined now. And *right* as the rain was so close to becoming a friend. How unfortunate.

I slipped on my dress and watched the rain tug on my tree outside, all I could think of was Dorian last night.

Dorian's stubbornness. Dorian's smirk. Dorian's wet hair. Dorian's jacket over my head. Dorian's soaked shirt. It completely tarnished the rain.

The curtain rods screeched as I pulled the drapes forward to cover the outside. *Focus.* I zipped up the back of the cocktail dress and dragged my tights over my legs. The sheer black fabric was sprinkled in tiny crystals that I had glued on years ago during

Christmas break after seeing a similar pair in *Vogue*.

I had stolen the tights from my mother's closet before she had left. For the first few years, it was difficult to look at them. To see something that was hers. Something she had worn when she was happy. A piece from her Before.

But sometimes it was easier to pretend that I had this great mother who left me garments as a token rather than a woman who up and left her daughter because I reminded her too much of her failed family.

The first time I wore them, my aunt had stared a second too long. She knew. Yet, she hadn't said anything. As per usual.

It felt like bad luck to wear them now.

Who would've thought the Townsen Dinner took place on campus every year? Well, not me. The school was capable of affording Buckingham Palace to rent if they wanted to (unlikely that was a legal option). But the grounds did have a magical touch to them at night that I hadn't experienced.

Anytime I was on campus late, it was to leave the library. And I didn't go prancing through the gardens after. But walking through them now, I wish I had.

The majority of the space behind campus was clean-cut lawn decorated with iron tables, chairs, and trees. It simply looked like a vast forest where fairies took advantage of the seating, only lit by the small sconces attached to the school's verandas. A werewolf or Mr. Darcy wearing a billowing coat could pop out at any moment.

"The Dinner happens in there." Sabrina pointed to the one lone stone building across the grounds. A pawn set apart from its chess pieces. "It's designated for events and other university-hosted things."

As the main campus's veranda ended, I swung my umbrella over our heads as we stepped onto the pavers stamped into the grass, like lily pads in a pond. My feet wobbled in my heels.

We followed the stream of students, filing into the building. Many of whom wore designer dresses. Archival pieces. Right off-the-runway pieces.

"Is that a chandelier?" Mia whispered, tilting her head back as we entered the lobby. Her box braids dipped down her ivory dress, a pearlescent hairclip twinkling.

"That's a chandelier," I responded, watching the grandiose gems refract light off the walls. "Really accentuates the spiral staircase, don't you think?"

Mia spoke in a terrible British accent, "I wouldn't go that far. The staircase is only made of a maple wood, nothing tasteful like a Parisian marble."

"Oh, a Parisian marble you say?" I twirled my fake mustache.

"*Guys*," Sabrina glared at us as she checked our coats at the desk.

"Her words are divisive. But her eyes are saying we're hilarious," I told Mia.

"Americans." Sabrina's hair bobbed as she shook her head.

Leaving our coats, we walked past the desk and up the spiral staircase. Sabrina's face quieted as we joined the group of luscious fabrics and tapping heels. Her neck arched every time a male with brown hair popped up in front of us.

"Do you think Dorian's already here?" she fretted.

"I'm not sure. But we'll have fun either way." I reached for her hand and squeezed as we reached the second floor.

"A ballroom with floor-to-ceiling windows. I think the

chandelier just became less impressive," I commented, taking in the view.

The ballroom was shaped like a half-moon, four long tables satisfying the back of the room along the windows. They were draped with black tablecloths and crystal flatware. At the front of the space, students were mingling, some even dancing to a small group of musicians playing violins and cellos.

"Are we sure we're in the right place?" I asked. "I knew Townsen events were ... lavish. But it feels like we've entered some Secret Student Society and they're going to chop off a piece of our hair for admittance."

"Oh, we're in the right place. I just saw Brad from Psychology II picking something out of his teeth," Mia pointed to Brad, who was indeed trying to get something out of his teeth.

"I need tea," Sabrina exhaled, going straight to a side table that housed a tea dispenser and porcelain teacups. I stood back at the edge of the entry way as Mia followed her for the cucumber sandwiches.

Where was he?

I didn't *want* him to be here. I wanted tonight to be easy. Easy would be fantastic. Chat with my friends, eat some sad excuse for a pie, convince someone's affluential, spoiled college kid that I was social yet professional enough to work for their CEO of a mother when I graduated. Not keep a third eye on Dorian all night.

But I didn't catch any left dimples or even a head of platinum hair. Most of the men wore the same attire: black dress pants that matched their black suit jackets with white button-downs underneath.

Then someone moved, and there was Dorian.

I saw the silver rings on his fingers first, and the crease of his dark brow next. His navy blue jacket was off, thrown over a chair somewhere. Shirt sleeves rolled up, revealing two tattoos. His smile was abundant. A painting of joy. His eyes were closed with heavy laughter. Strands of hair fell forward like branches as James held onto his arm trying to finish a story. It was how I found him the night we met, but wildly different in so many ways.

I hadn't realized how long I had been staring until his laugh ceased and his gaze caught me like an arrow to the chest.

Shit. Should I wave? Turn around and pretend like I hadn't been staring? The dinosaur trick? Maybe I—

His face bloomed into something earnest. I was expecting discomfort. A sweeping glance in the opposite direction. But he stared right back at me. Silver rings rubbed at the side of his neck.

Placing a hand in his pocket, I watched as his lips mouthed one word: *Wow.*

I shook my head, as if to say, *Do you ever stop?*

He rolled his tongue in disbelief. *You don't believe me?*

I know you.

His brows rose. *Really?*

Yup.

Maybe I know you.

Do you? I bit the inside of my cheek.

He tapped his watch. *You're already ready to leave.*

I pressed my lips together. *Point taken.*

He hid a smile. The lines beside his lips softened like butter as his smile dropped altogether.

Opening his mouth, I read the words he shaped out.

You look beautiful.

My heart thudded against my chest.

Thank you, I mouthed back.

His face was peaceful. No crease or smirk or fidgeting. It was romantic, in theory. It seemed genuine, in theory. Being told you looked beautiful could confuse anyone. It warmed you from the inside out like a sip of mulled wine running down your throat on a night where the windows were frosted over.

But I knew Dorian. I knew men like Dorian. They chased. Caught. Relished. And then moved on.

Watching it firsthand between your parents wasn't necessary but that's where I gained my patch of honor in *Spotting Typical Men*, stitched right onto my frontal lobe.

Each student here had assisted in providing me enough evidence of that only ten minutes later when we sat down to eat. Almost every head was turned towards Dorian.

The tables around us were loud with chatter, but ours was rowdy with whispers as people peppered him with questions about his dating life.

Princesses, models, actresses. There wasn't a category we hadn't touched on. New files were opening and labeling themselves in my brain the more everyone spoke.

So much for the students being academic titans that I would have to fight off with my planner and overheated laptop.

A phone rang and everyone quieted. I immediately caught strands of dark hair falling forward in my peripheral.

Dorian leaned over to whisper something in James's ear. James said something with a disapproving look before Dorian stood and walked out of the room on a call. Everyone stared at the empty seat and glanced at James.

"You think he'll come back, right? The dancing hasn't even begun yet," Sabrina asked, worry strung across her brow.

"I'm sure it's just a quick call," Mia assured her.

"It's probably Victoria," a girl across from us—Amber, I think—whispered.

"Who's Victoria?" another girl asked.

"She's Dorian's girlfriend," she responded.

The files I had been building in my head suddenly burst from their cabinets. A *girlfriend?*

Sabrina's fork clanked against her plate.

"What's her name?" Mia sat forward instantly.

"Victoria Sutton. Her and Dorian have been off and on for years," Amber took a loud slurp from her straw. "If he hasn't been seen with anyone, then he's probably with her again."

Sabrina was either swaying beside me or my vision was blurring around the edges from the built-up resentment uncurling behind my eyes.

I needed to slow down on the mulled wine.

I immediately pulled out my phone and began typing Victoria's name into—

"No phones." My heart caught in my throat as a man in a tweed suit appeared out of nowhere, plucking my phone away.

"Excuse me?" I twisted in my seat, clutching the back of my chair.

"We have a no phone policy at Townsen Events." His voice dragged low as if to say *obviously*.

"Since when?"

"Since 1705 when the college was founded and phones didn't exist," he responded with a smug smile.

"I just needed to check my email." I reached for my—

He moved his hand away. "If you want to use your phone, you can go outside."

I stood up and took the phone, striding towards the doorway, down the stairs, and back outside. I was too prideful to not *not* go outside now.

Alright.

Fortunately, the rain had come to a halt. But it had left the grass a soppy mess. Mud was kicked up over the stone path we had originally followed. Glancing at my heels, I pivoted, taking the (cleaner) path to the right, where it ventured into the trees.

Crickets chirped and slow streams of water dripped off of the leaves I passed under. The soft lull of the string music was faint as I found a small pond reflecting the light of the moon and took a seat on its neighboring bench.

The phone screen blinded me as I finished typing in *Victoria Sutton*.

Twenty-two years old. Also in her last year at Townsen University. Model. Social media star. Swore by green juice for puffy eyes.

She was pretty. Blond hair, pale skin with a bright blush to her cheeks.

I scrolled on, searching for some sort of headline that—*ah uh*. There it was: *Is Victoria Sutton Seeing Dorian Bla—*

"What are you doing?"

I jumped up and smacked my phone against my chest, clutching it tight. "Jesus, you scared me," I yelped, my throat tight.

Dorian threw his hands up. "Didn't mean to."

My shoulders fell. "What are you doing out here?"

"I had a call," he responded. "What are *you* doing out here?"

"I was taking a phone call too."

"Who were you talking to?" He crossed his arms.

"My aunt."

"You said you don't talk to your aunt."

"When did I say that?"

"Last night. At the bookshop."

Shit.

He spoke again. "What are you doing outside then, and why does it involve holding your phone to your chest like a stolen bar of gold?"

I immediately dropped my hand from chest, letting my phone hang at my side. "I just needed some fresh air."

"In the muddy grass?"

"Perhaps I enjoy grass in its post-rain state. You don't know me."

A second of silence past. Another chirp of a cricket. Until Dorian's eyes darted to my phone and his hand leapt.

"What are you doing?" I shrieked, jumping backward, stunned by how close he just got—both to me and my phone, which was now in his hand.

The rich smell of sandalwood and espresso surrounded me now. Another clean garment ruined.

The phone illuminated his face. His eyes darted across the words. They scanned, read, and then stopped.

"You were looking up Victoria? Why?" he asked. There was no emotion. It was as if he served a ball to my side and simply wanted me to hit it back.

"Mia had mentioned her," I answered.

"And you care?" A crease of surprise spread across his forehead.

"No, of—"

"Don't lie." It was like my attempt at a groundstroke fell flat, underwhelming him.

I narrowed my eyes. "I'm not ly—"

"Are you jealous?"

Blood rushed to my cheeks. "Why would I be jealous?"

"Because I think you think about that night too," he said quietly.

His eyes were doing that thing again. The thing where they shot a *zing* right through my spine. They were half-closed, one foot inside of a dream. As if they were writing a stanza of Italian poetry across my lips. It made the wind against the tree branches sound like soft guitar strums.

"Can I have my phone back?" I shot my hand forward.

"Answer the question." He pulled it away, taking a step back.

I groaned in frustration. "I can't believe you've somehow convinced someone to be your *girlfriend*." I took ahold of the phone.

"Victoria?" His brows furrowed.

"No, my neighbor Maureen. *Yes, Victoria.*"

"Victoria's not my girlfriend."

"Really?"

He sighed. "It's complicated."

He sounded just like my dad. *It's complicated*, he had told me the day he left us. I was twelve. *I have to leave. You'll be better off without me.* Apparently, his new wife and newborn twin daughters weren't.

"It's really none of my business anyways now that we're talking about it. Just. Give. Me. The. *Phone!*" I pulled like a ten thousand-dollar game of tug-a-war was on the line.

But then he pulled back with twice as much strength. And suddenly the phone was no longer in my grasp, and I was screaming as my hair was thrown in front of my face and the ground left my feet, falling backwards.

The pond water was colder than London's October rain. It

split the goosebumps on my legs, piercing right through my tights. My fingers immediately curled in as water rushed up my nose. It pried at my closed mouth and eyelids, trying to get in. It *hurt* it was so cold. I was trapped. Crying. Shut inside my old room all over again, blocking my ears but the waves were still roaring. Seaweed brushed my arms with a cold graze. Wrapping its fingers around my waist and pulling—

I gasped, gulping a cloud of air. My heart pounded in my chest as I clung to Dorian. My fingers buried themselves into his soaked dress shirt, gripping onto his shoulders. The muscles that made up my throat were rattling as I tried to get steady flows of air in and out, like the frame of a building being taken by a breeze.

His voice was muffled. I couldn't make out the words. The memories were louder. His hand breached my jaw as he took my face into his hands.

This was so much worse than being together in the rain.

"Adelaide, are you alright?" he asked. His eyes were wide, marked by remnants of the pond. They searched my face, marking checkpoints as they went along. "Please tell me you're alright."

Exhale. Inhale. Exhale. "I'm fine, yes. I'm fine, I'm fine." I pushed away from him, quickly finding the edge of the pond and pulling myself out. The only thing keeping me breathing was the sight of my phone safely on the grass.

"Adelaide, wait." My skeletal system jumped each time he said my name.

The water sloshed behind me. I turned to find his chest rising and falling in a chaotic rhythm.

I wanted to scream at him. I wanted to scream at him for ruining my dress and causing me to raise my voice an octave and making me question my feelings and I *so badly* wanted to shove him back into the water.

But I couldn't. Because all I could focus on was the absolute disarray in which his shirt was in because it was barely there. A transparent cloth stuck against his chest and abdomen from the water.

Suddenly, I was back in that night where I was pulling his shirt off. Another vexing reminder of what I was trying to forget. Another memento for me to deal with when I tried to fall asleep tonight, or saw him in class Monday, or watched Hugh Grant come out of the lake in *Bridget Jones's Diary* with a cigarette in his mouth.

I'd never watch that movie again.

I spun away. "I need to go."

"But—"

"Adelaide!" an urgent shout came, but in the opposite direction.

Mia. She rushed forward and then came to an abrupt stop, taking my wet appearance in. And taking in Dorian's a bit longer. "What happened to—"

I held my hand up. "We'll talk about it later. What's wrong?"

"It's Sabrina."

13

Don't Forget That There Are Eyes Everywhere — Adelaide

My mother used to play sitcoms or romance movies whenever she was home. It didn't matter if she was cleaning the kitchen, cooking dinner, blow drying her hair, or lining up her vintage watches on her nightstand to shine.

The TV would always display a cozy, suburban home, a studio apartment in the West Village, or a cottage nestled in the English Countryside, frosted with snow. The common denominator was that it was anywhere but here, in our stubby house where she and my father had made an attempt at the Dream Life. Buy a house with green shutters, get married in a church, and have a kid that'll look exactly like the mother but claim the last name of the father.

The longer I watched the suburban homes and cottages, the more I understood why she put them on. Those lives seemed so...peaceful. It didn't matter if your fashion magazine job was on the line or if the surprise twin sister you met at camp switched places with you. Because by the end, everyone was happy. We were missing that part of the equation.

When my parents fought, I'd slip out the window and run down the street to the park and sit in the wood chips with one of

Mom's fashion magazines. Pictures of glass perfume, lipstick bottles, leather purses, and voluminous dresses. I'd tear them all out and add them to the cork board above my bed.

Running away had a bad reputation. But sometimes, it was the only option. It offered me solace. Privacy.

That was a long time ago. Now, I was in my own personal sitcom, living in a cozy apartment in London. A gold-framed cork board branded with all of my favorite *The New Yorker* articles, 90s fashion photoshoots, Carolyn Bessette Kennedy's stylish candids, vintage watches, and postcards from all the English cities we explored over the summer. Just a step away from my version of the Dream Life.

But as wonderful as the apartment was, the walls were still thin. Thin enough that I could hear every wet sigh Sabrina let out last night. As well as each instance she rewound *The Notebook* before the old couple died.

From down the hall.

Several paces away.

The moment a bird chirped at 5:01 a.m., I shot out of bed and grabbed my sneakers. Two and a half miles in and Kensington Park Road's Victorian townhouses appeared as a slab of blurry white paint in my peripheral. The air was fresh. Brisk. Tugging at the pumpkin-orange and barn-red leaves on the trees. It heightened the smell of the crates of fresh flowers at Andy's Flower Shop down the block.

It was a wave of relief compared to the past nine hours.

The look on Dorian's face as I left him by the pond still pulled at a muscle in my chest. He was painted in disbelief. Arms slouched at his sides and brows pushed together in the center. As if *I* had done something wrong. As if *I* was the one who had waltzed right up to him, ignoring our rule to avoid one another. As if *I* had pushed him into the water.

I couldn't believe that society had been pushing this "women are confusing" agenda for so long when men like this existed. What a bunch of nonsense. All we had left was Marty.

I waved to Marty across the street. He waved back as I waited for the black cabs, cyclists, and cherry red buses to pass.

The smiling old man sat on the bench outside Big Ben's Bakery every Sunday morning with a croissant spewing chocolate like a tiny volcano. Hail could be falling from the sky while termites ate the seat around him, and he'd still be smiling.

I wanted to be like Marty. Rosy cheeks, a croissant in my hand, and zero thoughts about Dorian.

The one positive thing about yesterday was Sabrina getting a glimpse into who Dorian was: unavailable and narcissistic. Maybe not the latter but definitely the former.

When Mia had found me in a moister state than I had been previously, she dragged me inside where Brina was crying in the bathroom.

"He really does have a girlfriend." She had choked out the words, holding up her phone with a picture of Dorian kissing the blond I had just researched myself. It even made me choke.

"We don't know that," Mia reassured her.

"They're kissing!" she wailed, shaking her phone. My heart ached.

"Let's get you home," I said, taking her phone and tucking my arm under her shoulder, Mia followed the same movement.

"Whyareyouallwet?" she murmured, breaking up the emotion in her throat as we left the bathroom and stepped back onto the stone path outside.

"I saw a duck in the pond and thought it'd be fun to see if they acted differently from the ones in the Charles River."

She cracked a smile. A sunrise of a face breaking the ocean line. "Doesn't sound like a conducive environment for research since you interrupted their space. What'd you find?"

"I found that they react the same way when a tiny one tried to bite me. British animals obtain the same amount of politeness as my deli guy back home."

She laughed. "What actually happened to you?"

"I'll tell you another time." *When we're old and gray and you've forgotten who Dorian is.*

Her smile fizzled out once we returned to the apartment and she spotted my watch on the coffee table that "looked exactly like the one Dorian had worn that one time in—" The rest of the words became unrecognizable from the mixture of her accent and the tears.

We curled up on the couch—after I moved my watch—and wrapped a single blanket around us as if we were trying to test glow-in-the-dark bracelets, putting on the least romantic film society has ever watched.

Fast & Furious.

Brina was nodding off within the first half hour of the film, her cheek pressing into my shoulder. Mia held her head up as I scooted out from under her, replacing the space with a pillow. She slipped the bobby pins out of her hair while I worked on her mascara with a cotton ball.

She must've woken up and returned to her bed around 1 a.m. because that's when I heard, *He sent you letters, Allie!*

I folded my pillow around my head like a half-open sushi roll. *Come on, Sabrina. He's just a guy.*

I wanted her to be happy. But watching her cry over someone like Dorian was ... bittersweet. It pulled me away from the present and threw me into the past.

It was my mother all over again. Hours spent alone in her room. Porcelain dishware designated for guests collected dust. Even the TV collected dust. I hadn't seen any new sitcoms or romance films that came out until I was living at my aunt's.

Slowly, the photos of Dad disappeared from the fridge. Childhood pictures were suddenly missing faces. It was as if a murder had been solved and all the evidence was being disposed of. The smell of sawdust that lived in his clothes had dissipated from his closet.

He had ruined her life. And she, consequently, had ruined mine.

I wanted to grab her by the shoulders and shake her. *You're wasting your time. This will never do you any good.*

Sabrina was better off getting over him now. Today's pain would save her a lifetime of trauma.

I wiped the sweat from my forehead before I jogged across the street to Big Ben's Bakery.

"How are you doing, Marty?" I held my hand up to shield the rising sun.

"Enjoying this lovely Sunday morning with my croissant." He leaned back into the bench, laying a hand over his belly and raising the pastry as the sun warmed his face. "This is earlier than your usual time, ain't it?" He flicked his wrist to check his watch. "Early night?"

I massaged a muscle in my neck. "Late actually."

"Studying?"

I laughed. "For once, I wish. How's your itinerary going?

You're back to New York next week, right?"

"Sadly. Got to get back home to the cat and the business. I've only made it through about half my list though." He sat up to pull a folded piece of paper out of his pocket before handing it to me.

It was a page from a notepad with *Marty's Bagels* printed at the header. About six things at the top of the list were crossed out. The rest of the itinerary read:

- *Go on the London Eye*
- *Send a postcard back home*
- *Try something new*
- *Buy a shirt with the UK flag on it*
- *Use a telephone booth*
- *Kiss a Brit*

That last one seemed like something I shouldn't have seen.

"You still did a lot. I heard the telephone booths are really dirty anyways, so I don't think you're missing out," I said, trying to make him feel better as I put it back in his hand.

"That's the city for ya. There's an unhygienic downside to everything." He took a bite of his croissant, flakes sticking to his scrubby facial hair, watching a double-decker drive by. "You know what, why don't you keep this."

"The list?" The paper somehow back in my palm.

"Finish it for me. Let me know if the telephone booths are as gross as they say."

"You should keep this. Frame it until you come back to London," I urged.

He pointed his croissant at me. "It's your list now. Think of it as a piece of me so that you don't forget to visit my shop in New

York. Deal?"

"Deal." I smiled. "See you in New York, Marty. Have a safe flight home." I opened the door to the bakery. The bell chimed and wafts of butter and melted chocolate rushed forward.

"Make sure to write me when you've done everything!" he shouted.

"Fine!" I laughed as the door swung shut behind me.

"Adelaide?" A warm English accent startled me.

I turned in line and found—"Professor Emmerson?"

She waved me over before lifting a teacup to her lips and cozying into her corner table. A toasted blueberry muffin sat on her plate.

I almost pointed to myself. *You mean me?* But, yup, she was looking right at me. I left the order line.

"Sit, sit," she insisted.

I sat down in shock. She must've had a hundred students across all of her classes, at least. And we'd only spoken once: when I asked for extra credit during week two as a *just in case*. Other than that, I was just a raised hand that was never called on.

"I didn't mean to frighten you. I had saw you through the window talking to that gentleman. I never see anyone I know this early, let alone one of my students." Her cheeks wrinkled as she set her teacup down. The *clink* was muffled by the abundance of people ordering at the counter behind us.

"That was Marty. I usually come closer to seven, but he's been here every time. This was his last Sunday before returning to New York," I explained.

I folded and unfolded my hands in my lap. This couldn't have been worse timing. I was wearing a raggedy T-shirt that was three sizes too big, and I was ninety percent sure that there were two

Liana Cincotti

circles of sweat underneath my sleeves. I was not an angelic runner. Whereas she looked straight out of a home design magazine with a blue and white striped blouse, gold bangles on her wrists, and pink blush on her cheeks.

"I'm happy you're getting to know people, even if they're New Yorkers." She laughed with the vibrancy of a hydrangea bush. "It can be difficult to adjust being abroad away from family. Many of the students struggle with it the first month."

Couldn't have been easier, actually.

"It hasn't been too bad of an adjustment," I smiled, hoping that it sounded like, *I'm malleable. I can adjust to anything! Like a person necessary for an internship of someone you may know.*

"Something about that doesn't surprise me. The work you've been passing in has been exceptional, to say the least. Especially for a transfer student. I've been teaching some of the same students since they entered as first years and they've never grown. It's no surprise that you're here on a full scholarship. You work very hard. " She waved her finger the same way she did in class during presentations to make sure everyone was paying attention.

My chest filled like a balloon. Instead of helium or confetti though, it was packed with pride. "Thank you so much. The class means a lot to me."

"I can tell. I only imagine what you'll accomplish after graduation." She stabbed the muffin with her fork and raised it to her mouth. But she paused. "If you ever need a recommendation, I'd be more than happy to write you one."

The chair almost collapsed beneath me. "That would be incredible, thank you," I responded, trying my best not to sound like I just had my Sylvie Emmerson Fan Club dream come to life.

"Of course. Companies need marketers with an attention to

detail and work ethic like yours." She took a bite of the muffin and swallowed. "How have the rest of your classes been? Oh my, that bad?"

I pressed my lips together trying not to laugh. "It's manageable."

"Don't tell me my class is the worst," she asked, dreading the answer based on the *V* at the center of her eyebrows.

"No, no! Not at all." Her assignments were the sum of everything I loved about marketing. Branding. Slide decks. Content creation. Campaign brainstorming. The only downside was doing it all over again with Dorian. "Professor Dover's hundred-page assignment haunts me while I sleep."

"Oh no, you have Professor Dover?" She whistled. "*The Doom Paper* as the students call it. He assigns it every semester. I wouldn't worry though. You'll do just fine," she reassured me.

I'd feel fine when the assignment was done.

"Well, I've taken enough of your morning. I'll let you get on with the rest of your weekend. I'll see you in class tomorrow." She patted my hand, standing up and collecting her bag and a few papers.

"It was nice seeing you, Professor." I smiled.

"Enjoy the rest of your Sunday. Oh, and Ms. Adorno." She held onto the back of my chair and lowered her voice.

"Be careful about who you spend time with on campus. The Board is very … keen on how scholarship students act outside of academics. The professors are all very aware that most of the students would be perfectly comfortable if they didn't find jobs after graduation. But I know how hard you're working towards this. Who you associate yourself with can tarnish your image inside and outside the university. And you understand how important your brand is more than anyone. So I'd stay away from Mr. Blackwood if I were you."

14

"Adelaideeee."

I jolted in my seat as Mia's hand waved in front of my eyes.

"Hello there. Welcome back." She smiled as I blinked fast and hard, trying to remember why my computer was resting upside down on the table. Flipping it right side up, I was met with a blinking screen, like TV static in the 1960s.

Oh right. It had decided to ruin my life and stop working. I began randomly holding buttons down. That'd work, right?

It didn't.

"What are you doing?" she asked.

"Giving myself a five minute break."

"With your eyes closed?"

"Studies show if you take a nap for even just five minutes, it's enough to rejuvenate your creativity."

"Will that make your laptop work too?"

My eyes shot open. I huffed. "What had you been saying before? About plans?"

"Sabrina's dads invited us to a movie premiere, tomorrow night, can you believe that?" she shrieked.

"Shh, we're in a library," I warned.

The last thing I needed was for the librarian to kick us out. This was my only place of solitude for studying. Even when I was closed off in my room at the apartment with my headphones on, trying to study, I found myself giving in to watching *Strictly Come Dancing* with Brina or proofreading Mia's articles or chatting with their families on the phone during Monday night dinners when I should really be making headway on Dover's paper (as it was marked in my planner under every *Monday* in October).

She rolled on, lowering her voice just a spec. "Brina said we get to dress up and watch the actors walk the red carpet before the movie. We have to be at her parent's place for six in order to make the carpet at seven."

"When is this?" I asked.

"Tomorrow. I just said that." She gave me a disapproving glance. "Don't say—"

I squinted, preparing for the attack, leaning back in my chair. "I think I'm going to—"

"—that you're going—"

"—to have to pass." I shielded my face.

"—to pass." She sighed.

The setting sun coming through the wall-stretched windows was warm enough to put me to sleep. I could curl my arms up and use my overheated laptop as a pillow even with the intimidated look on Mia's face. Tall, gaunt trees craned for a view inside our hidden corner of the library. Their burnt orange and lemon ricotta yellow leaves were like claws trying to get at the books.

"Tomorrow is the last day of midterms and all I want to do after is read the past six Cultural Comments from *The New Yorker*, watch reality TV, stuff my face with the creamiest vanilla frappe I can find, and *sleep* before I have to do this all over again." I gestured to the calculator (for creating KPIs), stacks of papers (highlighted printed syllabi), two cups of coffee (that I still loathed) and a mutilated lip gloss tube (because I couldn't stop picking at my lips and needed to lather them in coconut goodness).

Her mouth was pressed into a line. "Is the project kicking your ass that much?"

"You really know how to comfort a friend, don't you?"

"I didn't mean it that way! But I hardly hear you say anything anymore that isn't 'planner, assignment, or SEO strategy.'"

My skin smelled like coconut as I dropped my head into my palms. "Midterm assignments have been overriding my semester-long assignments lately, so I've just had even less time than usual."

"What do you have left on your project for Sylvie? It's the project on watches, right?"

I nodded. I chose this small business that handmade watches in Scotland and engraved people's wishes on the back of the faces.

"My next step is to create content to put in the editorial calendar. I'll make some graphics, along with taking a day to go shoot photos. I'm not too worried about it, unless my decision to take some of the pictures on a disposable camera blows up in my face and the film ends up entirely blacked out. But if it goes well, then I'll end up with these perfectly vintage-like photos that'll match the timeless, elegant ambiance of the campaign. Imagine a catalog with film photos, a Bodoni italicized font, hints of beige and ice blue bordering images postcard style."

"No wonder Sylvie was so nice to you that morning. You're making the rest of us look like couch potatoes," she threw one of my erasers at my chest.

"I hope she doesn't forget about the recommendation. It'd be huge."

"Even if she did, I'm sure she'd still be *delighted if you'd ask*," she finished in a fake British accent.

"I didn't realize she sounded like the crumpled crab apple of a woman from *Snow White*."

"Are you referencing *the Evil Queen?* Did you just forget the name of the *easiest* Disney villain?"

"I am tired, woman, I told you," I argued in a hushed tone, trying not to laugh. Students sitting at the strip of tables against the windows remained stoic. No one passed us a second glance. "All I dream about anymore are spreadsheets, slideshows, drafted emails I've yet to send, and Maureen's stupid cat outside my balcony."

"Well, I wouldn't say that's *all* you dream about. Let's be honest here."

I glared at her.

"Alright, fine. We won't talk about it." She lifted her hands up in surrender. "Have you thought any more about what Sylvie said?"

"Every day. I can't stop thinking that if she knows about Dorian, then someone else must know too."

I had considered asking James about it. But that'd mean I was getting involved. And I was sticking by my rule to not get involved. Despite partially being involved.

"How would she know though? She's probably just making an assumption because you guys are in the same class, and he sits right in front of you."

"That's possible. But why wouldn't she have said something earlier then? It's the middle of October." I twisted the pearl bracelet clasped around my purse strap. "I'm nervous she saw us at the Townsen Dinner outside."

"I mean you both made quite a *splash*."

"I don't think you're funny."

"You totally do. You're just clouded with marketing jargon. Even if she did see you with him, it's not a big deal. She's obviously looking out for you."

"There was just this…tone in her voice. It was different."

"The Evil Queen different?" Her brow rose.

I threw my eraser back at her, knocking it off her shoulder. "It was odd. My gut is saying it was odd and that's the only word I can come up with at this point."

She blew out a breath of air. "Maybe Sylvie wants Dorian for herself."

"Sylvie's in her fifties," I deadpanned.

"Don't shame age gap relationships with older women and men of adult age, Adelaide. This is Dorian we're talking about."

"Dorian is twenty-two," I deadpanned, *again*.

She continued on. "I've even seen my journalism professor whispering about student gossip with other professors. Dorian's name always comes up. Gossip may be frowned upon 'by the Board,' but the staff is just as into it."

"Mia, I think that the gossip around here is getting to your brain."

"Fine." She shrugged her shoulders and began collecting her pastel set of highlighters. "Don't listen to the *reporter* in training. I will let you finish up and think about this situation more in peace. Your blueberry keychain is beginning to look tasty which means I need to get back and eat."

She stood and shook her backpack, making enough room to slide her laptop in. "I'll see you in a few hours?"

I lifted my laptop screen. Still black. It seemed like I'd be handwriting for the next hour.

"Yeah, I'll head out soon. There's leftover butter chicken in the fridge up for grabs by the way."

"You're the love of my life, Adelaide." She twirled, her arm outstretched with a binder in her hand, almost completely whacking a bust statue off its pedestal.

I shot up from my chair—as if to somehow catch the statue from five feet away—right as she pulled her arm back like a rampant dog on a leash before anything could happen.

"I will be going now," she said quietly, tiptoeing out of the library.

Adelaide. Adelaide. Adelaide.

Dorian's voice was everywhere. Soft and swooping. His soothing tone spoke in cursive. It hooked onto my ears and hugged the back of my head. It even grazed my spine.

Adelaide. Adelaide. Adelaide.

I wanted to lean into it. Bottle it and attach it to my purse to listen to when the sway of the trees and the smell of the ink on a page weren't enough to calm me. I wanted to know what it tasted—

Adelaide.

My shoulder blades struck the back of the wooden chair. Long pieces of black hair hung in my face like an ink wash painting. I swiped it away and was still met with darkness. I couldn't even see the trees outside the windows. The only light in the library came from the antique lamp on my table.

"Holy shit, I fell asleep." I pushed my sleeve up to find my watch. "What time——"

"Quarter past eleven."

My chair legs jutted against the hardwood floor as I found Dorian sitting on the table beside me. The last time I saw him, he was drenched.

"Holy shit, I wasn't dreaming," I responded, feeling mystified.

His eyebrows rose. "Excuse me?"

"Nothing."

God, he looked handsome when he was taken aback. Get it *together*.

"When did you get here?" he asked, saving me from any other sleep-related questions.

"Three, I think. I was studying for my Consumer Behavior midterm that's tomorrow but then my laptop stopped and—*shit*, my laptop. I was supposed to fix my laptop." My voice strained.

I whipped open the screen and was greeted with my reflection. An earring hung upside down, snagged in a piece of hair, while another strand was stuck to my lip gloss. I brushed it away and clicked a few buttons. Nothing changed.

"Come on, come *on*." I had an exam in the morning. This could *not* be happening.

Oh wonderful, here came the Overworked Stress Tears filling my throat.

"Hey, it's alright. I can fix it," Dorian offered, his voice soft and reassuring, pushing off the table to lean over my shoulder. His face right beside mine, his shoulder neighboring mine. I could smell the coffee on his black sweater.

"I really don't think that's a good idea," I argued, emotion still clogging my throat as I turned to face him.

"Do you want your laptop to work?" He twisted. His lips

almost brushed mine. It was so fast; I couldn't tell if I had imagined it. My heart replaced the emotion in my esophagus. Something told me I was just tired because he looked unaffected, waiting for my response.

"That's what I thought," he said, and faced the laptop, pressing a few key combinations I had missed. "Does the screen shut off often?"

"Not usually. It's been glitchy for the past month though. I think it was from the rain when we …" I let the words drop off. He knew what I was referencing.

"There's probably some water damage then. This should only take a minute."

He reached for his back pocket, returning with a set of keys. I watched as he sat the laptop upside down and unscrewed the back of it with a house key.

"How do you know what to do?" I asked, genuinely curious.

"My dad works with a lot of video production equipment. There were always cameras and computers lying around the house. Compared to everything else, a laptop is the easiest thing to fix," he explained.

I nodded in acknowledgment, unsure of what else to say. He said it like his dad wasn't an award-winning director. Nothing pompous about it.

I sat back and watched him work, careful to not brush his shoulder with mine.

His presence was more poignant than I remembered. Like a blank wall decorated with a single painting. It was difficult not to frantically twist your back to look at it or reach your hand forward to graze its brush strokes. Avoiding it for two weeks didn't help either.

Side effects included: staring longer than usual, counting the number of moles on his neck and the outgrown curls above his ear, and having the urge to ask why there was always paint under his nails.

Jesus.

His *girlfriend* probably thought the same thing.

Something was possessing me. I was a victim of a horror movie; possessed and cursed.

I had been dodging him since the pond incident and now I was facing the consequences.

I'd tell him that the bookstore was slammed with customers or that I had nonstop bloody noses or was contagious with something he'd never heard of or that I couldn't leave my apartment because the mice in the walls were freaking Sabrina out.

(There were no mice.)

Between Sabrina's tear-filled night and Sylvie's comments, I was overwhelmed. Even now, a part of me was nervous Sylvie had eyes in the books watching us.

"Let this sit for a few minutes and it should be good." His words poked through my thoughts. He sat against the edge of the table, facing me.

An internal piece of my computer was resting on his jacket.

"That's it?" I looked at him in disbelief.

"Well, that and you have to rub its back and take it out to dinner."

I laughed and his mouth kicked upward. That dimple appeared on his left cheek.

"Easy, I'll cook it a frozen meal tonight for all its hard work," I responded.

"Oh, you thought I meant the computer? I was talking about

me. You owe me damages for the past two weeks of no tutoring."

I laughed, *again*. And then he laughed from the reaction on my face. It was joyous and wonderous. The laughter of a boy who was chasing after a butterfly. The same laughter he shared with James.

The library quieted as we caught our breath. He looked at me with an unreadable expression before redirecting his gaze.

"To be honest, I would like to make you dinner. And I know. I know, it's out of the question, and you have no problem telling me no." He shook his head, twisting the ring around his thumb. "But I don't understand why you've been avoiding me."

His head shifted, and so did his glance. I was pinned by his eyes.

I knew the answer: Sylvie and Sabrina.

But why did it feel like there was this third answer bubbling at the surface each time he looked at me? One that had to do with the fact that I could count the number of inches between our lips and the time it would take to grab his belt loop and pull him forward.

I needed something else to stare at. I picked the window behind him like a coward.

"The Townsen Dinner was a difficult night for Sabrina. She's needed me the past few weeks."

It wasn't a complete lie. Sabrina did want more movie nights than usual. But she always wasn't getting over Dorian like I had hoped.

"Did she have a difficult night or did you?"

"Well, I didn't exactly have the best night either. Ending events in ponds isn't my first choice."

"You're avoiding the question."

"How am I avoiding the question?"

"Because you were royally pissed off before that."

"That's no surprise, I usually am when I'm with you."

"Do you say anything you're genuinely thinking when you're around me, because it feels a lot like you're covering something up."

"And what would that be?"

He opened his mouth and shut it. I waited as he searched my face, calculating his response.

"Nothing." He leaned back. I hadn't even realized we had begun to ease forward.

He returned to the laptop, placing the piece back in.

"I'm sorry about your dress," he said as he twisted the key, screwing the piece in.

"It's fine. It was just a dress." *Said no one ever.*

"I could buy you a new one."

"I don't need you to buy me anything, Dorian."

"I know, Adelaide. I don't *need* to do anything, but I want to." He flipped the computer over, opened the screen, and—

"Oh my gosh, you fixed it!" Relief flooded my chest as my wallpaper of Elizabeth James's home from *The Parent Trap* appeared. My shoulders finally loosened. "Thank you, I really appreciate it."

"It was my fault anyway. I'll bring an umbrella for the next walk."

"I should probably get going." I stood, reaching for my bag on the table. "Oh sorry," I apologized as I extended my arm across his lap to grab my bag. This was weird now. Why did I make it weird?

"I can get it—"

I interrupted him. "No, that's al—" The contents of my bag hit the floor.

We both crouched down, scrambling to pick everything up. I was stuffing things back in—for once not caring if something was crushed—so I could get out of here. Whereas he was refolding papers and brushing them off.

"You really do make to-do lists for everything," he mumbled.

"What?"

"You have your London itinerary in *to-do list format*." He was amused reading the note.

I reached for it, but he pulled back. "I don't have a London Itinerary," I countered.

"Whose list is it then?" He held up the small note, a bagel logo at the top.

"Oh, that's Marty's."

"Marty?" His amusement fell. "You're sharing notes with other guys, but I can only communicate with you via email?"

"Marty is the man who sits outside my bakery."

His eyes narrowed. "And he gave you this list?"

"That's what I just said."

"That sounds like a lie. I need to ask Marty myself."

"Well, you can't."

"Why not?"

"He went back home to New York."

"This all sounds very convenient for your lie."

I yanked the note back. "Believe what you want. It's not mine."

"Fine, I'll throw it out for you then." His hand launched at the paper.

"You can't!"

He responded with satisfaction. "So you did make the list!"

"I didn't! I'd never"—I scanned the list—"go on the London Eye."

His lips parted. "*You haven't been on the London Eye*, and you've been here five months?

"It's a giant spinning wheel of metal that's eerily close to a body of water."

"Have you done any of these things?"

My eyes snagged on the last line. He followed my gaze. *Kiss a Brit.* Blood crawled its way up my neck.

"I guess you can cross that last one off." He scratched the back of his neck. "Especially if you've kissed any other—"

"I haven't. Focusing on class only, as I've mentioned."

He nodded, taking his bottom lip in between his teeth in thought.

Chirps and tweets from bugs against the windows were clearer now. An unhelpful audience that loudened our silence. I stood up from the floor. He followed.

"Well, this'll be a good way to think about things that aren't class." His eyes darted to mine and then back down.

He handed me the laptop; I passed him his jacket. Then he picked up my bag and I checked my emails on my phone one more time. Our usual post-session ritual.

Part of me had missed it the past two weeks. But logic told me that it was simply a needed distraction from running around.

"Come on, I'll walk you home," he replied, pulling an umbrella out of his bag.

Liana Cincotti

15

Don't Learn About His Hobbies — Adelaide

"We most likely won't be back until one because we have to meet my dads at their place first. Then we'll head to the red carpet and the actual movie and after, well, the afterparty." Sabrina was rambling.

She tended to ramble when she was nervous or guilty. Currently, it was the latter. Because looking at her roommate (me) who was dressed like the epitome of the Tired College Student (the flannel pajama pants and an over washed T-shirt uniform), made her feel like she should've tried harder to convince me to go.

"Brina."

"Addy."

"I. Am. Fine. I'm actually more than fine. I had my last midterm and now all I want to do is watch cocky people go on cringey dates and fight about whose villa is larger," I explained before tediously pushing a bobby pin into her hair.

I tilted her head down to make sure the pins were parallel before letting her get up from the coffee table. Her light blond hair complemented the glittery lavender A-line dress, along with her iridescent eyeshadow and teardrop earrings. She looked like a gumdrop. A gumdrop with a frown.

"If you look at me like my dog died one more time——"

"But you're going to be all alone. On a Friday night. In London! What if you need something and don't know where to go?" she stressed.

"We've lived here since June! She'll be fine!" Mia shouted from her room. "Addy loves to be alone, she's like a little grandma."

You crack down on homework and suddenly Summer Adelaide is forgotten and has become the grandma of the group.

"I really wouldn't mind some time by myself," I emphasized.

"You're sure?" Brina whispered.

"Yes. Now you're going to be late!"

She grabbed my wrist and read my watch. "Crap! We'll see you later!" she shouted into my ear as she hugged me.

Mia gave me an enthusiastic wave before they were out the door. I watched the picture frames rattle on the walls before pushing myself off the couch.

"Time to start the night." I slugged back a gulp of my milkshake as I shuffled into my bedroom with my slippers.

I had an entire night to mold the couch cushions with the shape of my body as I thought about nothing but Jenny's taste in men with tattoos and poor conversational skills on the island.

My desk drawer screeched as I dug around for my maroon nail polish in the sea of neutrals and stormy gray blues.

Meow.

The polishes jumped in the drawer under my grasp.

Maureen's stupid cat was sitting on my balcony railing again.

"How are you even balancing on that? Your single thigh is larger than the width of the railing."

His meow lowered an octave.

"What type of greeting did you expect? If you'd like to sit in peace, go to your balcony."

He bared his canines and hissed.

"Fine, we'll do this the hard way." I reached for one of my magazines, stepped onto the balcony, and began fanning him. Then he turned his face.

"Kurt, come on. Go away, please! This is my only night where I don't have to do *anything*. Do you understand how rare that is? No, of course you don't, because you're a cat."

I rolled up the magazine and nudged his butt. The more I nudged him, the more he shifted. "Yes, there we go. Keep going."

He hopped away onto my windowsill, between mine and my neighbor's balconies, and … sat down.

"Are you seriously going to wait for me to leave? No way. I'm not getting up from the couch once I'm sitting down."

I poked at his belly, trying to get him to hop to the neighbor's balcony.

"I. Can't. Deal. With. Your. Cat. Hair," I huffed with every poke. I wedged my foot between the railings to prop myself up. My lower stomach squished against the baluster. "Go. That. Way. Come. On!" I gave him one more final push and—

I screamed as my feet left the balcony and the cement of my windowsill flew towards my face. I squeezed my eyes shut and threw my hand out as fingers latched onto my hips, tugging me in the opposite direction.

"Jesus Christ, Adelaide, *what are you doing?*" Dorian breathed out a sigh full of disbelief.

My chest churned out air like a broken air mattress pump.

"I," exhale, "Kurt," inhale, "room," exhale.

"Someone was in your room?" He was *horrified.*

I shook my head. "No, no. The neighbor's cat, Kurt."

His stomach deflated. I fell deeper into his chest.

If I could count his breaths, it was time to get off.

I pushed away from him, stepping to the other side of the balcony.

"You were leaning over a railing *for a cat?*" he asked.

"He's covering my clothes in his fur!"

"Bloody hell, I was thinking you were saving the cat." He massaged his forehead. "I will buy you new clothes, Adelaide, if it means you're not fighting with a cat and risking falling twenty feet."

Wait. "What are you doing here?" I crossed my arms.

He bit on the inside of his cheek. "I need you to look over my project."

I held my finger up. "Oh no, no, no." I laughed and stepped off the balcony. Returning to my drawer, I rummaged for a base and top coat.

He followed me. "You—"

"Close the balcony," I interjected. The balcony door screeched shut.

"It's still been two weeks since we last met—and the library doesn't count."

"How unfortunate." I wiggled my fingers around in the back of the drawer.

He exhaled. "I really—God, let me help." Then his body was leaning over mine.

My eyes could've been shut, and I still would've felt him there. Even without the rich scent of his sweaters and jackets. No contact between us was necessary. It was simply *him.* My body was so hyper aware of him. Like a page expecting the drag of ink. I could've been unconscious, and I would've felt his presence.

He followed my hand, his arm running along mine like paint on a canvas, until his fingers were on mine, feeling for the bottle. I retrieved my palm hastily. He wriggled his hand until the polish was free and in my palm.

"Thank you," I shut the drawer, put the polish down, and picked up my milkshake. "And I can't, I'm busy." I took a sip.

"Really?" he asked. He glanced down at my fuzzy slippers. But it sounded more like *relly* with his accent.

"*Relly*," I repeated, referencing the milkshake.

He raised a brow as if to say *oh, we're doing this now?*

"Is there alcohol in this?" he questioned.

Before I could respond, he was leaning forward, strands of his hair flopping forward as he took the straw into his mouth and sipped. His Adam's apple bobbed. Then he was standing back up with one swipe of his tongue across his lips before I could let the image simmer any longer.

"Nope, you're just making fun of me while sober," he commented. "Change your slippers, we're going."

"Going where? I just told you I'm busy." I shook my shake.

"We're checking something off your to-do list and going over my project because that was our deal. Go throw on some real clothes, it's my turn to teach you something tonight."

Dorian wouldn't budge. Not on the walk down the stairs. Not in the car when I held the milkshake out the window after he tried stealing a sip. Not even his driver would tell me.

"You'll enjoy it, don't worry," he kept saying.

So I didn't worry or ask any more questions. Only traced the hem of my maxi skirt and tried not to feel the weight of his gaze as he watched the movement until the tires halted, stopping in front of a red brick townhouse smooshed in between identical buildings painted a variety of grays and whites.

I heard the tree's dew drip onto the car's roof before I noticed Dorian opening my door and reaching for my hand. In public. In the middle of London.

I remained in the car. "Anyone could see or take a picture," I reminded him.

A photo of him leaving a cologne launch had appeared in my feed a few days ago. Days before that, a tabloid was reporting on his choice of loafers that he wore to our class on Monday. And last week, he was at a charity event speaking to author Bella Lola (who was *very* single apparently).

I didn't ask for any of this information. The public simply cared enough to put it in magazines and wake me with its middle-of-the-night notifications.

He braced the car frame above me, leaning down. There was so much leaning. So much cutting into my space. I was beginning to get dizzy.

"I haven't forgotten. I come here every week, so it won't be a problem. I know everyone who owns these buildings anyway." *I'd take care of it*, were the words left unsaid, but I got the message.

He pushed off the car and offered his hand. Reluctantly, I accepted as he placed his other hand between my head and the car frame, stepping out.

Once we buzzed into the building, our footsteps bounced off the empty oak hallways. The sound was quickly replaced with French music and chatter as he opened the last door.

An art studio?

I breathed in the woodsy smell of charcoal pencils and took the punch of the oil paints.

I didn't know what I was expecting. Maybe a restaurant that only made food I hated. Or a university party where every student was waiting with their phones raised to take a picture of us and send it directly to Sabrina and the Board.

It was anything but a shirtless male model sitting on a stool in the center of the room with easels and chairs surrounding him like a recreation of the solar system. The planets around him were made up of a mixture of people. Some looked like accountants with their ruffled blouses. While others resembled fashion interns and grandparents. Each one was twisted away from their canvas to talk to the person beside them. Warm smiles and rosy cheeks everywhere.

"Hey Poppy," Dorian greeted a woman who had tiny violins for earrings and a blush pink pixie cut.

Her face exploded into a smile. "Dorian, you're never this early—" Her words snagged once I stepped beside him. "You brought a friend! Oh, how wonderful." She clapped. "The more the merrier. Get a stool from the back, we'll get started now. I'll let you fill your friend…"

"Adelaide," I filled in her gap.

She smiled. "I'll let you fill in Adelaide on how we do things here." Then she left to pass out a few cups of brushes.

"Go sit, I'll grab another seat." He gestured to the lone seat.

I nodded, moving to the small stool perched in front of an easel. I was fortunate that our seat was to the side of the model. It felt wrong to stare him in the eyes or be staring at him in the … backside.

Another stool tapped the space beside mine. I scooched over, making room for him.

"I can't believe you have a hobby. Especially not *this* hobby." I was dumbfounded.

"I have to be interesting somehow. You don't even find me being British interesting," he responded, a smile tugging at the corner of his lips. "I dragged James the first few times because I was so nervous they'd kick me out for being horrid."

"You really paint?"

"Do you think this is a front for a recreational football team?"

"This just doesn't seem like something you'd do!"

He rolled his eyes. "And someone as type A as you doesn't seem like the type to hoard stuff and then hang it on expensive pocketbooks."

I clutched my bag. "They're souvenirs, not *stuff*."

"Everyone have their brushes?" Poppy asked over the music. Everyone raised their brushes, including Dorian.

I put my bag on the ground and pulled out my lapt—

"Not yet." He took the purse and put it beside him, away from my reach.

"But I need to go over your work—"

"We can do that later. This is the 'try something new' of the list, so you do have to try it first."

"How do you know I haven't done this?"

"I think it's fairly evident you don't make much time in your schedule for…fun." There was a smug look on his face. He knew I couldn't argue.

"Dorian, did you give our guest the rundown?" Poppy reminded him from the other side of the room.

"Doing that now."

"The rundown?"

He turned his body to face me. "Poppy takes creativity very seriously. So when you're in here, you can do anything you want that'll garner some type of inspiration. Sing, dance, paint the model, don't paint the model, close your eyes. Take off your trainers and paint with your toes if you wish. As long as you've painted something."

"Do people do that?" I hope they had highly fragrant candles nearby.

"Arnold, once." He pointed his brush at a man in his sixties wearing a tie dye bandana. "He takes things quite literally when they come from Poppy. He fancies her quite a bit."

"Oh god, does she know?"

"You say it like he's committed murder. What's wrong with a crush?"

I could've written a dissertation on it. Ran my own TedTalk on it.

Crush, like love, was a sweet, romantic word for lust. Crushes were The Chase portion of the lust. That well-known Pursuit rather than the actual person or relationship.

Crushes were exciting because they were completely fictionalized. They led to unreliable, energetic lust.

I felt it whenever Dorian grabbed onto my hips or stared at my lips or looked into my eyes when he wanted an honest answer.

It wasn't that lust shouldn't be enjoyed. But this unpredictable version that made you question your emotions and their motives? That's where it went downhill.

I settled for a simpler response that wouldn't lead to my TedTalk: "It's *embarrassing.*"

"Of course it is." His brows crinkled together. "It's *love*. Everything about love is embarrassing. You're pining over someone who's across the room hardly thinking of you. That's incredibly embarrassing. But I also think there's something romantic about being secretly fond of someone in a way that only you know."

I never heard him speak so seriously. He seemed to even shock himself.

The air in the room was thick. Not middle-of-October-air or even the expensive heating unit hung behind me. But this heavy unidentifiable *thing* between us. The thing that made me want to ask *more* and ask *who*.

"Have you never had a crush?" he questioned.

"No." I brushed my hands on my skirt.

"I don't think I believe you." His words dragged my gaze back up.

"Why would I lie?"

"Because you don't want to be embarrassed." He watched me carefully.

"It's a good thing I have nothing to be embarrassed about then."

"I guess so." His eyes flickered across my face until he was satisfied. "Well then. Do you want to start?"

I handed him the pencil.

He pressed his forearm to the paper on the easel and sketched the silhouette of the model. He started with the arch of his back and the curve of his neck. Then he shaped out his side profile, trying to get the arch of his nose just right. Within a few minutes, angled arms, bent knees, and a thoughtful face were drawn.

"Alright, you're up," he said, putting the pencil down and flipping the notepad to a new page so that his drawing hung over the easel.

"I thought we were working off your drawing."

"You have to make your own. It's the first-timer rule." He handed me the pencil.

"Dorian, I will look like a toddler compared to you."

There was a pull at the corner of his lips. "Why don't you paint something then. Not the model. Just anything. Anything you want."

Want.

Looking at him now, his head bent to meet my eye and the knowledge of our knees barely touching, he was what I wanted.

What I wanted to paint, of course.

To explore the color of his eyes with the selection of brown paints with a hint of orange to achieve that brightness. I wanted the satisfaction of running a sharp line of paint across the paper to fulfill that need of holding his jaw. I wanted to try retracing his tattoos from memory to figure out if my dreams had been distorting them for the past month or if I had them memorized down to each curvature.

I cleared my throat. I stretched my arm across his lap for the brush. He instantly moved. I took that as an offer to scootch in rather than a reaction to my proximity in order to maintain sanity.

I dipped it in the blue and then realized— "Are there any smocks?" I glanced down at my white shirt.

"Poppy doesn't believe in smocks here. She thinks if paint ends up on your clothes, then it's proof of your passion."

"Poppy has obviously never owned a favorite shirt before."

"Adelaide, her favorites obviously have paint on them."

I suppressed a smile. "What are the chances she's willing to give one of those up?"

"She'd probably give you the shirt off her back if it was in the name of art. I did bring something though." He rifled through his bag and pulled out a T-shirt.

"You've got to be kidding. Is your name on the back too?" I asked. It was a gray short-sleeve with a British flag at the center— one of the items on the list.

"I can make that happen."

"I'm sure you can." I took the shirt before he could take it back to some embroider that's worked in his family for a century. That or he'd probably paint *Blackwood* on the back.

I pulled the shirt over my head. The cotton fabric was soft and worn, the woodsy aroma surrounded my nose as I dragged it over my face. The collar sucked all of my hair in like a vacuum, strands trapping themselves in my mouth.

"How much of a tourist do I look like now?" I asked.

He brushed my hair to the side, meticulously pulling it from the collar without it tugging or knotting. He pushed the last piece behind my ear.

"Very much so," he answered. "But London looks good on you."

"Where did you get this?" I questioned, looking down at the graphic.

"My closet," he responded. He was biting the inside of his cheek to keep from smirking.

I shook out my hair and picked up the paintbrush, trying to ignore the blush on my cheeks. "You're the worst."

I dipped the brush in the blue and mixed it with a bit of white and green on the palette attached to the side of the easel. I outlined a house, leaving space at the top for a roof. I brushed short strokes in a horizontal line until the home was fully sided. It truly did look like a toddler's painting.

"I like your souvenirs by the way," he commented.

"I like that you draw," I admitted.

"Because it makes me seem like less of a snob?" he guessed.

"No, because you draw with vulnerability," I said. It might have been the most honest thing I had said to him. From the quiet look on his face, I could tell he was thinking the same thing. But I wasn't sure what that meant for me.

16

Don't Think About Dating Her — Dorian

"You're throwing your life away," Victoria spat from above me.

She texted me that there was an emergency while on my way back from Adelaide's after the art studio, so I came immediately.

If I knew that my life choices were the emergency, I would've walked slower. Maybe grab an acetaminophen and a drink to relieve the headache that was forming in my right ear where she was shouting as I fixed the lock in her door that her landlord refused to fix. The packaged deadbolt on her counter made for a good distraction during this conversation.

From my kneeled position on the ground, eye-level with the lock, I unscrewed the old deadbolt with the drill.

"Are you really just going to throw your future away?" she questioned.

"By wanting to open a gallery?" I asked. I was so tired. She must see it.

"Yes!" she shouted.

"This is what you wanted to talk about? I haven't seen you or heard from you in three months and *this* is what you've been thinking about?"

She skipped half of my question. "Because it affects the both of us."

"Affects us how?"

"Are you joking? Rye, what you do affects our future. What I do affects our future. Which, by the way, do you know how embarrassing it was to hear about your post-grad plans *from your mother?*"

"I'm sorry. You've been busy. I didn't think it was worth mentioning." Since up until ten minutes ago, I thought we weren't together.

"Of course I want to hear about it. You're supposed to discuss big-life decisions with your partner."

"There's not much to discuss. I'm moving in with James after graduation so I can use my own flat as the gallery space. I have it all planned out." I placed the new deadbolt on the door, lining it up with the holes.

She scoffed. *"You're going to move?* Seriously? To live *with James?* When your parents could just buy you another place? That's ridiculous."

"Yes, Victoria." Were we standing on a spinning scratched record?

I put one of the screws between my lips, and strung the other through the hole, fitting the drill in the divot. Then onto the next screw. She began talking louder as the drill shrieked.

"You're ruining your life by not considering joining your father's production team! This art thing is a joke! What are you going to do? Sell your paintings? It's embarrassing!"

I stopped the drill. I bit the inside of my mouth. *She's just upset you didn't tell her. You'd be upset if she kept something from you.*

She has, you idiot. Gregory, Drew, Lewis, Alfie. There's probably even more from this summer.

"The deadbolt is fixed. Have a good night." I opened the door, threw the rubbish in her bin, dropped the drill on her counter, and grabbed my coat from the ground. I took the stairs down to the lobby two at a time, praying she wouldn't follow.

Once the goosebump-raising air hit me outside, I exhaled. It wasn't enough to cool the heat on my neck and sides of my face, but it was something. A droplet of rain against the hot pan that was my body.

Embarrassing. She thinks I'm embarrassing. Maybe I was. Maybe that's what happened to a person who kept going back to someone who didn't love them.

What should have been the sound of the lobby door shutting behind me was her voice instead.

"Dorian wait." I turned. She was pulling her blond hair from the restraint of her coat.

Sometimes if I looked at her long enough, she began to look like the girl I fell in love with at seventeen. I could see the light freckles that polka-dotted her nose fighting for space through her makeup. Imagine the smile that lifted on her face when she saw me. Pretend that her next words were going to be supportive and sweet, the way they used to be.

But it was just going to be an empty apology.

She folded her arms tightly against her chest. "I didn't mean to upset you."

"Well, you did Vic. But I can't change how you feel. If you want to spend entire summers pretending I don't exist and continue to hate my life choices, then that's fine. But I don't want it."

"Don't want what?"

Liana Cincotti

"This. Us. I'm exhausted."

"You're just going to give up? Five years and something gets tough, and Dorian wants to give up, yet I've been here for you through everything. *Really?*"

"You know this isn't the only thing. It's been like this for *years.*"

"No." She shook her head, and her eyes developed a glassy glow. "You don't get to just leave. Who else will deal with the publicity and scrutiny and still stick by you? No one. No one but me because I know you. I've always known you."

Maybe she did know me. Five years did that.

She'd been there through every scandal, every speculation. When people in class stared at me and when tabloids ripped me apart, she was there. She had a right to worry about the future.

So when she leaned forward to kiss me, I gave in. Sank into the comfortable space I was accustomed to because no one else would ever offer the same. Because I had no other choice.

"What are your thoughts on a Halloween party?"

"James, are the Americans hypnotizing you? Writing subliminal messages into your journalism notes?" I ruffled the papers between us on the library table. The reflection of raindrops bouncing off the windows behind me slid against the notes.

He swatted my hand. "I just think it'd be fun. A conversation I had with Adelaide made me think of it. My mother agreed—wants to use it to celebrate the retail launch for Beverly now. We could make it a masquerade rather than some tacky costume party."

"My presence is contingent on whether or not I have to handle caterers and mingle with your mother's friends."

"You don't enjoy talking to Gretchen?"

"Is my sleeping during my conversations with her not obvious enough?"

"You could start drooling and she *still* wouldn't notice."

"I'm not sure if that's a compliment to my looks or a hit at my acting skills …"

He rolled his eyes. "To answer your question though: no Gretchen and no hosting duties. But you do have to show up in a suit. A shirt included."

"That was *one time*. I didn't anticipate on taking a nap in the middle of your mother's Christmas party and waking up with my shirt missing. Whoever made those drinks was insane. And to be frank, I think you enjoyed it since you mention it so much."

He tipped his head back and laughed. After a moment, when our laughter fizzed out down, he asked, "How's tutoring with Addy going?"

Addy? Suddenly, there was a thick blanket thrown over the mood. I felt stiff but continued to write down the research Adelaide assigned me to look for.

"It's good," I replied.

"That's good." He nodded. "Have you guys been getting along?"

Getting along? Was she telling him we weren't?

"Yeah," was all I said before returning to my notes. I tried to ignore the heavy silence, but it was petulant, dancing on my tongue. I wanted to tell him how I was feeling. How *she* made me feel. Anxious. Admired. Agitated. Adored. Acknowledged. A complex canvas with layers of paint that couldn't be traced back to their first brushstrokes.

I needed to hear that I wasn't insane. Because the way my skin shivered as Victoria kissed me last night felt like the embodiment of loneliness. I walked home with a fishhook grip on my conscious, filled with guilt.

Guilt for caring for Adelaide. Guilt for not considering Victoria. Guilt for hoping she'd let me go.

I couldn't navigate why I was feeling this way.

I had to tell him about everything that happened last night.

Then he spoke. "I hope it wouldn't be awkward then if I asked Adelaide out?"

My pencil snapped. The lead flew across the table, leaving a short, thick line in my paper—proof of what he just said.

"Adelaide? I didn't realize you were interested in her," I said.

"I didn't know if it'd make things weird, but I've been seeing her enough to know that there's a correlation between her and my heart palpitations." He laughed. It was small, focused on his lap where he picked the skin around his nails. "So you don't mind then, since you guys are getting on well. I know Victoria's back anyway so …"

If we were in the campus kitchen, I'd assume the shooting pain in my chest was from a fork pressed into my chest. But no. I leaned my head into my palm to stop the swaying and prepare myself in case this was some early-on heart attack. I'd sure provide a doctor with quite a bit of entertainment.

The cause of the attack, you ask? Best friend fancies the woman I'm dreaming about.

"Of course not. You should pursue her," I said. I didn't recognize my voice.

"You're sure?"

I nodded.

"Alright, I will then." He leaned back as if he was preparing to get up and ask her this second. But he sat forward and restored the steadiness of his voice. "Now that that's over with, what'd you do last night?" he asked.

I paused.

I couldn't tell him now. If I told him I took her to Poppy's, then he'd know Adelaide meant something.

He knew no one saw me paint. It wasn't supposed to be for anyone. The moment you created art and shared it, everyone took it as an invitation to tell you how to make it better. More interesting. To critique and commoditize it. To make assumptions about it that weren't supposed to be made.

Art was meant to be enjoyed. To provoke. Not to be pulled apart and judged stroke by stroke.

But Adelaide just watched. The same way I watched her run her finger over her computer screen to breakdown definitions and explain analytics.

"Nothing much," I told him.

17

November was only a week away. Which meant that I had to switch out my red gingham duvet for a heavier cotton blend. A fun seasonal change.

November, unfortunately, also meant one month until final exams and the semester-long projects were due.

Right when I needed time to slow down so I could catch my breath, it was running away and dragging me with it. It was even changing the view outside my window to a late, wet October filled with vibrant orange leaves, dark concrete sidewalks, and a commitment to slip its cool air through the seams of my window.

Lately, time had trotted away just as quickly as when I was with Dorian. After visiting the art studio, the silent space that usually passed between us during tutoring sessions had dwindled.

We discussed weekend plans, late-night thoughts, childhood memories, and embarrassments, like the time he and James went on their first annual Italy Christmas trip where Dorian ended up with his first tattoo. Neither of them knew any Italian, but that didn't stop him.

"I thought I could understand enough," he had said. "But one thing led to another, and I ended up in a tattoo shop, telling the artist he could tattoo whatever he'd like. I swore up and down to James that I knew what the artist was saying. But an hour later, I had a tomato tattooed on my upper thigh."

I laughed at both the story and his pronunciation of *toe-mah-toe*.

For a split second, I almost asked him to show me. But the logical half of my brain kicked in before he could unzip his pants to show me his upper thigh.

"Non parli Italiano?" I asked with surprise. Wasn't there some requirement for all rich kids to grow up knowing every European language?

His eyes had lit up. "Parlo dieci lingue. Italian just happened to be the last." My heart lurched. I pushed my hand against my chest as if I could calm the beat. "How do you know Italian?"

Then my heart stilled. Like a hummingbird trapped behind a window.

Two words I avoided for over a decade: my dad.

But his face was so calm, and he was so close. His hand splayed out on the desk like he was reaching for me. That pocket of energy in my chest surged again. Suddenly, the words were out. I was an open book, and my pages were losing ink.

"My dad loved to listen to Italian music whenever he was home. It was on so much that I had memorized the lyrics but had no clue what they meant. When he got home from job sites, he'd go over the words with me, until one day, I could translate everything in the Italian dictionary back to English," I shared.

I didn't say where he was now. Or how he'd stolen the life my mother imagined. Or how he made her someone I despised and uprooted my life.

Liana Cincotti

There was something cruel about your parents deciding to bring you into the world, and just choosing not to be with you in it.

It was easier to talk about it as if I was telling a story, rather than recalling my life. Like how Dad would cut my peanut butter jelly sandwiches into star shapes. Or how he'd sing to Mom in Italian when she cooked his favorite panko-crusted chicken, picking me up to dance in the kitchen.

I had stopped there. Dorian didn't push.

He opened his phone and showed me pictures of paintings he was working on.

They were beautiful. Delicate. A series of watercolor and oil paintings. Corners of living rooms. Windowsill flower boxes. Men drinking coffee at the cornerstone cafes. Hands pulling books off of shelves.

"These are beautiful, Dorian," I said, imagining what they looked like in person if they were already this beautiful through a screen. "You should sell these. They should be in people's homes."

"Oh, I don't know."

"I would cover my entire room in them," I gushed.

"You would?"

"*Of course.* I could even help you promote it. Reach out to galleries about their newsletters. Organize a branded website with the paintings."

He absorbed the offer before moving on.

One of the paintings was for his older sister Jasmine and her pottery studio in the South of France. Despite her living abroad, they spoke every week. Much of their conversations revolved around their mother's dating schemes and finding ways to irk one another.

"She knows all about you," he mentioned. It wasn't phrased in a romantic way. But my stomach still dipped the way a golf ball went over a hump in a mini golf course.

On the walk back home from the bookstore last night, I jumped over puddles. He held the umbrella above our heads with his left hand. I clutched onto his right, reluctantly, in order to avoid falling a *second* time.

"What will you be subjecting me to next? I tried painting, I have a T-shirt with a flag plastered across it," I listed them off.

My patent leather flats smacked against the pavement as I hopped. His rings dug into my fingers as I squeezed tight, careful not to fall, but let go immediately once my feet were back on the ground.

"I'm thinking the postcard one," he responded, his eyes snagging on one of the many postcard carousels we passed. All the tourist shops sold the same ones. Cheesy variations of the British flag with oversaturated images of the monuments. One of them was pinned to the cork board above my desk.

"I'll have to find one with a pastry on it for Marty. He'd love that," I thought aloud.

"I was actually thinking you could send it to your aunt," he responded.

"I see what you're doing, and I appreciate it, but no. My aunt and I don't have that type of relationship."

"But maybe you could."

Before I left for class this morning, there was a blank postcard in my mailbox with a sticky note.

I'll bring you a stamp when you're ready.

Twelve hours later, there was a collection of pen dots in the top left corner of the postcard. It looked as if I forgot how to spell.

Or how to use a pen.

I picked up the pile of clothes from my chair and moved them to the end of my bed. His shirt with the British flag was in there. Even covered, I couldn't stop thinking about it.

The legs of the chair squeaked in debate as I sat.

"I don't want to do this either," I grumbled.

The postcard resting on my desk was giving me a headache like an unopened Pandora's box. I had zero desire to touch it though; its existence made my head throb. I'd rather dangle from Big Ben's clock than dip a toe in the past via a postcard.

There wasn't a word in the English language that I could start with that sounded right. "Dear Auntie Laila" was too formal. Especially for an aunt who was in her twenties the last time I saw her. I also hadn't called her "Auntie" in ten years. It was difficult to call your aunt anything when she stopped acting like a relative the moment her older brother decided to move on from his family.

Unfortunately for her, she was my only other relative in the area. Twenty-five years old and trapped caring for her fifteen-year-old niece.

Another ink dot appeared.

What were you supposed to say to someone who despised you for upending their life with your presence, but was the only family you had left?

I had no clue.

The drawer screeched as I opened it wide and dropped the blank postcard in, shutting it hard enough to hear it hit the back of the desk: a place I wouldn't have to think about it.

"Jameson," I bowed my head from across the hall.

"Adelaideson." James mimicked my manner, pretending to tip his imaginary cap.

"We're starting to scare the first years," he commented, motioning to a few girls giving us odd looks.

Correction: they were giving *me* the odd looks. He received daydreaming glances and arm-grabbing attention.

"I think it has more to do with you being part of the *we* in that statement than anything else," I explained.

"What's that supposed to mean?" His dark brows furrowed.

"It means that you're watched." Thick coat sleeves swiped my arms as we navigated the hallway.

He shook his head. "Maybe when I'm with Dorian, but other than that, I'm quite left alone."

"James, my friend, you forget yourself," I sighed.

"Oh please, tell me, *friend*," he laughed.

"You may not be forward and proud like Dorian—"

"Are you calling me shy and insecure?"

"I haven't finished! Forward, extroverted people usually take the limelight, but that doesn't mean no one is paying attention to you. You're the heir of a *very* iconic fashion house. And you're well-dressed, polite, and handsome."

He *was* handsome. The autumn sun coming in through the tall corridor windows bounced off the angles of his cheeks. A blush painted his pale jaw. It made his skin and platinum hair pop. Like a glittery red heart on a white envelope.

"What I'm trying to say is that you shouldn't be surprised that people pay so much attention to you. Dorian isn't the only one everyone's looking at."

He skipped over the parts about himself and went straight to Dorian. "You underestimate him. He may seem like that, but he's not."

Dorian almost never came up in our conversations. It was as if we had an unspoken agreement to never bring him up, especially in public. But the more I saw him, the more my initial ideas of him were scratched out and replaced with question marks.

"Do you mind if I ask you a question?" I asked.

"Why would I mind?"

"Because it involves your friend's personal life." I smiled innocently.

"Alright, let's hear it. I'm intrigued."

"What is going on with Victoria?" I asked.

"Victoria Sutton?" he guessed.

"Are there other Victorias?" My face was hot.

He shook his head. "No other Victorias. What do you want to know?"

"Are they together?"

He pressed his lips together in a line. "It's complicated."

"Oh my gosh, you two are the same. Do you plan your answers?" Dorian said the *same thing* by the pond.

"I'm being honest! Victoria is a complicated woman in general, let alone in terms of their relationship."

"So they are together?"

"No, they're not. She's just very … persuasive."

"Are you telling me that she seduces him into being with her?"

He pressed his fingers into his brows. "I'm trying to say this without completely embarrassing my mate and putting words in his mouth." There was a pause, and then he continued. "Dorian met her when we were seventeen. She was the first person he truly dated. I could see it on his face when he fell in love with her. And when he loves something, it consumes him. She consumed him.

Dragged him to every celebrity event, pulled him into every picture, said his name to whomever in order to benefit from it. She used him, and it took a while for him to realize that. But every few months, she manages to pull him back in."

My first reaction was to swallow the irritation crawling up my throat like a thorned vine piercing every muscle it passed. The idea that someone had been dragging him along for *five years* made me sick. It created an anxious patter that made it difficult to breathe and I didn't know if it was because I was beginning to care for him or because ... I didn't know.

My second reaction was logical. He was a guy. A support of The Chase. That constant *want*. Victoria may have used him originally, but now it sounded like he was using her for the benefits of a relationship without the relationship.

"Speak of the devil," James muttered.

It was like we summoned her.

Long blond hair swished back and forth as Victoria Sutton turned down the hall in a tweed skirt. She looked just like her Wikipedia page. The quintessential model. Tall, thin, high cheekbones, full lips, perfect posture. Someone who greeted you with two air kisses on the cheek and had hair from a shampoo commercial.

It took only one second. One second that Victoria spent giving James a smug smile, and me, an odd look. One I couldn't piece together. One I couldn't spend long enough dissecting.

Her floral perfume hit me before she was facing her phone again, turning down the hall.

"She knows you hate her, doesn't she?" I asked.

"One hundred percent."

I turned to him. "You can't actually put up with this."

"There's not much I can do. Dorian loves her."

18

I knew what James said yesterday. The conversation was involuntarily filed away in my brain, right in between my Strategic Brand Management syllabus and the wine cellar scene from *The Parent Trap*.

I knew what he said. *She used Dorian. He had realized.*

But that was difficult to comprehend when there was an image of Dorian and Victoria making out on my phone under the headline:

"Dorian Blackwood is Greeted with Romantic Return from Girlfriend After Her Three Months Abroad" — London Today

There were several images, actually. Angles really. Like some preppy, collegiate magazine spread.

One of her grabbing onto his bottom lip with her teeth. One with her hands under his shirt. Another with her whispering into his ear. And another and another and another and another.

I flipped the phone upside down and smacked it against the desk beside the register. No more screen time.

"What's wrong?" Mia asked, slicing the tape down the middle, and opening another box of books. I took the scissors after, hunching over to do the same.

"Nothing," I responded with a closed-mouth smile, shredding the tape and dropping the scissors back into her hands.

"You saw the photos, didn't ya?" Dotty asked, coming from the backroom with a list of invoices.

"What photos?" Mia perked up.

I let a curtain of hair hide the right side of my face from Mia as I gave Dotty a death glare.

"I thought you were avoiding the boy. I didn't think you cared!" Dotty defended herself.

"Boy?" Mia questioned.

Dotty rifled through the papers on the desk until she found a vibrant magazine, handing it over to Mia. "Page twenty-six," she clarified.

"Holy shit. That's the girl—Victoria." Mia looked to me for an explanation.

The cardboard box snapped under the scissors. I quickly pulled them out and returned them to the desk. "It's his girlfriend. It's normal to kiss your girlfriend."

"But he's obviously interested in you," Mia urged.

I stood up and took a pile of books with me, walking as far away as I could get.

Unfortunately, the store was small.

"You have to talk to him about this. It has to be PR or something," Mia argued, her voice getting closer.

"I'm not talking to him about his relationship." I snuck into the corner where the history books were.

She followed.

"But there has to be an explanation—"

138   *Liana Cincotti*

"I am not going to waste my—already—minimal time getting romantically involved with a man who will be interested in me for approximately four weeks before he gets bored," and finds another girl, and takes all of my favorite places to eat, my favorite words to say, the people I enjoy seeing after class, and the recipes I've handwritten to share them with her and leave me without anything.

"I don't think he's like that," Mia said softly.

"Really?" I took the magazine that hung in her hands and reminded her of the photo.

She was at a loss for words.

I shook my head and shelved three books. "People are only interested in you for as long as you're new."

I didn't need an unfaithful boyfriend or to be divorcee to know that. Dad's woodchip-ridden scent that had followed me to London in my old pajamas was a souvenir in itself.

"He's not coming today then, I assume?" Dotty asked, peeking into the aisle.

I felt guilty for telling him I was busy. Especially because the last few sessions had been great. Really great. As if we were becoming friends.

But that was the problem. We couldn't be friends. Because all I could think about were the un-friend-like things we had done and what a horrible friend to Sabrina that made me.

Now that I was learning more about him—his hobbies, his habits—it only added more weight. More interest.

I could feel myself leaning in more. Memorizing the freckles on his throat and the annunciation that his accent carried on certain words.

I needed distance. A reminder of real life and the

consequences that came with it, perched on my shoulders waiting to dive like resentful ravens. "No, he isn't."

Mia interjected, "Well, about that. I'm actually staying late tonight to make up hours from going out last Friday. And I knew you brought your nice purse today and there's no room for an umbrella in there. But I didn't want you to walk home alone in the rain so—"

The front door chimed, opening.

In walked Dorian, an umbrella hanging at his side. Wet specks polka dotted his navy blue sweater, a change from his usual black and grays. I hated that I noticed that. That I liked it.

His gaze swept across the room, from Dotty to Mia to me.

The corner of his mouth ticked upward.

"Hi." He smiled.

"Hi." I smiled back, the muscles in my face going rogue.

"Ready to go home?" he asked.

"How did Mia get your number?" I spoke over the rain as it pattered the umbrella above us. I attempted to hold onto the handle, but the difference in our height made our arms seesaw back and forth. He peeled my hand off in debate, holding it above me.

"I gave it to her when you started skipping out on our meetings a few weeks ago and began walking home by yourself again." He gave me a level look. "Think I'd forget?"

"One could've hoped." I shrugged my shoulders. "I could've walked home with Mia—"

"Mia is working late tonight." He responded with a smug smile. *Try again*, it said.

"You're smarter than you look."

"Is that how you've assessed me?"

"Assessed you? What's that supposed to mean?"

"It means that I've caught you staring at me a few times."

"I have not."

"Oh, we're lying now?" he cocked an eyebrow.

"Everyone looks at you, you're *the* Dorian Blackwood," I waved my hands.

He rolled his eyes. "I know why everyone else looks. I want to know why *you* look."

"We spend three nights a week studying together, Dorian. There's nothing flirtatious about me making sure you're paying attention."

"You're a terrible liar."

"What do you want me to say? That you're insanely hot?"

"If that's what comes to mind, then yes."

I smacked his arm but laughed anyway. A quiet pause built between us as our laughter died. Swaying trees and rustling leaves frazzled by the rain filled the space. But it wasn't loud enough for me to ignore the sound of his breathing or the beat of his footsteps.

"How's your laptop working?" he asked.

"Good, thankfully," I said appreciatively. "How's your art class? Arnold any closer to asking Poppy out?"

"It may be another five years until Arnold gathers up the confidence to talk to Poppy, let alone ask her out."

"There's no way that's possible."

"You obviously know nothing about Arnold."

"His crush will fizzle out at some point."

"Says who?"

"Says the attention span of men."

"I think you're talking to the wrong men then."

The umbrella shuddered slightly. I glanced up at him expecting a smirk, but there was none. Earnest was the only word that came to mind. His face softened. No pull at the corners of his lips or tension in his jaw. It carried all of my attention to his eyes where all of the light came from. Just as the windows bled light in the dark now.

I focused on my Mary Janes, bringing us to a normal walking pace again. His face made my cheeks ache. As if I had eaten too many madeleine cookies.

He cleared his throat. "Did you talk with James yesterday?"

"Why?" I startled. *Did James tell him I asked about Victoria?*

"Didn't know if he told you about the Halloween Party."

"Since when were there Halloween parties in the UK?"

"Since you told James how much you love them apparently. But based on the look on your face, I'm missing something?"

What an instigator. "I'm not one for holidays. But I'd love to hear about the party when it's over." I smiled before he could ask.

He didn't care. "Mia and Sabrina already told James yes."

"You're despicable."

"Just thorough."

"Where's the party?"

"James's mum's home right outside London. Tomorrow night." As we approached a puddle, he caught my hand so I could hop over. I attempted to detach myself from the feeling until my hand was back at my side. "It's invite-only, so no one else from Townsen will be there. You'd even get to wear a pretty dress."

"I'll think about it." I wouldn't. Thinking about it would be precarious. It would mean I wanted to say yes.

We turned down my street. My tree waited at the end of the

block.

But he stopped abruptly, pulling us to the side under the black and white striped awning of Brina's favorite floral shop, away from those passing by. It was closed now, its black windows acting as a mirror.

"Come with me. Be my date," he offered. He dropped the umbrella at his side.

I wanted to say yes.

But my answer had to be no. I couldn't let *wanting* steer my life. I'd end up like my parents if I did.

"Dorian—"

"Hear me out. It's a masquerade. No one will know it's you. No one would know it's us."

"My friend loves you," I reiterated.

He stepped closer.

My throat tightened. The bones making up each structure in my chest wavered like a coastal cottage cracked by the salty ocean air.

The telephone booth across the street watched us. The lights inside flickered as if it was frantically waving a hand saying, *What are you doing?*

I don't know. I really don't know. His hand is on my forearm and it's draining me of all my logic.

"Based on the way you're looking at me right now, I'm starting to doubt that's the reason." He shook his head. Rain droplets flew from the ends of his hair.

"It doesn't matter what my reason is. *You have a girlfriend.*"

"I do not." His eyebrows drew in.

"I saw about twenty articles that said so."

"You sure know nothing about a fake headline for someone

working in marketing."

"You're *kissing* someone in them."

"That doesn't mean anything," he pressed.

"Do you hear yourself?"

"It. Doesn't. Mean. Anything."

"Prove it then," I argued.

One moment his eyes were skipping across my face like a pebble in a pond. And the next, his hand was leaving my forearm and taking the back of my neck, pulling me in.

I didn't have time to react. There was no time to react when Dorian Blackwood looked at you like that.

His lips met mine and I gasped despite myself. It felt like all the lights in London exploded.

His hand tugged the hair at the nape of my neck, and I leaned into his hold, kissing him back without hesitation. I reacted as if this was habitual. Like my subconscious—who had been designing my dreams for the past two months—kicked in and took hold of the pedal. Heavy-footed, it pushed to the floor.

I was drowning. Back in that pond outside the school and he was bringing me back to shore again. Holding me up, cupping the sides of my face. The drumming of the rain on the sidewalk was a distant sound compared to the roaring in my ears.

We're kissing. We're kissing. We're kissing and I don't want to pull away.

His lips were soft and sweet and consuming and decisive.

Like feeling the seasons turn from summer to fall, when the goosebumps spread, the air chilled, and the trees changed. It was beautiful and steadfast. Then one night, you were placing the hot skin of your palm against the frosted window to cool yourself down from the heat of the hearth.

But I couldn't cool down. Every surface of my body that he touched was on fire. Every surface of my body that he *wasn't* touching was on fire. Anticipation was the brink, and I wanted to dive in.

I grabbed onto his jacket and pulled him against my chest.

He groaned. His lips parted just enough in the proclamation, and I was instantly parting mine. I wanted more. I needed more.

His hands left my face and ran down my back, making their way to my hips. It was primal—the way he held onto me, the way he kissed me. But there was also a sense of care. Caution.

I couldn't think on it further. Not when we were accelerating.

His tongue ran over my bottom lip and his heart thumped against mine as I finally explored the clean smell of his hair that lived on the T-shirt he had given me two weeks ago.

It was painful, how familiar it all was.

"We should stop," I murmured between breaths.

"Should we?" he asked against my lips.

God, his voice was so attractive, and I found myself leaning onto my toes to reach more of him.

"I've thought about this every day," he whispered.

I had thought about this every day too. I had thought about the way his hands clutched onto my hips. And how he kissed with his head tilted to the left. The way he unwound, letting all of his truths spill out as if I force-fed him some serum.

I wore these thoughts like a Scarlet Letter since that night in August. They smeared my face every time I looked at him.

Now, they were officially stitched into my skin. Paint glued to a canvas.

Suddenly, the sound of the rain became clearer. I could hear it bouncing off the awning above my head. I could hear the creaky sound of the front door of our apartment building opening down the block. The pot smacking against the stovetop in my kitchen where Brina was most likely making us dinner right now in the only place I had called home in eight years.

I was guilty.

If I wasn't guilty before, I was guilty now.

I knew what Dorian meant to Sabrina this time around and I went ahead and kissed him anyway and *enjoyed it*. I already let myself think about *him* and *us* for *months*.

And now I was acting on all of those thoughts.

I pulled away, suffering from labored breathing and the look on his face. The evidence of us kissing was in the dark color of his lips and the dishevelment of his hair. I hadn't even realized I had been running my hands through it.

I clutched my chest. I couldn't muster up words in this state. I couldn't be logical right now.

"I need to go," were the only words I could come up with. I turned—

He reached for my hand. "Adelaide, wait—"

"No." I squeezed my eyes shut. "This was a mistake. You live a very different life than mine, and even if you didn't, I have a life that can't exist with you in it."

"You don't mean that." His grip loosened on my palm. "We can make this work."

"Make *what* work? This isn't personal, but I don't care to build any type of connection. I have no interest in building any type of relationship with anyone. So don't waste your time because I'm not capable of loving you."

His face fell.

I didn't know why I was surprised, because that was my

goal—to get him to back off.

But I didn't realize how much it was going to puncture me in return.

For once in my life, I understood what it must've felt like for my father to have left my mother. And for my mother to have had to face it despite believing something else entirely.

19

"Mia, I'm not going."

"But it's Halloween!"

"I hate holidays!"

"But you have to come!"

"No, I don't!" I raced away from her. We were running in circles around the fountain outside Buckingham Palace—our favorite place to sit and have breakfast before our shift on Saturdays.

I was surprised we hadn't startled any guards yet. (We definitely spooked a few tourists.) Maybe we looked too idiotic to be worth the hassle of being dragged to the dungeon.

"Why not?" she whined, stopping.

I halted, turning around to face her from several feet away. "Because there's only six weeks left of the semester and I have—"

She took several rushed steps forward. "No, no, no. What is it *really?*"

"What do you mean?"

"Right there. That. You're pulling at your earring. You're hiding something." She pointed at me with narrowed eyes.

I crossed my arms. "I am not that easy to read."

"Did something happen last night before I got home? Yes! That's it. Explain. Now." She took a seat on the edge of the fountain, waiting.

Reluctantly, I joined her. The water *pinged* behind us as a child threw a coin in.

"Did you and Dorian get into a fight?"

"Possibly."

"What was the fight about?"

I covered my face. "Boutuskissing."

"Huh?" she leaned in.

"Itwasaboutuskissing."

Her gum fell out of her mouth. "You *kissed!*"

"Be quiet!"

"You kissed and waited *this* long to tell me?" She stood and began to pace.

"There's really no need to pace. It's only been like twelve hours."

"I can't believe you kissed him. *Again!*"

"Well, he kissed me, if we're going to get technical about it."

She paused her pacing. "I *knew* he liked you. I just knew it. This changes everything. Before it was just some one night fling. But now you two know each other and you've kissed with all of this knowledge of another and prior intimacy—"

"Are you done?"

"Wait. How did it lead to an argument? Was it bad?" She was horrified by the idea.

"I wish." I massaged my temples. "He asked me to be his date tonight."

Realization swept her face. "This is why you won't go? *You told him no?* Why would you do that!"

"Why do you think?"

"Shit." She paused. "Maybe it's time to tell her, Addy."

I thought about telling Sabrina constantly. I thought about what she would say. How she would react. How maybe it was possible she wouldn't hate me and would understand the situation. But now I had kissed him *knowing*.

The pictures of him and Victoria destroyed her. There were so many tears; her lipstick drying up and falling off her lips like dead rose petals.

How would she feel knowing that her *best friend* had been doing the same thing?

"She'll hate me, Mia." My voice thickened.

Her eyes softened. "She could never hate you."

"I hate me."

She bit the inside of her cheek. "Did Dorian take the rejection well?"

"As well as he could've. I said some horrible things though. And he just … stood there and took it. He probably hates me too. It'll be better this way though. We can return to hating one another until the semester is over."

"I think you're underestimating the power of tension."

Ten hours later, the pads of Mia and Sabrina's feet were smacking against the hardwood floor as they rushed to get dressed. Trying one another's shoes on, swapping purses, asking for advice on which teardrop earrings looked better with their masks. (Diamonds on Mia, emeralds on Brina.)

Hairspray and perfume pinched my tear ducts. They zipped

back and forth into my room, searching through my thrifted accessories. I watched from the couch with my June edition of *The New Yorker* reading a story on "The Dread of Getting Dressed."

"Dreadful it is," I hummed, watching Brina take her vintage silk-wrapped headband off for a tenth time. I shoved myself further into the couch cushion, letting my hood knot my hair.

"Ta-da!" Mia announced, tugging Brina (who decided on the headband) into the hallway.

The theme of the ball was black-tie with jewel tones. Sapphire, crimson, emerald, et cetera.

Mia had her box braids pulled into a low bun to show off her backless magenta dress with a halter neckline. While Sabrina stood in a deep emerald dress made of chiffon.

I clapped. "You guys look beautiful! Why are you moping?"

"Because you should be coming." Brina's glossy pink lips turned down.

"I'll be—" The buzzer inside the apartment went off. "Did you invite someone?" I sat up abruptly. They exchanged a look but showed no sign of opening the door.

Pushing myself out of the crack of the cushions and putting my slippers on, I opened the door.

"James?" I asked, perplexed. He had sage green suit on, and his hair was pushed back. He always looked dapper, but he managed to upstage himself now.

For his party. That he was supposed to be at right now.

I turned for an explanation, but my roommates had disappeared.

James took in my appearance with a confused look. I brushed down my hair with my hand. "Where is your dress?"

"What do you mean?" I asked.

"The masquerade ..." The space between his eyebrow crinkled with confusion. "I came to get you all."

"Did Dorian not tell you I wasn't coming?" I whispered, gripping the door as I leaned forward. *That stubborn, persistent, rigid man.*

"He did. But I thought Mia had convinced you to come."

"She didn't." The energetic look on his face slipped. "I'm sorry. It's really better if I stay back."

"That's ridiculous. You have to come."

Mia shouted from down the hall, "Addy, you turn twenty-two in two weeks! Have *fun,* live your life. We're in London!"

"What Mia said," he agreed.

"Even if I wanted to come, I don't have anything to wear." I turned to walk away but was stopped by Sabrina and Mia.

"So ... we did a thing. It doesn't exactly match the theme, but we thought you'd look beautiful in it." As she finished, she pulled her hands from behind her back, revealing a dress. It was a floor-length silver gown made of silk. Almost like something out of a Roman museum. It looked like stone with the bateau neckline and a completely open back.

I looked to Mia for help. I couldn't accept this.

Say yes, she mouthed. Her eyes creased at the sides with care.

"Go get dressed," Sabrina said lovingly, handing the dress off.

The skin on my back was left entirely exposed, from the nape of my neck to the bottom of my spine. The cold leather of James's car seats chilled my shoulder blades for the entire drive.

I anxiously adjusted the strands of hair hanging outside my low bun. This was a horrible idea. A dreadful idea. It was being jotted down in the book of poor decisions. Right beside dying my hair blond when I was fifteen and returning Dorian's kiss.

"Wow," Sabrina and Mia sighed harmoniously as we pulled up to the property.

When Dorian said the masquerade was taking place at James's mother's home, he had failed to mention that the home was not a house.

We were pulling up to a mansion that was surrounded by acres of rolling grass and a driveway that ran the length of the home.

We followed a line of cars that were dropping guests off in jewel-toned gowns and velvet suits, all donned in masks.

My heart pounded louder each time a new guest stepped out. My eyes scoured every head of hair and jawline, questioning if Dorian would come.

"Adelaide." James's voice cut me off. He was holding my door open, giving me his hand. His green mask was already in place.

I pulled the small silver mask over my face and took his hand. "Thank you."

"You alright?" he whispered.

I nodded. I needed to get my eyes on Dorian before I could relax.

"You never mentioned that you lived in castle," I commented.

He laughed. "Maybe it's because I don't live here."

"But you used to," I guessed.

"Well, yes I did grow up here," he said unwillingly.

"Why move? It's not too far from campus."

"Living with one's mother while also trying to have a social life and build a career isn't exactly ideal."

"I don't know, I think the idea of having a mother who wants to know about those things sounds like a gift."

"You're telling me you enjoy having your mother meddle in your business?"

"If she ever had, I would've welcomed it."

He looked at me with a long, weighted stare. The solemn stare the moon gave me every Halloween as kids ran by the house; parents holding onto pillowcases and disregarded capes.

A look that pulled at the corners of my lips. The same regretful look professors gave me when they asked if my mom was proud of my high test scores.

The sooner the uncomfortable questions came up, the sooner we could file this topic away as One to Never Speak Of.

His words were rickety, shaking like a fence with a rain-rotted picket. "I didn't mean to—"

I took his hand. "Don't let me trip up the stairs. This color would be impossible to get stains out of."

With Mia and Brina behind us, we followed groups of guests as we ascended the staircase that opened up the home. A high-arched ceiling with a skylight greeted us at the entrance. We passed painted portraits and framed photographs of runway shows and …

Holy shit. I forgot.

I spent my entire life cutting out dresses and purses and perfumes from Beverly's newest campaigns to add to my mood boards above my bed. I dug through every pocketbook section in every thrift store in hopes of finding an original Beverly. I even did last year's branding project on Beverly's re-introduction of their 90s shoulder purse collection.

And now I was in the home of the longest running Chief Designer of Beverly.

I drank each image in, trying to memorize them all. Photographs of the 1995 Autumn/Winter show. Of the original design of their crescent purse. Of their newest campaign with Luna Aldridge. Private, personal images seen only by the people in those images and this house.

I pressed my hands against the silk on my hips to dry my hands.

I should've taken more time to do my hair. Paid more attention to the way I styled myself. I should've worn my signet ring or maybe just more deodorant. I didn't even match the theme for God's sake. I was a flute of champagne in a room full of lavish red wine.

James welcomed guests, shaking hands every few minutes as we made our way to the end of the grand hallway where we were emptied out into a Cinderella-sized ballroom that bled into a dining room. It was filled with spinning fabric and bright smiles. Feathers, sparkles, silk. Open balconies peppered the sides of the room, looking over the rolling green hills.

"Finally, Jameson! I've been waiting for you. What took you so long?" A woman in a ruby red dress and black lace mask immediately approached us.

I stopped short. Cressida Breyer was in front of me. *Chief Designer of Beverly* Cressida Breyer.

"I was picking up Adelaide and her friends, remember?" James gestured to us.

I prayed she couldn't see the beat of my heart through the silk.

"*Oh.*" Her attention turned to me.

I stretched my hand forward with a smile. "It's so nice to meet you, Mrs. Breyer, you have a wonderful son."

She smiled. It was James's smile. Sweet and kind.

Large diamonds overtook my palm as she returned my gesture. "What a lovely dress."

Cressida Breyer likes my dress. "Thank you," I responded as if I was a sane person.

"If you don't mind, I need to find Dorian so I can make my announcement. I left that poor boy with my notes."

Sabrina's entire presence beside me crackled like a firework. I didn't have to turn to see her blush.

"I'm going to find the bathroom," I lied.

With haste, I made for the first balcony I spotted.

20

Don't Dance with Him — Adelaide

One moment, I was checking my watch like I had a pumpkin carriage to catch, waiting for enough appropriate time to pass so that I could leave. The next, I was pretending to be interested in the man who entered the balcony after me to talk about the weather. Dreadful stuff. Doppler radar specific.

But I couldn't escape. Not with Dorian out there.

Hence why, when he leaned into kiss me, I let it happen.

Both random, and uncalled for, I know.

It was fine. Nothing to write about in a diary with invisible ink. My cheeks were warm, but it wasn't anything compared to Dorian's grasp and Dorian's urge and Dorian's lips.

It was a distraction. Purely a distraction. A way to hide and not be bothered and not continue to look for *him* in the crowd.

The frigid air nipped at my exposed back as the man deepened the kiss, tilting his head.

I'm not inebriated enough for this.

"Wait." I pulled away before he could find a crevice of my mouth to explore. "I think I—"

A hand from behind grabbed onto my arm and pulled me out

of the cold air and back into the ballroom before I could realize what was happening.

The hand was attached to a man with rich dark hair and clad in a well-fitted navy blue suit.

Along with a freckle at the back of his neck that I stared at three times a week.

"*Dorian*," I whispered with fury. He kept going. We were almost at the center of the ballroom now. Voluminous dresses brushed against my ankles as pairs gathered for the music to begin again. I touched my face to confirm my mask was still in place.

He stopped once we were at the center, his hand falling on my back lightly. It was so much worse than just pressing deeply into my skin. Now I had to remain rigid and refrain from leaning into it. His other hand slipped into my right palm delicately, as if he was holding a pocket watch.

Then the music began, and my chest was against his.

No smirk or rebuttal. The bored look that was partially covered by his navy blue mask surprised me. No secret italicized message to infer.

"I'm not sure if you noticed, but I already had company," I commented as the music rang.

"I don't think he wanted your company anymore," he responded matter-of-factly. "And I don't think you wanted his, by the look of it."

"Says the one who dragged me out here." I narrowed my eyes.

The skin on my back cooled as his hand left. His thumb grazed my cheek as he lifted my mask up. He asked, "Are you questioning my intentions?"

I swatted his hand away and pulled the mask back down. "With a track record like yours, I think I am."

He scoffed. "I think you're the one with questionable intentions."

"And how is that?"

"You show up here, despite rejecting my invitation, throw it in my face by kissing another man in this—this, I don't even know if this counts as a dress—then you act like you don't even know me." He wouldn't look at me. His gaze brushed my shoulder. "Frankly, it should be illegal for someone to wear a dress like this. This is an elegant event. It's really not appropriate."

He was flushed. It was comical. Dorian Blackwood was *embarrassed*.

"I don't remember asking for your opinion but thanks for that. And also, I didn't plan on coming," I defended myself.

"Yet here you are."

"I'm not happy about it either."

"I'm glad we can agree on something."

"Me too," I responded firmly.

The violins plucked fast notes. I inhaled sharply as I was released and pulled back, my spine against his chest. I stared straight ahead, for something, someone to focus on that wasn't Dorian's face beside mine.

I caught James's face in the crowd talking with Mia and Sabrina.

"Did James tell you I was here?" I asked.

"What?" He turned me back around.

"James—is that how you knew where to find me?"

"I didn't need anyone to tell me how to find you," he clarified. "I saw you leaning against the balcony. Your back is practically painted in my brain."

Looking at him was a mistake.

I swallowed the emotions. Or at least I tried to. But my emotions were stubborn. Unwilling to go down. Because one look and I was falling back into our trysts. Into last night's kiss. Into August's night. Into every dream that had spoiled my thoughts.

The urge to kiss him was so potent that I had to look to the ceiling.

It'll pass was the only thing I could tell myself to alleviate the yearning in my gut.

Once the music finished, I was unraveling myself from his grasp and taking quick steps away. His focus on my back was blazing.

21

Don't Get Jealous Around Her — *Dorian*

One moment I was fetching James's mother's speech and the next I was finding Adelaide Adorno's body wrapped in another man's hands and her lips enveloped in his.

There was a mask shielding the top half of her face. It didn't matter though. I could spot her from a mile away. I could see it in the curve of her jaw and the freckle at the bottom of her back.

Jesus Christ, that dress was low.

She was pressed up against the railing of the balcony. And she was kissing him back.

She was kissing him back.

I couldn't watch. But I couldn't stop either. It was making all of the muscles in my back stiffen and trapping my focus on her. On him. On her. On him *touching* her. On her *kissing* him. Kissing him the same way she had kissed—

I took strides across the ballroom.

What is she doing? What am I doing? What the bloody hell I am doing?

Well, it looked like I was pulling her off of him and forcing her into the ballroom so that she couldn't scream at me.

The air from the balcony pushed at my suit jacket.

Instinctively, I grabbed her arm and his grasp on her released. For a dazed moment, she followed my footsteps into the center of the ballroom without a word.

Not the original plan but frustration was running the show and there was no going back now.

No one turned a head. Dresses swished back and forth in conversation. We simply joined the next group of guests planning to dance.

"*Dorian.*" There it was. She was pissed.

That made two of us.

I turned once the music began, taking her against my chest. I slipped my hand into hers while the other hovered over her exposed back to lead the same four steps as the rest of the crowd.

"I'm not sure if you noticed, but I already had company," she stated coldly.

I resisted looking at her and spoke to the air. "I don't think he wanted your company anymore. And I don't think you wanted his."

"Says the one who dragged me out here."

Was she really going to act like she was enjoying that guy's company?

I succumbed and swept my gaze over her face.

What a terrible mistake.

Her lips were swollen to a deep burgundy. And her big, spellbinding eyes were cut into dramatic slits; narrowed in determination. If I searched lower than her face, then all of my anger would fizzle out.

The original conversation I had planned—the one where I'd tell her I never wanted to see her again and we could throw this whole tutoring thing out the window just so I could save myself some embarrassment—diminished.

Because looking at her now—holding her, reminding myself of the coconut smell in her hair and the perfect *V* that connected her top lip and the bite her of words—was a mistake. I didn't want to go.

She yelled at you, I reminded myself. *She made a mockery of you in the middle of the street about coming as your date and being involved romantically and now she was here, kissing someone else.*

But last night, she had also kissed me like she missed me. The same way I've missed her on this instinctual, primal level.

Her eyes pierced every part of the room with intention. I'd do anything to have them in my direction. Even if it meant facing a few cuts.

She was such a difficult person to read.

Always focused, always carrying a rebuttal. But I could never figure out what thoughts were carved under those looks. Especially not with the line between her brows being covered.

I tilted my head down and slipped my thumb under her mask, nudging it off her face.

"Are you questioning my intentions?" I argued.

She brushed my hand away so quickly that I missed my opportunity to read her.

"With a track record like yours, I think I am," she said.

"I think you're the one with questionable intentions."

"And how is that?" Her eyes narrowed.

I inhaled. Exhaled.

There was no calming the caged bird flapping its wings inside my chest when I was both close enough to see the angry crinkle above her nose as I told her she was wrong and yet still close enough to kiss her. Her eyes were piercing through me, daring me to go on.

"You show up here, despite rejecting my invitation, throw it in my face by kissing another man in this—this, I don't even know if this counts as a dress—and then you act like you don't even know me. Frankly, it should be illegal for someone to wear a dress like this. This is an elegant event. It's really not appropriate."

"I don't remember asking for your opinion but thanks for that," she huffed. "And also, I didn't plan on coming."

"Yet here you are." I looked away.

"I'm not happy about it either."

"I'm glad we can agree on something."

"Me too."

Her lips remained tightly closed until I was releasing her and pulling her back into my chest. Then her mouth opened.

"Did James tell you I was here?" she asked.

"What?" I needed to start keeping count of how often she brought up James.

"James—is that how you knew where to find me?"

"I didn't need anyone to tell me how to find you. I saw you leaning against the balcony. Your back is practically painted in my brain." I hated how much I had her memorized. I hated how much overtime my brain was running to remember her while I slept, injecting it into my dreams.

I expected retaliation. But nothing came. Only a bright rim of gray painted around her iris that lit with surprise. As if I told her I knew her deepest secret and planned to release it on dove-delivered letters.

She searched my face and then plagued every thought by staring at my mouth.

My hand twitched on her lower back.

What if she was lying? What if she did want this?

I'm not capable of loving you, she had said.

The music halted and she was creating distance between us faster than I could think.

22

Don't Sit In Between Them — Adelaide

Spotting Mia and Sabrina in the crowd, I followed their path out of the ballroom and into the dining room where three long tables fit for serving an army spanned the space.

A hand brushed my wrist as I passed over the threshold. I jerked it back, expecting to find Dorian.

"There you are, we never got to dance," James said, his mask pushed over his hair.

"I know, I'm so sorry. I really just needed some air," I winced, hoping he, and everyone else, hadn't realized I was with Dorian.

"It's alright, there's always another ball or gala to dance at." He laughed. "Come, let's sit."

Before I could find Mia or Sabrina, James was pulling out two seats at the center of the table for us.

"Have your thoughts on holidays changed yet?" he asked.

"Oh Jameson, I'm not that easy." I smoothed out the hair on the top of my head as I pulled my own mask off.

"Come on, you can't say you aren't having fun."

"Maybe a little." I pinched the air.

He laughed, shaking his head. His smile twinkled under the

chandelier.

I reached for his hand on the arm of the chair. "Thank you for inviting me."

"It wouldn't have been worth coming if you weren't here." He squeezed my hand back. His gaze skipped from my face to a space behind me. "There he is. I haven't seen you all night!" He stood, taking a few steps from the table.

"Sorry, I was busy arguing with—"

I turned around at the sound of his voice. James stepped to the side just enough, halting Dorian's sentence.

"Adelaide, how nice to see you tonight," Dorian commented.

"Good to see you," I responded with a closed lip smile.

"Who were you arguing with?" James asked, taking a seat again.

Dorian took a step forward, right as an older woman filled the seat beside James. He looked at me, and then the open seat beside me.

Oh no. *Please, no.*

He slid the chair out and sat down, looking as if he was taking a seat beside the dreaded Aunt Margaret he mentioned once.

How quickly I had fallen to Aunt Margaret status.

He took his cloth napkin and folded it over his leg before leaning towards me—*towards James* to answer his question. I pressed my back firmly against the chair. A button from the cushion pierced my spine. I'd let it drill a hole through my skin though.

"I was arguing with this girl. I had invited her to come last night, but she turned me down and showed up anyway," Dorian explained.

Dammit, Dorian.

"She's here, right now?" James was abashed. Then *he* leaned in. I could smell his woodsy cologne and see the rich brown of his hair growing in at the root.

"Yup. And I found her kissing another guy."

"*What?* You need to point her out."

"Actually, I think you know her—"

"I can just move so you both can speak," I offered eagerly, trying to end this conversation.

Placing my hands on the side of my chair, I pushed myself up—

"*No,*" they blurted out. Their hands landed on my legs. Dorian's right hand on my left thigh and James's left on my right. All of my blood rushed to my lap. Their hands projected catastrophic levels of heat into my skin despite the fabric of my dress dividing the grasps.

"Okay …" I agreed, sitting back down.

They immediately retrieved their hands.

With a cleared throat from James and a slug of wine from Dorian, I was left ironing the silk on my lap with my hands.

James spoke up. "Um, so, the weather has been really great despite it being the end of October and everything—"

Buzz. My phone screen lit up.

"Thank god," Dorian muttered.

I reached for the phone.

Mia: Everything good over there?

My head snapped up, and I found Mia sitting directly in front of us—two tables down, twenty feet away.

Her eyebrows rose as she stared at both boys.

Me: Am I providing you with ample entertainment?

Mia: Almost too much. I don't know if I can fit this all on Monday night's call. My cousins will have lots of follow-up questions. Like if throuples are common in England.

Me: There is no throupleness happening over here.

Me: Does Sabrina see Dorian?

Mia: Luckily, no. She thinks you're talking with James. She's busy chatting with his mom anyway.

Me: YOU'RE SITTING WITH CRESSIDA BREYER?!?

Mia: Should I have mentioned that first?

Me: Mia.

Mia: I'm kiddingggg. I actually asked her about summer internships because I know how you think eight months in advance for everything. Beverly "typically puts out internship listings in November" and "favors high GPAs and a personable cover letters". But they're only hiring one public relations intern…

Me: Shit.

Mia: Why don't you tell her you're interested?

Me: And get a leg up because I'm friends with her son? I don't think so.

Mia: Why do you have to be so moral??? People use connections all the time. Nepotism is the cause of generational wealth.

Me: I'm not using James! I want them to hire me because they're impressed by me anyways.

Mia: Fine.

Mia: You could always talk to James.

Me: We're not saying anything to James.

Three dots appeared and disappeared.

Me: Say it.

Mia: You should consider asking your aunt. She used to work for a company like Beverly. Maybe she still has her cover letter.

I stared at the phone. She was right. But I didn't want to.

Asking for help meant revealing that I couldn't do everything on my own and admitting that to her. It meant owing her one more thing on top of the tower of things I already owed her for living under her roof.

But I wanted this internship. It was the stepping stone to my Dream Life. I just didn't know if I was willing to ask for help when I had come this far without it.

The sound of glass hitting the tablecloth pulled me from my phone.

I looked up and realized Dorian had left.

23

Don't Let Him Stay in Your System — Adelaide

"This can't be real," Jane uttered.

"It's not possible!" Lottie gasped, looking over Jane's shoulder.

Book Club found out about page twenty-six. Apparently, Dotty left it on the desk the night Dorian walked me home during Mia's late shift.

Apparently.

Evelyn took the phone from Jane and put her reading glasses on. "This must be altered," she swore.

"That scammy AI they keep talking about!" Cora realized.

Beatrice reached over her armrest and stole the phone from Evelyn.

"I'm not sure what that's supposed to mean but that boy's hands are *low*." Beatrice lowered her glasses.

"You're sure these are from October? Maybe they're old photos," Cora hoped. It reminded me of what Dorian had said: *You sure know nothing about a fake headline for someone working in marketing.*

"Cora, he's wearing the same clothes Addy saw him in that night," Dotty deadpanned.

"I liked him," Evelyn sighed.

"I still like him!" Iris raised her hand.

"Me too!" Lottie raised her hand too.

Dotty rolled her eyes.

"Time's up!" I announced, pushing out of my seat and taking the magazine—back.

At least last time I only had to see a few photos. This time was hell.

Roughly twenty-five dark, blurry images of Dorian and Victoria outside of her apartment scattered in this *one* article. I could see the paint on his fingers from our night out.

The image turned over the contents in my stomach. Her hands in his hair. His hands on her waist. Her hands. His hands.

The same hands that were on my lower back last weekend on Halloween.

Even now, the frames of his and James's palms were still nailed into my thighs.

Last weekend was an omen. A wakeup call. I was getting too close. Too involved.

The filing cabinet in my brain that took notes on everything about him had been shifting to a Mason jar, relocating to my chest. It was filling itself with colorful notes scribbled with words he liked to use and postcards on stories he told me and scraps of fabric from the clothes he wore the most. Jam packed with private things I shouldn't know about him.

He was building. No longer just a single-layered person, but a scrapbook-stacked human whose habits I was memorizing.

These pictures were good for me. Tonight was good for me. Dorian not showing up for tutoring all week put me on edge, but it was probably for the best. James showing up to walk me home this week made me feel worse somehow.

Between thinking about Dorian and refreshing the Beverly Careers page every twenty minutes, this unresolvable anxious knot wouldn't stop twisting in my chest.

"Maybe it's because you turned him down!" Jane reasoned.

"Yes!" Lottie liked that idea. "Did you tell him you like him yet?"

"I do not like him!"

"Don't act like we didn't notice how smitten you were when he was saying how smart and beautiful you are," Beatrice responded.

"He did not say beautiful." He had said *pretty*. Lampshades were pretty for God's sake.

"So you do remember!" Beatrice pointed her knitting needle at me.

We were currently knitting socks. Evelyn just found out she'd be a grandmother and believed the baby would grow up with a poor immune system if they didn't have enough socks.

For reference, I had no idea how to knit, but I was trying like my life depended on it. I didn't half-ass a craft.

"That means nothing, Beatrice." I pointed back at her, droopy loops of yarn hanging off my needle.

"Do you remember Reginald?" Dotty spoke up.

"How could I forget? He was in our flat for a month," Iris complained.

"The American that had a boat?" Lottie asked.

"And a missing a tooth?" Jane shivered.

Dotty nodded. "Besides the point. I met him in a pub one night years ago. We were having his great conversation about a band we both saw in the nineties. He was so handsome. Smelled like popcorn and scotch. Then the fire alarm went off and everyone funneled out into the street, and I lost him. Thought about him for weeks after. Never thought about a fella so much before. Don't you think I see him at the corner shop down the street a month later? He put away everything in his hands and took me out on a date. Never cared about him since."

"What are you getting at, Dotty?" Evelyn asked.

"Shouldn't have asked," Iris shook her head.

Dotty looked at me. "It sounds like he's still in your system. You know what they say about that?"

"Ah yes. You need to start a new hobby," Cora nodded.

"How did you even end up in this group?" A sock landed on Cora's head.

Nine days into November. Every window in the university had no choice but to welcome the autumnal colors. We were surrounded by acres of land that longed to be let in. The tips of trees surrounding the property were kissed by the sun, granted orange and yellow colors. The colors bounced off the walls in the university.

The leather of my loafers skimmed the carpet as I walked into the library Monday morning before Sylvie's class. With midterms over, it was empty. Even the librarians' eyes were half closed when I walked in.

But hiding in here gave me an excuse to 1) avoid possibly bumping into Dorian before our class, and 2) finally having the chance to get some test shots of these watches for the content calendar.

Dropping my textbooks on the table in the furthest corner, I unlatched the clasp and set it over the leather of my bag, positioning my camera. A little to the left. A little to the right. Capture the hardwood in the back. Right there should be—

"Can you believe he's with her again?" a girl asked.

My phone immediately hit my bag. I rushed to pick it up, as if it would erase the noise.

I turned but didn't see anyone. Completely empty.

"It's so boring. We practically have a Kennedy on campus and he's not even single," another girl spoke up.

My heart thumped. *Dorian*.

Their voices were coming from straight ahead. Like they were speaking to me.

The studying nooks.

The nooks were hidden behind the wooden panels to the right in the wall. I put my phone down and inched forward towards the first nook.

The door was wide open. No one inside. Just extra books stacked high, filling the single bench and legroom.

"About that …" a different girl commented, and it was *close*. Hair-raisingly close. It pushed my heart into my throat.

Logically, I jumped into the empty nook, closing the door slowly to ease the squeak, and hid. I didn't even have to push my ear to the wall to hear them. They were in the spot beside mine.

A pause passed. No one spoke. *Did they hear me?* I leaned my head against the wall.

Suddenly, there was a shadow under the door. Two shoes.

Shit, shit, shit. No hidden doors to escape out of, no corners to crouch in, no air ducts to jump in.

I had nowhere to hide, but the knob turned anyway.

24

Why was she standing against the wall like that?

"Why are you stand—"

Her eyes lit with the same rage she had when I pulled her from the balcony on Halloween. It was both terrifying and surprisingly invigorating.

Maybe even more terrifying now as she latched onto my wrist and yanked, pulling me into the tight space and slapping her other hand over my mouth.

"We have to stop meeting like this." I pulled her hand off my mouth, thinking of when we were stuck behind the couch in the bookshop.

"Be quiet," she whispered, reaching past me to shut the door.

I got a strong whiff of the sweet coconut-scented lip gloss she wore. It gave me a headache that would reappear once my head hit my pillow tonight.

We were uncomfortably close. My hands itched to pull her closer. I could even count the number of gems in her pendant at this proximity.

"Why?" I asked.

"Because I'm investigating."

"Investigating? Investigating what?"

"If people know about us."

"So you're snooping."

"I am not snooping," she argued

"Says the one hidden in a closet with her ear pressed against the wall like a retired detective."

"I don't even know what that means." She pinched the bridge of her nose. "And it's a reading nook. We're in a reading nook."

"You're not helping yourself here."

"Says the one stalking me."

"Stalking you? You sit in the same spot *every day.* I walked about three feet to find you."

She looked me up and down. It made the muscles in my hand flinch. My brain was having trouble dissecting that the look was not to actually *look* at me but to analyze me.

"Stop looking at me like that," I told her.

"Like what?"

"Like I followed you in here when you're the one up to something. If anything, it'd seem like you were luring me here. If you wanted to be locked in a room with me so badly you could've just—"

"Sorry, that was my aunt. She texted me the picture." Some girl's voice came out of nowhere and Adelaide's hand was back over my mouth.

Listen, her eyes said. She removed her hand and pressed her ear against the wall. I followed.

"What did you hear?" another girl said.

The original voice responded. "My aunt was there, and she swore she saw Dorian dancing with someone else and—"

"Not Victoria?"

My heart thudded. Adelaide looked at me with wide eyes.

"Definitely not Victoria," the girl confirmed.

It's fine, I responded, trying to relax the curve of stress between her brows. Students gossiped all the time.

No, it's not, she glared.

"So what? It was a masquerade *ball!* All there is to do is dance!"

"Exactly. She was the *only* person he danced with—for the entire night. No Victoria in sight."

"What if it was his cousin or something?"

"Well, there's something else *if you had let me finish.* She said it looked like they were arguing."

"I argue with my cousins all the time."

"She said that his hand was very low on her back—the girl's back not my aunt's."

"Obviously," someone deadpanned.

"And let me preface this by saying that her dress was completely backless."

Adelaide avoided my gaze now. I should regret the hand placement, but I didn't. Holding her like that was enough of a fix for the withdrawals I had been having since kissing her.

"*Woah!* Why wasn't *that* the first thing you mentioned?"

"How low?"

"I don't know, Kate! Want me to call my aunt and ask her to point on a diagram."

"Yes."

"So he's not with Victoria anymore?"

"Dorian Blackwood is back on the market," someone hollered.

I exhaled.

"It's never too soon to start campaigning to be his date for The January ..."

Jesus Christ, they were already talking about The January. The last thing I needed was a gaggle of girls bombarding me for the next two months over needing a date. James would love to hear this.

A door creaked and footsteps spread the carpet. No more noise came from the neighboring nook.

Adelaide squeezed by, every part of her body brushing mine to get out of the tight space.

"You need to figure out who saw us so we can shut this down," she commanded.

"Adelaide—"

"*No.* Don't follow. We need to walk out separately."

"Don't be like that."

"Be like what? *Difficult?* I'm not having my entire future blow up in my face over gossip that revolves around *a man* who can't keep his hands off of every woman he sees."

My shoulders fell. "Fine. Isolate yourself. Come up with one of your plans. I don't care."

I turned and left.

If she was going to believe what everyone else thought, then fine.

25

Don't Underestimate Gossip — Adelaide

I underestimated British society's interest in the Blackwoods and the power of gossip.

"Dorian Blackwood Is London's Most Eligible Bachelor Again" — *The Scandal Sheet*

I read the article at least twelve times. And then I passed it to Iris, Dotty, and Mia, before they looked at me with worried eyes and sent me to the café down the street to take a tea break.

The article commented on the status of Dorian and Victoria's relationship: "not as solid as our sources had believed." And followed it up with evidence from the masquerade: "Blackwood was spotted devoting his attention to a young woman, who was not Sutton, the whole night."

Gossip in nooks spread quickly.

I took another sip of the bitter tea in front of me to calm my stomach and remind myself of one very important thing: no one knew it was me. There was no description of me or even the color of my dress. Apparently just the mention of another woman in

Dorian's presence was enough gossip to publish an article that'd rile Britain's dating pool.

Coming to a café was a fun idea in theory. The same way going on a run was a fun idea in theory, until it started raining and you were being partially threatened by your professor.

Since catching Sylvie at Big Ben's Bakery, I was too scared to go back. The idea of seeing her and she immediately realizing that I'd been with Dorian—many times—since her "advice," made me ill. She'd look me right in the eye, recognize my inability to follow rules, and email the Board. Then they'd rip my telephone booth keychain right off my cork board, put me on a blacklist for every tourist shop that sold a Paddington Bear, and tear up my passport. I'd never be allowed back in England and my dream of working at Beverly would disappear.

Maybe that was dramatic, but they may as well at that point. If my tuition wasn't covered, then I couldn't afford my degree.

I shivered at the image—and from the door to the café opening and letting another cold gust of wind in.

No Sylvies here at least. Just a variety of university students in cable knit sweaters with scarves thrown over the backs of their chairs while they tapped away on their laptops and pretended to read emails.

One girl at the table in front of me wasn't even pretending. She was three articles deep into this Dorian Mistress Drama. (That's what they were calling it.) One night together and a kiss months later and I was a mistress now.

I hadn't felt this sick since June when Sabrina and Mia almost got me onto the London Eye.

I opened my laptop and clicked onto Beverly's Career page. They finally released their summer internships last night.

There was only one PR internship, but there was also a marketing analyst, branding intern, event coordinator, and a social media marketing internship available.

Would it be desperate to apply to all of them?

Ugh. I added that to the list of questions I had.

"Is this seat available?"

"Actually—" My head snapped up to say no but it was—"James!" I pushed the chair forward with my foot, urging him to sit. "How did you know I was here?"

"The group of women down the street that sent you here," he laughed, sitting and unwinding his scarf. His silver hair was in disarray and his skin was pink from the wind as if he ran over.

"Ah, so you were looking for me?"

"Well, of course. How else would I know how your photos turned out?"

I groaned.

"Come on, we didn't finish our conversation yesterday! I need to see Mia's watch modeling abilities." He rubbed his hands together.

"I wasn't exaggerating when I said she forgot how wrists worked," I complained, handing him my phone.

Dragging Mia to the campus gardens this week to model my watch for my presentation was my only option. Sabrina had said no before I could even finish asking.

"They can't be that—*how does one even bend their wrist like that?* Why is she curling up her fingers in all of these?" He burst into laughter.

I leaned forward. "I don't know! I didn't even bother pulling out my actual camera because it was so bad."

"What was her reaction?"

"Eagle-pitched laughter, followed by her urgency to ask you or Dorian."

"Me and Dorian?"

"You know a lot about fashion, so you have a very artistic eye. And Dorian is plastered across half of London on cologne ads." I waved my hand.

"I tend to forget about that," he said. "Well, I'm nowhere near a model but I'd obviously help. We'd both help."

"That's very sweet of you, but that's not what I meant. I'll figure it out." I smiled appreciatively.

"He's been dodging me all week too, if it makes you feel better," he reassured me. Not that I needed reassurance.

I told Dorian to stay away from me. Whether he was choosing to ignore me now or was busy figuring out what flavor Victoria's lip gloss was, I didn't care.

"He tends to isolate himself when everyone's talking about him. I'm going to assume you know about the article seeing as you were … ya know. It may be everywhere right now, but it'll blow over. They always do, so don't think too much about it," he advised, reaching for my palm and squeezing. I squeezed back. "You have a project to worry about anyways."

If Dorian was catastrophic storms, then James was the light rain that followed. His voice always quiet and comforting like small patters of rain droplets against your window on a summer night.

"When do you need your photos by?" he asked.

"Next Friday." Right before my birthday.

Next weekend I had plans with both Iris and Dotty, and Mia and Brina. If I missed either because of assignments, they may actually drag me out the door with my laptop glued to my fingertips.

"Dorian and I have some red carpet event this weekend. You could stop by then, if that works?" he asked.

Could one even "stop by" a red carpet? "James, that sounds like a huge inconvenience."

"I'd actually have something to look forward to if you came. Not that Dorian isn't great company, but you know what I mean."

"I really don't think he would appreciate me showing up in the middle of that," I argued.

"You guys can't avoid each other forever."

He was right. It had already been two weeks. I couldn't avoid him forever. Especially when I was so worried about him keeping our promise intact.

"He wants to see you," he finished.

That pierced my chest like a serrated dagger through the skin. It was lodged in there. No chance of getting those words out now. Not until I saw him for himself and was able to determine if that was true.

"How about this: come early before I even meet up with Dorian. That way there's no pressure to see him," he offered.

"Did I ever mention that you were my favorite human?"

"Not nearly enough." He attempted to hide a satisfied smile. "It's at Leicester Square. I'll send you everything you need."

"If you change your mind—"

"I won't. Now I'll let you get back to—well, working? What are you doing right now? I thought you were supposed to be on a break."

I looked at the internship listings on my laptop and then glanced back at him.

I could ask him right now. Ask him if Beverly would notice if

I applied to more than one position. Ask him if I should include my volunteer work or sacrifice it for my hobbies, since there was only room for one when my internships took up the rest of my resume. Would Beverly want someone who was passionate about helping the community or had an interest in fashionable DIYs?

"Just proofreading," I lied. Another lie with another friend. "Is there anywhere nearby to get a stamp?"

26

Don't Button Up His Shirt — Adelaide

I almost committed a federal crime by stuffing my hand in the post box and pulling out the postcard addressed to Auntie Laila. There was a reason they made the slot so skinny—so you couldn't second guess your decision to send your emotionally distant aunt a postcard full of odd niceties and questions on the application process for a fashion house.

The second James left the café was the moment I realized that I needed to suck it up if I wanted this internship. The applications didn't close until February 1st, so I had two and a half months. I either had to ask James, ask my aunt, or continue to navigate unanswered Reddit pages.

Hi Auntie Laila,

I know we haven't spoken in a while. I'm actually in London right now studying abroad (hence the weird stamp) but I just wanted to reach out and say Happy Belated 32nd Birthday. I know you've studied abroad here too and enjoyed it. I'm hoping to remain in London when I graduate in May, but I need an internship for the summer. Beverly—the luxury brand I used to talk about—is hiring. I know you've worked for a fashion house before, so I just had some questions on applying to one, if you had the time?

— Addy

Now we'd wait. I'd either get a response, or I'd never hear from her and cement our relationship as what I'd always known it: ruined.

Leicester Square was packed with the chatter of onlookers and bustling with reporters and photographers. The premiere was sandwiched by tall buildings and shops, forced into one street filled by the red carpet. Movie banners covered the windows on the building above.

After pushing through the crowd and finding someone with an authoritative enough look to show me the entrance, I was in.

One hotel lobby, an elevator ride, and a pointed finger from a man in a black suit at a walnut door, and I was left alone outside James's room.

I knocked on the door and a shuffle of shoes on carpet followed.

"Are you Adelaide?" an older woman in a pantsuit asked.

I nodded and she moved to the side to let me in.

Smoke—no, steam actually—filled the room as a man ran a steamer over a burgundy dress jacket. The plumes of steam were pushed around by everyone pacing through the room taking phone calls, cleaning up makeup mirrors, zipping up suitcases. Then there was a woman holding a notebook, running through a list with James.

All of the color in the room came from his ribbon pink cheeks and silver hair. They popped vibrantly like strawberry-flavored candies against sand with his burgundy tailored pants on.

I stood by the door, unsure where I was supposed to fit in.

James's gaze ticked up. "Adelaide." He smiled, stepping away. "Did you have an easy time getting in?"

"It was—" I was cut off by someone's phone ringing.

"I just need a few moments, if you don't mind?" His question swept the room. Everyone quieted before filing out. "Sorry about that."

"Remember that thing I said about being an inconvenience?"

"I wanted them gone, that had nothing to do with you!"

"I'm going to leave and get tripped on the way out."

"Good thing this hotel is carpeted then." Soft creases formed around the corners of his lips as he stifled a laugh.

I snorted. "I'll be fast then so I can meet my fate."

I pulled the watch off my wrist and handed it to him. He put it on as I took out my phone and the single-use camera.

"I was thinking something like this, and then this." I showed him my example photos. One with a hand in the pocket, and another with a hand adjusting at the opposite sleeve.

"Got it." He nodded.

Getting down on one knee, eye level with his hip, I snapped some pictures with my phone, and then more with the camera. With his hand halfway in his dress pocket, I adjusted his thumb.

He flinched.

"Sorry, I forgot how cold my hands were. Can you just relax your thumb a bit?" I asked, shutting one eye and pressing the other to the viewfinder.

He cleared his throat. "Do I look okay?"

"You look very attractive James, don't worry."

Liana Cincotti

"Well, that's very nice to hear, but I meant in the photos."

"Oh, sorry." I laughed briefly.

"You look very attractive as well." He looked down at me. His words weren't light or breezy. Rather a strong gust of wind that pushed your hair back. It made me blink to regain my focus.

"Thank you," I said softly, looking up at him. I brushed my knee off and stood.

"Could you move your hand like this and hold your lapel?" I placed my left hand against the right side of my chest.

"Like this?" he asked, awkwardly pinching the material.

"Can I?" I hovered my hand over his.

Despite his "okay," his hand was still tense as I shifted it down and uncurled some of his fingers. His palm was smooth, clear of any calluses or ink that often painted the side of his hand.

"Adelaide." That strong gust again. His tone pulled my chin up.

"James."

He searched my face. The chestnut brown of his eyes was so different from Dorian's dark orbs. His reminded me of a mahogany bureau mixed with vintage paper. Kindness lived in his color.

He opened his mouth and closed it, before parting his lips again. "I'd like to take you on a date."

Oh.

Either one of my ribs detached from its cage and dragged against my heart, or the look on his face hurt *that much*. Beautiful, sweet, kind James. Beautiful, sweet, *kind* James wanted to go on a date. And I had to say no.

"I'm sorry." The words fell from my mouth.

His mahogany eyes grew but looked anywhere but my face.

"Oh. No, it's—it's fine, of course."

"It has nothing to do with you—"

"Really, it's alright—"

"No, no, I mean it, it's not you. I don't date. I don't do the whole love thing." His brows rose. I was royally screwing this up. "Not that I'm saying that's what you're looking for! I'm just trying to say I don't do any of that."

"You don't do love?"

"I do not," I said. "It's um … it's easier that way for—"

"You don't need to explain yourself to me," he said quietly.

Buzz.

He reached for his back pocket before glancing at the phone and accepting the call. "Hey," he answered.

A pause as the person on the other line spoke.

"She left a while ago, sorry. Why, what's wrong?" He walked the length of the room, listening.

"Mhm, mhm, okay. One moment," he hummed. Pulling the phone from his ear, he asked, "Is there any chance you know how to sew?"

"I can hand sew like a basic stitch, why?"

"Do you have anywhere you need to be after this?"

"No …" I hesitated, still rattled by his previous question.

"Thoughts on helping Dorian?"

"James." I glared at him. "I'd rather stab myself with a spoon."

"That doesn't sound that bad."

"You'd think, but it actually makes it much more painful."

"Can't avoid him forever," he reminded me.

I exhaled. "What's the room number?"

I used to have common sense. But now I was standing outside Dorian's door like a frozen lamppost with a small sewing kit in my hand from the hotel's nightstand, waiting for an assistant or manager or hairdresser to answer my knock.

The door finally swung open. I was met with Dorian, who was in the middle of buttoning up his untucked shirt.

It was a horrendous surprise. One that clutched my throat and ripped the air out, leaving me without any knowledge of how the English language worked.

"Adelaide." He was taken aback. "What are you doing here?"

I held the sewing kit up. "James sent me. And I'm assuming from the look on your face that he didn't tell you ..."

"No, he did not. Were you just with him?"

I couldn't navigate the look on his face. It was like trying to traverse a map of London upside down. His parted lips said to come in, but the crease between his brows said to go left and exit.

"He was helping me get those pictures for my project," I explained.

He nodded his head and moved to the side, letting me in.

Shutting the door behind us, the quiet was loud. Uncomfortable.

He sat on the ottoman at the end of the bed.

"I'm surprised you don't have a million people running around in here." I attempted to make conversation.

"I like to be alone when I get the chance." His voice was gruff, turned down at his shirt, trying to finish the tiny buttons.

"I'll make it quick then." I put my bag down beside him.

"You know that's not what I meant. I prefer you in every room." He looked up and it felt so vulnerable. His body being below mine was a cruel memory. The arch of his neck to meet my gaze made my blood pump faster.

The artificial light coming in the through the windows from the lights in the street kissed his face and pressed into the angles of his cheeks.

I couldn't isolate this person from the one I had kissed. I couldn't watch his mouth move as he spoke and not think about when they were pressed against my lips.

"Well, that's good, because I'm not that great at sewing so it will take me a second," I confessed. I couldn't help but laugh as he struggled to squeeze the buttons into the tiny slits. "This is ridiculous, let me help you."

I pushed my hair back and kneeled on the ground.

He cleared his throat, backing up, his hips hitting the bed. "If this is your version of seducing me," he took a breath. "It's working."

"Dorian," I shook my head.

"Yes," he exhaled.

"Stay still." Taking the sides of his shirt into my hands and gripping each button, I pretended that this had absolutely no effect on me. That the proximity of his face to mine did nothing to my nervous system and that his warm breath against the crown of my head didn't make my hands shake.

Maybe this was all my subconscious's tactical excuse to get me closer to him.

I pulled my hands away once the buttons were in, avoiding using his legs that caged me in to stand back up.

I looked for an article of clothing that appeared torn and needed sewing.

"It's just the jacket—the button fell off," he explained,

standing up.

"Can you put it on?" I asked.

He nudged the jacket over his shoulders and held the button out for me.

"One second," I stopped him, threading the needle first. I pulled the black string through and took the bottom of his jacket, carefully stabbing it through where the button should be.

"Now the button." I held my hand out, and he placed it between my fingers. I let the first hole of the button fly down the string before I steadied it in place and pushed the needle through the next hole.

"How have you been?" he asked. His voice was soft and quiet.

"I've been alright." Mine came out just as warm and small, like a teacup full of English Breakfast tea. For once, it seemed like neither of us felt like arguing. We were two boats treading water unsure of whether to dock, nervous to knock into one another.

I continued, "I wrote that postcard actually."

"You did?"

"I did. This morning. Even went and bought a stamp and put it in the post box."

"Wow. How do you feel?"

"I stood in front of the post for five minutes debating how dangerous and illegal it'd be to stuff my arm back in and grab it."

He laughed. "You could've called me."

"You're willing to commit a federal crime?"

"I would've shown up with a coat hanger and gum if you asked."

"A hanger and gum?"

"Unravel the wire hanger, stick a piece of gum to the end, push it through the box."

I gasped. "You're a criminal mastermind."

"How do you think I'm capable of driving without a license?"

I smiled, suppressing another laugh. "I feel better about it now though—sending it," I said. "You were right."

I reached for the tiny pair of scissors and cut the thread at the knot. Tossing the scissors back in the bag, I moved the button around to make sure it was secure.

"You should be proud of yourself," he said tenderly.

"I don't know about all that."

"You should be. You reached out when you didn't want to, but because you knew it'd be good for you. That's something to be proud of."

"Thank you," I responded earnestly.

"I've missed seeing you this week," he said.

"We have class three times a week together," I reminded him.

"That's different. I sit in front of you."

"Well, if you start showing up at tutoring again then that won't be a problem." I directed my gaze at his tie, feeling the urge to fix it.

"I wasn't sure after the library incident if you'd want me to."

I opened my mouth and then closed it. I had played the kiss in the rain and the masquerade and being stuck in that nook with him so many times that it grew more dramatic each time I thought of them.

"We have a deal, I haven't forgotten," I said, and flattened his tie.

His hand wrapped around mine on the fabric, forcing me to look up. "Just because we have a deal doesn't mean I don't respect your boundaries."

I wish I could avoid his gaze. But he was magnetic, constantly

Liana Cincotti

pulling me in, even when he didn't mean to. Then he trapped me with that hauntingly handsome, serious look.

"Got it?" he asked.

I nodded.

"If you're okay with me coming Monday, then I will. You don't have to say now. Just let me know beforehand. Or during. Whenever you want to see me, I'll come."

"Alright," I responded, too dazed to muster up anything else.

"What are you doing Saturday?"

I laughed. "We don't meet on Saturdays."

"I know. My question still stands."

"Well, it's my birthday."

"I know." His lips lifted with a slight smile. "That's what I was getting at: do you have any plans?"

"Who told you it was my birthday?"

"What makes you think someone had to tell me?" he contested.

I rolled my eyes. "I'm going out with Dotty and Iris."

"Will you be busy the whole day?"

"I'm not sure yet, why?"

He shook his head with an embarrassed smile. "Because I'm trying to ask you out, Adelaide."

My shoulders fell.

"No, I know what you're going to say, and I didn't mean it like that. You've dealt with me all semester and we've seen each other almost every day. I don't want to miss your birthday. I want to be there. As a friend."

A friend. I guess that's what we became in a weird, twisted turn of events.

There were so many things wrong about saying yes. But he

wasn't going to take no for an answer. And honestly, I didn't want him to accept my no.

"I'll be working for the day, so you can join us for dinner after, if you want," I offered.

"When and where, I'll be there."

"Bookstore, six o'clock."

27

Don't Buy Her a Birthday Gift — Dorian

"We're just friends," I clarified, *again*, over the phone as I sat in Poppy's closed studio, hours after the premiere, still in my dress pants.

I needed to clear my head.

My mind was whirling with thoughts of *her*. Talking to her. Watching her lean over me. Feeling her hands on my chest. Having her in between my legs.

She was like an intricate piece of Fine China hidden in a vintage shop made up of complex swirls and patterns that I couldn't perfectly recreate in my mind. And every time I saw her, I was more enamored, finding more things to explore. From the way she tilted her head when my words were unexpected to the way she brushed hair from her face when she was impatient.

I wasn't one to study. But I knew the wave-like ups and downs of her voice as if I studied them for centuries. I could predict the meaning of each one with my eyes closed if asked.

"I don't think you even believed yourself there," Jasmine refuted. The sound of her pottery wheel spinning stirred in the background.

"What do you want me to say? That I've fallen madly in love with her and think about her every waking second as if she's poisoned me?"

"Brother, I'm proud of you for finally being honest with yourself."

"How's Tristan? That dirty sock smell in his hair go away yet?"

"You just had to bring it up, didn't you?"

"I'm sure Mum would *love* to know that you're dying to see him again—"

"I'm just being honest with you! If you don't want me to be honest, then fine! But there's nothing wrong with being interested in her."

I paused the brush on the canvas, letting a large blob of cerulean blue paint accumulate in the middle.

I had an encyclopedia-length of reasons why it was wrong to be interested in her. The first being that I had an unhealthy addiction that was looking, listening, and touching her. An addiction she had no interest in. Letting it simmer wouldn't help by speaking on it.

Jasmine accepted my silence as my disagreement.

"Have you spoken to James about it?" she asked.

"James and I don't talk about this stuff." I rolled out my neck and then searched for a smaller brush in the unorganized stack balancing on the stool beside me.

"You mean you don't talk about Adelaide-related stuff."

"That's not what I said."

"I know it's not what you said, but it's what you meant."

"They're friends. I don't want my opinion to affect that."

"The opinion that you're interested in her?"

"Why did I even bother calling you?"

"Because you wanted my wisdom over getting her a birthday gift."

"What a terrible idea. I must've had a stroke. Call me an ambulance, will you? It's the least you could do."

"Where should I send it?"

"Poppy's studio."

"What are you making now?"

"That painting for your living room."

"Cerulean blue, right?"

"As cerulean blue as it get," I replied, staring at the canvas covered in half-finished cerulean blue vases. The few lamps switched on in the studio flickered yellow light over the painting.

"Why don't you paint her something?"

"Because that's weird, Jasmine. And I already got her a gift anyway."

"Why did you call me then!" Her pottery wheel shrieked.

"Because I bought the gift when I was half asleep weeks ago and now that it's open and sitting in my kitchen, I've realized it's oddly personal, so I need other ideas."

"What did you buy?"

I briefly explained what the gift looked like and that I got the idea based on something I saw hung on her cork board in her room.

"Dorian, she'll love that."

"That's the problem. If she loves it, then I'm not doing a great job at proving the 'friend' thing."

"Maybe just flowers then," she suggested. "Oh! You could get her the November birth flower."

"What's the November birth flower?"

"Peonies."

"I don't know." I switched the brush to my other hand to scratch my forehead. "That seems a bit romantic."

"Nooo, not romantic. No one buys flowers for romantic purposes anymore."

"Dad buys Mum flowers every week," I deadpanned. "Are you trying to set me up?"

"You're a hopeless romantic, I don't need to do that. You do it to yourself."

"I am not," I argued, accidentally flinging paint onto the floor in the process.

"Being a hopeless romantic is a sad life."

"Are you calling me hopeless now?"

"No. I'm calling you senseless." The eyeroll was evident in her voice. "Dad's obsessed with Mum, so of course he buys her flowers all the time. It's possible Adelaide's never received flowers before."

Something told me that wasn't true.

She continued. "I'm telling you. If you walk in with flowers, the first thing she'll do is smile when she sees you."

That would definitely be a first.

It was risky. But that's how things tended to be around us.

28

One week later, I not only had the photos for my project, but a finished hundred-page Globalization paper, a twenty-second birthday to celebrate in London, and a nerve in the back of my brain that forced me to think of Dorian Blackwood every hour on the hour like a grandfather clock. There had to be some recluse intern running around in my head pressing the Think of Dorian button. Maybe a forgotten paperweight.

Knowing that I was seeing him in about ten minutes made it worse. Every time the bookstore door chimed open, my head snapped up.

I lacked the privilege of distraction seeing as I finished all my work for the semester and applied to every open marketing internship for the summer in London (except Beverly). I'd ask about next semester's workload if I knew the professors.

Digital scrapbooking was my only option. Mood boarding was out of the picture at the moment. It was hard to get a magazine around here that didn't include Dorian's face within the pages.

I've been throwing together various scrapbook pages on my laptop since July after Mia showed me her physical one stuffed with pastel ribbons, notes, tickets, lace, and stickers that looked like stamps.

Her mom had made it for her before she left for London. Mia was meant to fill it with photos while she was here.

There was a twang of jealousy in my chest. A curling, twisting pain that felt more like heartbreak and less like envy. Her mother's handwriting was on every page. Hair ribbons that were saved for over a decade. Original copies of report cards. An unspoken inscription of family support.

I remember when I was told I'd be valedictorian in high school. My first thought was about the speech. The dreaded speech at graduation. If it weren't for the university scholarships, I would've let my GPA drop just enough to miss it.

Graduation day, I stood at the podium with my speech. I looked out at everyone's parents, siblings, cousins, and grandparents. They all held plastic-wrapped roses and cards pushed into bright yellow envelopes. The objects possessed me. I knew each one would end with "love, Mom & Dad." They were the worst part. Each person would have that card forever. A card that listed their accomplishments that their parents got to witness.

I couldn't look away from them. I was stuck.

Everyone was going to walk across the stage to accept their diploma and smile for their mom's photograph that would exist on their family home's mantel for forty years. While my aunt sat in the crowd by herself.

I was appreciative that she came but it would've been easier if she just wasn't there at all.

I had reached out to both of my parents because I felt obligated to. Maybe they'd want to see me. See how my hair had grown out. How I got my ears pierced, even though they were slightly off centered because they had gotten infected and needed to be repierced, that one time they weren't around for. Maybe they'd want to see how I got his lips but her nose. But they never came. Never answered my emails or my voicemails.

Only seven days had passed since I sent Laila my postcard, but I still worried. Customs can take a while—or so I was told.

"There's no way she's received it yet," Sabrina had reassured me. "She'll definitely text you when she gets it anyway."

That wasn't something we did. Example one: no word from her today and it was her niece's birthday.

Not that I cared. I hated birthdays. I hated all big occasions.

I was surrounded by the ghosts of who should've been there every time. Sometimes the ghosts would fade to the back in a crowded room. Stick to the walls. Stretch their heads over shoulders.

They were always there. Reminding me that no matter how many hours I worked, how many friends I made, how many job acceptances I got, I still wouldn't have a scrapbook.

I inhaled.

Two ghosts hovered. Hidden away in the backroom, they accompanied the birthday balloons Iris and Dotty had waiting for me.

I shut my laptop, put my headphones on, and brought a stack of returned books to their correct shelves to pass the time. I slid each book alphabetically by author onto the shelf above me, careful to keep them from falling on their side in the gap. I continued on that pattern until something moved in my peripheral and my hand froze.

The music faded away as I took in the absurdly attractive man standing at the front desk.

Whichever part of my brain was in charge of receiving words and breaking them down into meaning had diminished. The only meaning I could understand was Dorian.

Dorian in a suit. Dorian checking his watch. Dorian holding flowers. Holding peonies.

His presence strung me like a violin bow and kept me still as if I was captured by a haunting melody.

Then I was staring at him too long and he was turning, his eyes instantly catching me. His posture corrected.

I immediately became aware of the shortness of my dress and the chip in my nail polish and the small strand of hair that wouldn't rest on top of my head.

Wow, he mouthed.

I rolled my eyes. *Typical.*

You like it, a full smile that squeezed out his dimple said.

I couldn't help but smile back.

Right as I took a few steps forward, he followed, the two of us meeting in the middle.

I checked my watch. "You're early."

"Am I?" he cocked an eyebrow.

"By a minute," I confirmed.

"If I were a minute late, you would've left without me. I know you better than you think."

"Well, I'm happy you got here on time. Wouldn't want you to miss my birthday."

"Oh, I wouldn't dare."

"Surprise!" Cora, Evelyn, Jane, Beatrice, and Lottie cheered, standing from the restaurant table, spooking many of the elders dining around us in the jazz bar.

They all moved around their chairs and greeted me with a hug one-by-one, the pungent smell of sauce and cheese mixing with the smell of their floral perfumes.

"Don't you look beautiful," Cora commented, touching the hem of my black short sleeve mini dress and pointing to my knee-high leather boots that I had picked up from a sample sale years ago.

"The smartest twenty-two year-old in Britain." Jane kissed me on the cheek, pushing Cora out of the way.

"Happy birthday, sweetheart." Evelyn and Beatrice squeezed my arms, scooting around Jane.

"Aw, those flowers are beautiful," Lottie commented on the peonies in my hand, complementing Iris and Dotty.

"Oh, we didn't do that," Iris explained wide-eyed.

All of the women twisted, half-in, half-out of their seats.

"Well look who the cat dragged in." Beatrice stood as Dorian walked in from paying the cab.

I leaned forward on the table. "Don't make it weird," I begged. "We're sorta acquaintances now."

"Acquaintances?" Jane gawked. "That can't be right."

The rest of them jumped in to say something, but I cut them short. "*Please.* You can say anything you want at December's book club."

"No funny business," Dotty warned them before Iris pointed a finger at the lot.

Lottie rolled her lips in. "Fine."

"We won't say anything," Cora held her hands up right as Dorian made his way to our table.

I caught the surprise on his face from the unexpected group

of women. But he reeled it in.

"It's nice to see you, Dorian," Evelyn smiled kindly as everyone sat.

"You can say that again," Jane mumbled. I shook my head praying he missed that.

"It's nice to see all of you again," he responded, pulling out two chairs, gesturing to the one on his right.

Oh.

I quickly accepted the seat before I could analyze the situation. With that, he sat beside me and listened intently to Lottie complain about her daughter's new boyfriend. And then he laughed with Evelyn as she told stories about the time she turned twenty-two. And he understood Cora's complaints about the rising prices of oranges at the grocery store.

I was so focused on him that I forgot I was even here, and not just watching him from afar.

"Is this the first time you two have been out together?" Beatrice waved a finger between me and Dorian.

"Yes," we lied as if we rehearsed it.

"Well, isn't that nice. Don't you think so, Jane?"

Jane gave her an odd look. "Yes …"

"We come here whenever we want to get out. It's a great place for dancing," she explained.

Then Jane caught on. And so did I. *Evil, evil woman.*

"Do you go dancing often?" Jane asked Dorian.

"Not really, no," he answered.

"Well, the least you could do is ask Adelaide to dance."

We looked at each other in horror. Our track record with dancing wasn't great.

I spoke up. "That's not necessary—"

"I'm not one for dancing—" He shook his head.

"You're the youngest ones in this restaurant. Whatever you do, the old timers around here will be impressed," Beatrice urged.

"I'm not really a jazz fan," I tried to reason.

"Dance, dance, dance!" Jane began cheering and my stomach plummeted as if someone had tipped my chair back and let my head crack against the floor. Dorian's face mirrored the same alarm.

One second, our entire table was cheering. Next, the customers around us were clapping.

29

Don't Mention His Upper Thigh — Adelaide

The chair beside me scuffed the floor. Dorian was up and extending his hand.

"Dance with me," he said.

"I don't have much of an option, do I?"

"Not really."

So I rose and took his hand, satisfying everyone around us and torturing myself in the process. We left our table and joined the small group of couples dancing in front of the jazz musicians. The older couples all swayed to the soft saxophone and lull of the singer's voice.

His hands filled the space on my waist while mine occupied the back of his neck.

"Are they watching?" I asked, my back facing the tables.

"Oh yeah." He nodded, looking past my shoulders.

"What are they doing?"

"Making snogging faces."

"You're kidding," I said in horror, twisting so I could see our table.

Not a single one of them was looking at us.

"You're the worst." I shoved his shin with my boot, replacing his satisfied smirk with a scrunched brow.

"Christ." His leg faltered for a split second before he was meeting my eyes again.

"It was a nudge, not a kick," I argued.

"Says the one with a working shin."

"You're a baby."

"Am not. You're stronger than you look," he defended himself. "And I'd know because you try to lead when we dance."

"I like to think I'm good enough to lead, Mr. Blackwood."

"And I'd let you lead me wherever you'd like, Ms. Adorno. Maybe without a stiletto in my leg though."

"I'll try harder next time."

"Next time it is." He nodded.

In my heels, I could see him so much better. Sitting across from him three times a week in the dim light of the backroom removed any chances of taking in the true brown of his eyes and the stubble he consistently shaved above his lip.

"What are you thinking about?" His head had a slight tilt.

The shape of your brow. The scar close to your scalp. The broadness of your shoulders. The way you say my name. The light that's cupping the right side of your face.

"The word for when artists depict light in a painting," I responded.

His brow rose. "Chiaroscuro."

"Of course you'd know that."

"Of course that's what you're thinking about right now." He rolled his eyes.

"Fine, what are you thinking about?"

"You don't actually want to know. You're just asking because

I asked."

"True, but now I want to know."

"I'm thinking about how you've stepped on my foot three times already."

"No, I haven't." I backed up anyway.

He pulled me back in. "Maybe I lied." He winked.

My knees were weaker than the spine of a two-hundred year-old book. The only way I know how to play it off was opening my mouth. "You're derailing the conversation. What's on your mind?"

"Why the price of coffee has increased so much lately."

"Dorian."

"Adelaide."

His eyes met mine in a moment of thought. They were dark. Conflicting. As if he hoped he could just pass the words swirling around in his mind through a look rather than voicing them. Then he paused on my mouth and regret instantly hit my throat.

I stared at his full lips, debating the consequences of kissing him.

Get him out of your system, my personal group of therapists had said during book club.

Maybe there was some type of truth to that. The last time we had kissed was four weeks ago and I already needed another fill.

"Are they looking at us now?" he asked.

I ripped my gaze away from his lips and glanced over his shoulder. "Yeah, actually. They're all staring at your ass."

He twisted immediately without loosening his grip. "You liar," he narrowed his eyes. But a charming smirk escaped his lips. "It's concerning how much you enjoy humbling me."

"If not me, then who?"

"My sister, my mother, James—"

"James does not humble you," I argued.

"That's what he wants you to think."

"I'm thinking that has more to do with *you* than it does him."

A pause. Then, "You're quite fond of him." He watched me as we swayed, waiting.

"He's become a really good friend," I said softly.

"What category does that put me in?"

I pressed my lips together. "To Be Determined."

"Why's that?"

"Because I still can't read you."

"Ask me something then. Anything."

I pressed my lips together. "What do you think of me? Truly. Because I can't figure it out."

That's the question? his eyes said.

That's the question, I nodded.

"I'm just surprised you don't already know," he responded.

"It's obvious?"

"I thought so." He paused, as if he was waiting for me to tell him I was joking. "What do you think of me?"

"Oof, that's a loaded question."

"God forbid I ask the same thing. Fine, what's something you like about me?"

"I find the tomato tattooed on your upper thigh incredibly hot."

He turned away to laugh but I didn't miss the dimple appearing in his cheek.

"Dorian Blackwood, *are you blushing?*"

"You would too if someone's hand was on your arse," he admitted.

"My hand is not on your ass!" I lifted my hands off his body immediately.

Laughter shot out of him like a canyon. "I was referencing the older woman behind me. Now who's blushing?" He took my hands and returned them to his shoulders.

"It's because you're looking at me like that."

"Looking at you like what?" he asked as if he was innocent.

"Like you have something to say. Do you have something to say?"

"I always have something to say."

"Well, what is it?"

"Well, it's really not appropriate at the moment."

"I just said your thigh tattoo was sexy; I think we're past appropriate. You have to tell me."

"No, I don't," he debated.

"You do. Birthday policy."

"You loathe celebrations. Since when did you start upholding their policies?"

"It doesn't matter when there's no expiration date! Now tell. I doubt the woman behind us with her hearing aid half out is listening."

He shook his head determined. "I'm not telling."

"Come on," I pouted.

"Adelaide," he gave me a level look.

"It can be my birthday gift."

"I think you look beautiful, that's all."

I never understood what people meant when they said words carried weight, because people almost never meant what they said. But right now, I got it. Because his words felt so full, so serious, that if they were physical entities, I could hold them in my hands, and they'd pull me right down.

I cleared my throat. "How's that inappropriate?"

"I gave you the censored version, that's why. I also don't think you're supposed to find your friends beautiful."

30

Don't Watch Him Go — Adelaide

Outside the restaurant, rain was throwing bare branches around and bowling pieces of trash down the sidewalk.

"Well, that's a lot of rain," I observed with some slight dread at the front of the restaurant, clutching my flowers. I liked these boots.

Dorian's face seemed to mirror the same thought, watching the weather as the music and tables bustled behind us.

He proceeded to open the umbrella.

"What are you doing!" I grabbed his hands and stopped him.

"What do you think? I'm getting the umbrella ready because it's downpouring!"

"That's bad luck!"

His gaze jumped between me and the weather outside.

"Fine. You wait here, I'll open it outside," he said.

"Dorian—"

"You better give me your number after this—no more communicating via email!" He ran out of the restaurant and was completely soaked before the umbrella was open and over his head. He returned to the door and bridged the gap above us.

Liana Cincotti

"How do I look?" he smirked, a laugh on the edge of his lips as rain droplets turned strands of his hair into sopping curls.

"Exceptionally wet. That look is pretty in right now," I replied, stepping under the umbrella and letting the door shut behind me.

"Is it?"

"Slicked back hair, wet makeup—"

He tilted the umbrella away from my head, letting a line of rain in.

I shrieked, jumping forward into his chest, laughing.

"Let's be nice to the bloke with the umbrella."

Our walk back home was too short. While twenty-five minutes of dodging puddles and being hit by windy waves of cold rain wasn't ideal, it ended our conversation too quickly.

The tree outside my balcony dripped dew onto the umbrella.

"Thank you for coming. And bringing these." I gestured to the bouquet.

"Thank you for inviting me."

"Pretty sure you invited yourself," I reminded him.

"Semantics." He shrugged, the ghost of a smile on his lips.

"Well, goodnight then."

"Goodnight," he said softly. A thin stream of water ran down the edge of his face. I stopped it with my thumb, surprising us both.

A clouded look spread across his face as he searched mine. The silence that tended to spread between us was always uncomfortable. But this time, it gave me a moment to breathe him in. As if I was in a museum trying to pull the meaning of a painting from its use of light.

I counted how far I'd have to lean forward on my heels to reach his lips. Then I tried to calculate how many *what was I doings* would pass before they were replaced with the complete and utter chaos of *desire.*

I cleared my throat and abruptly backed away. "Goodnight," I repeated.

"Goodnight." He nodded, backing up.

I left the bubble of our umbrella and stepped under the awning above my apartment entrance, pulling the door open.

The heating unit in the small lobby hit me and the door shut. I took three steps upstairs before the urge to get one more glance at him turned me around.

I found him in the rain still, under the tree.

Don't do it. Don't do it.

I ran back down the stairs and opened the front door.

"What are you doing?" I shouted over the rain.

"I'm waiting for you!" he yelled back, the rain shadowing his words.

"Waiting for me to what?"

"For you to get into your flat!"

"But your shoes—"

"Adelaide, I'm already soaked so just get inside!"

"You're so demanding!" I threw my arms up, letting the door shut and running up the steps.

The rain said hello on my apartment windows as I pushed the front door open. Its hellos grew louder as I ran into my room to open the balcony.

The wind whipped my hair as I looked below at Dorian.

See, I'm safe, my arched brows said.

Liana Cincotti

Stubborn, he shook his head. Rain was coating his hair. He resembled a shot from a romance film. With one hand in his pocket and the other holding the umbrella at a slant, he didn't care if it was covering him anymore.

We just stared at each other for a moment before he pulled his hand out of his pocket and wedged the umbrella under his elbow. Cupping his hands together, he passed a glance between his hands and me.

You want me to do that?

He nodded and dug something out of his pocket. Walking right underneath the balcony, he tossed the item high in the air, catching me off guard. I threw my hands out and cupped the item between my palms as if I was trying to grab a guppy leaping from a pond.

Stepping back under the cover of the balcony above my head, I opened my hands and found a telephone booth keychain. It wasn't the red ones I passed every day on my way to campus though. This was painted a blue-gray and had small streams of green that ran from the top to resemble vines. It matched the keychains hanging from my purse.

You did this? I let it dangle from my fingers and stared at him in awe.

It's just something small. He scrunched his nose.

My chest filled with earnestness. I was a teddy bear stuffed with handknit hearts.

I twisted, glimpsing at my purse. Before I could second guess it, I grabbed one of the keychains off my bag and ran out of the apartment, retracing my steps to his outside.

"What are you—" I cut off his question with a suffocating hug.

The umbrella shuttered above us. Then, it fell altogether at our side as he wrapped his arms around me.

I breathed in the cold rain smell coating his hair and let the side of my face absorb the scent. My hands found the back of his neck and my heart found his. I squeezed, and he squeezed back.

"Thank you. *So much*," I whispered. "That was the best birthday I've ever had."

With one hand secure on my lower back, his other smoothed out my hair, twirling strands at the bottom.

"I'm so glad," he exhaled. "I'm so glad."

I could remain here all night. The rain could dissipate my clothes, soak the leather of my boots, and prune my fingertips. I didn't care.

My toes ached as I pushed up on the balls of my feet to hold onto him.

Pick me up and kiss me, I wanted to tell him.

Swallowing one more gulp of this moment, I reluctantly pulled my hands from his hair. But not before clipping my Red Sox hat keychain onto his belt loop.

I kissed the side of his neck, felt him shiver, and ran back inside. I practically floated up to my bedroom. From my balcony, I watched him pull the umbrella back over his head. In a haze, he stared at the keychain attached to his hip.

Then he looked at me.

He opened and closed his mouth before shaking his head like a flustered kid. The smile on his face was no longer shy.

My heart raced as if I was struck by some shock of electricity.

Happy Birthday, Adelaide, he mouthed. And then he left. His figure was slowly taken by dark sheets of rain, like a tugboat tethered to a ship in an ocean. I felt myself leaning forward.

What if I went back outside? Took the stairs two at a time and got to the sidewalk before he could get too far?

I let the rain hit my face in thought. The old black paint of the railing chipped under my palm.

I'd run to him, catch his sleeve, grab his attention … and then what? Tell him what? Do what?

I think I like you. I think I really like you. I can't stop thinking about kissing you.

What am I doing? I stood up straight with the haste of a spark.

I let my head fall back and closed my eyes, hoping the rain could wake me. Hoping it could wipe these thoughts away and cure me.

I'm lonely. I just feel lonely.

And he has a girlfriend, you absolute dumbass.

"*Ugh*," I groaned in frustration and pushed the balcony doors shut.

I clipped my new telephone booth keychain to my purse before I could think it over. Tugging off my boots and draping my coat over my desk chair, I walked into the hallway.

My feet stopped. Two cinder blocks attached to my legs as I found Sabrina on the couch.

Mia had said they'd both be out late with Sabrina's dads. But there Brina was, quickly reminding me of what a horrible friend I was.

The guilt in my chest was debilitating. The last time this much emotion clogged my throat was when I told my aunt I'd be moving out indefinitely to live on campus. She said goodbye and let me move in by myself while I watched siblings and parents carry their children's belongings into their temporary homes.

Something about seeing Brina half-asleep, her head falling into the cushion with such peacefulness, made the guilt so much worse.

I approached her quietly, my feet spreading the area rug. A printout of a highlighted periodic table was on her lap and there was a movie on the TV illuminating the dark room, casting a light across her face.

"Brina," I whispered, resting my hand on her shoulder.

"Hm," she grumbled, squeezing her eyelids together.

"You have to get to bed. You have a final in the morning."

She slowly opened her eyes but didn't make an effort to move. "This is my favorite part though," she sighed, trying to focus on the movie.

I turned to watch. The live-action *Cinderella* was playing. Cinderella stood at the top of a grand staircase in her blue ball gown. Then it cut to Prince Charming looking up at her in awe, meeting her at the bottom of the stairs.

"I want that. That's my dream," she whispered.

You already have so much, I wanted to tell her. *Parents, comfortability, security. How's that not already a dream?*

"It's a movie, Brina. Just a fairytale." I brushed her bangs out of her face.

"I know. But someone wrote that movie. And that writing couldn't have all been fictional. Something real must've inspired it."

I closed my mouth and watched the scene with her. Prince Charming pulled Cinderella in and out of his chest, letting her sparkling skirts spin around her ankles.

"One day, I'm going to have a husband that looks at me like that," she thought aloud, words muffled by the cushion. "And we're going to have kids and live in a beautiful house with blue shutters. We'll make pies together, take the kids to flute recitals, create Christmas traditions, and compile new stockings when we have grandkids. We'll grow old together, and even when I'm eighty, he'll still look at me like that." She exhaled, her eyes falling shut again. "It'd be perfect if Dorian turned out to be that person."

Air stopped moving through my lungs.

"I'll let you finish your movie." I brushed her back one more time and then stood, walking back into my room.

She loves Dorian. She loves Dorian. She loves Dorian.

I like Dorian. I like Dorian. I like Dorian.

I was spending too much time around him. That had to be it. I was confusing a budding friendship for romantic interest. Just because he was attractive didn't mean that *I liked him.*

I closed my door and let my nervous breathing run through my chest.

One day, I'm going to have a husband.

Why was I forgetting that Sabrina and Mia were going to outgrow this apartment one day and build homes? Build families.

If that's what she viewed as her Dream Life, then that's what I wanted for her. But part of me couldn't help but think where I was supposed to fit into her life.

It was selfish. They should be happy. I wanted them to be happy.

I sat on my bed feeling numb. The memorabilia hanging from my walls overwhelmed me.

For years, I had this idealistic image of what a perfect life would be: a job that consumed me in the best way possible, and a home that was forever mine. Not a place I'd have to move out of one day or a house I'd get comfortable in only for it to be taken away. Just a home for me.

But having friends warped that.

Now all I could picture was being alone without them. Utterly alone.

Alone in a home I paid for with the job I worked hard for in college to qualify for, which required restless nights in high school to achieve. The home I dreamed of filling with my souvenirs and successes.

Brina and Mia were my only family. But they'd also be busy building their own families.

I couldn't even begin to think of Dorian or James in the same circumstances or else I'd succumb to the rolling in my stomach and vomit.

He left these things because they reminded him of us, my mother had said as she stared into Dad's bureau drawers, filled with his clothes and sawdust. *He didn't want us, so he left his belongings to become things.*

Ever since then, I packed my things like a squirrel in the winter to protect my life and my joy and prove to myself I had memories worth keeping, only to feel like they were all slipping away now.

I stared at the frames filled with film photos and postcards above my desk. Then my lamp strung with keychains and my bureau attacked with handwritten notes.

They were always comforting. Pieces of my life I could hug tightly to remember I had so much to be grateful for. That I had experienced so much of the life my parents never had in their twenties.

But the items loomed over me now.

They were a reminder that, one day, all of my things would be just that: things. They wouldn't be handed down to a child or displayed in a museum. The items stuffed with my joy and the happiest times of my life would be things that no one wanted, in a

Liana Cincotti

bureau with excess sawdust.

I was a reflection of the things I carried. So what did that mean if the things I collected were destined to be tossed away?

Was I just a collection of the things no one wanted?

31

Christmas music played in the living room and the cinnamon candle (that had been burning long enough to make me dizzy) slinked down the hallway as Mia and Sabrina packed to go home to their families for the holidays.

The longest time we've spent apart since June, but it'd be good. I needed to remember how much I enjoyed being alone. With shifts at the bookstore every day and issues of *The New Yorker* to catch up on, I was hopeful.

My only Christmas wish was for Dorian to stop popping up in my head like a never ending montage that a romance director would definitely make use of.

Oh, and to land a job for the summer, of course. A close second.

Sitting on a pile of blankets in the hallway between Mia and Brina's doorways, I scrolled through job listings in London, hunting for one that paid anything and would hire an international post-grad student.

"Which number are we on?" Mia shouted from her room.

"Twenty," I groaned.

"You've applied to twenty jobs just today?" Sabrina gawked—from her room. I only heard their muffled voices as they sifted through clothes to pack.

"I want to curl up and die. It feels like I'm trying to win the lottery. But in this circumstance, I actually have the winning ticket, and no one is willing to even bother looking at it, let alone giving me the cash."

"I don't think I understand that metaphor …" Mia said.

"She's qualified but no one will respond to her resume!" Brina clarified.

"Hmm. Did you reach out to Sylvie about the recommendation letter? The semester is over now so it's probably the perfect time," Mia commented.

"I want to reach out when I'm ready to apply to Beverly. I don't want to waste her recommendation on a job I don't love."

"Is there a runner up position?" Sabrina asked.

"Maybe the watch business I did my project on—Grace & Gears? It's a digital marketing position rather than PR. But I sent them the full plan I put together for Sylvie's class. Thought that'd be nice since I spent three months on it," I grumbled. They'd most likely skip over that too when they found out my graduation year.

"I'll deal with this problem when I actually get the degree," Mia said.

"Hopefully I can get an internship with an interior design agency before I get stuck in some lab job. I thought if I got the degree in biology, I'd be able to pursue design anyway. But according to my dad I need to get a job in it now," Brina sighed.

"How dare he," Mia feigned agreement. We assumed this entire semester that Andrew would want Brina to get a job in biology if he was paying for his daughter's degree.

"Has Noah said anything about it?" I asked.

Sabrina crawled over to her doorway with a pile of sweaters and began folding. I pushed my laptop to the side and joined.

"He's always been the calmer one of my parents," she exhaled, brushing her bangs out of her face. "He thinks I should give the biology job a try. He doesn't understand that just because I understand STEM, doesn't mean I want to do it every day until I can retire."

I folded a pastel pink sweater and moved it into her pile. "You should start applying to design jobs. Find one that pays well and then you can prove to your dad that it's a legit career. I can help you look for jobs even."

"Maybe I will then," she nodded. "Thank you by the way," she extended her hand, stopping me mid-fold. "I'm really lucky to have you."

I returned her earnest smile but the heavy guilt coating my stomach overshadowed it.

"Can you pass me that blazer?" Mia shouted.

"Where do you plan on going that requires a blazer?" I asked. Standing from my failed blanket fort, I picked up the plaid blazer and tossed it to her where she sat in her closet with her suitcase.

"What if I have a job interview or a hot date?"

"Do you have a job interview or a hot date?"

"No but what if it happens spontaneously!"

"I think you're overpacking."

"Not compared to Sabrina!"

"I'm going on *holiday,* you're going *home!*" Sabrina shouted. "You already have clothes at home—there are no clothes for me in Paris!"

"She has a point," I muttered.

"She has no point, watch her come back with a new wardrobe," Mia argued, waving a shoe in the air.

"No Paris gifts for you!"

I laughed. "I'm going to miss you two."

"You know my offer still stands. You can come back to Washington with me," Mia responded in a sing-song tone.

"My offer stands as well! Why don't you come to Paris with me?" Sabrina asked eagerly.

Because I'll get attached. Attached to you and your family more than I already have. And I don't think I can withstand to lose that many people.

"Next time. I'm not prepared enough. I'll keep Iris and Dotty company while you're both gone," I reassured them.

"If you see James or Dorian, you *have* to tell me!" Sabrina shouted.

"I'll definitely let you know if I somehow run into Dorian Blackwood on the street," I said.

"Has James mentioned him recently? Or said anything about Victoria Sutton? She hasn't been seen with Dorian in a while. And seeing as she didn't even bother showing up to the Townsen Dinner or the Halloween party, it couldn't be *that* serious." She shook her head, folding a tweed jacket. "That article did speculate that he was single again." She slapped the top of my hand to get my attention. "You must keep me updated if you see him or if James mentions him."

"Alright!"

I couldn't stop *thinking about him*. Our last week of tutoring was brief. I made an effort to change the topic anytime it wasn't related to the exam. Even his texts were difficult to ignore, especially when I had *wanted* to give him my number after he pulled that umbrella open. The blue-gray telephone booth keychain was hidden in my bag at the bookstore so that he wouldn't point it out.

So much guilt.

Guilt for betraying Brina.

Guilt for pushing Dorian away, *again*.

But I was *terrified*. This urge to touch him, to tell him how handsome he looked, to ask him about his plans for Christmas break with James to Italy. It was suffocating. The less I saw him, the more I dreamed about him. The only solution was to completely close myself off. Once finals week ended last week, it was easy on the tongue to tell him that I'd be busy. Even with the Red Sox keychain hanging from his trousers.

I shouldn't have to make an excuse. Our deal was complete. He'd probably call or text, maybe even show up to throw something at my balcony, but he'd give up at some point.

Brina dragged her designer suitcase into the hallway. Crisp whites, pale blues, light greens, and pastel pinks sprinkled the brown interior as we carefully packed the piles away.

"Adelaide."

I registered her serious tone and looked up.

"I'm worried about you."

I grew a soft smile. "I'll be fine here, don't worry."

"It's not that." Her short blond hair swayed as she shook her head. "I know you enjoy your alone time and can take care of yourself here. It's what you're avoiding by staying here that worries me."

"Avoiding what?"

"Going home."

I returned to packing the clothes away. "You know I don't consider that home," I shook my head. Two months since I sent that postcard and still no response from my aunt.

"I meant your parents."

It was as if she stabbed the portion of my heart that had been decaying for the past nine years. A sharp knife against a ragged, wrinkled heart that didn't know how to pump blood anymore.

I stared at her in disbelief. "You can't be serious."

She continued, "What if you let them back in your life? They could've changed. *They're your parents*. They love you."

"People don't change, Sabrina. You have an incredible family, but mine will never be that way. They don't care. One of them left to have new kids while the other gave up because she enjoyed sleeping and drinking more than she did parenting. I refuse to believe they acted that way because *of love*. Love just gives the people close to you an excuse to inflict pain without consequences. I'm trying to forget about them but forgiving them won't do that."

"You're letting them control your life, Addy."

That was *rich* coming from her. "*How?* They have no idea what's even going on in my life."

"Because you've completely shut yourself out from any chance of attachment and now you won't even admit when you're in love!"

My mouth fell open, and the cinnamon smell suddenly made my stomach turn.

"I know you're in love with James and I can see you trying to pull away from it and don't try to tell me you're not because *I know*. I've seen the way you tense up at these events that he's at and how weird you act the days following. Or how you go out when Mia and I have plans because the next morning on the way to my 8 a.m., Maureen likes to mention the pretty boy who walked you home" *holy shit*—"I also don't think you've been sleeping well because of it since you're drinking coffee all of a sudden and you hate coffee. You're letting your preconceived notions of love and relationships affect this when you could be taking a chance."

I shake my head incessantly. "No, oh my god, no."

"There's no point in lying because I do the same thing with Dorian. I get it. It's hard to sleep sometimes when we see him from afar at these events. Then I don't stop thinking about him for days."

What do I say? What do I say? What do I say?

"Sabrina, I'm going to say this as clearly as possible: I am not in love with James, and I'm not interested in James. He is my friend and nothing more."

Her shoulders softened as if I was in denial. "I saw the way he looked at you on Halloween. He couldn't take his eyes off you."

Probably because I was avoiding his best friend the whole night.

I fell backward into the pile of blankets, giving up.

Her hand patted my knee. "Don't let your past ruin your future."

32

Don't Upset Maureen — Adelaide

Boredom was finally starting to seep in with Mia and Sabrina gone. After two weeks of *The New Yorker,* morning runs in the snow after the sidewalks were cleared, applying to every job possible, and eating the same chicken and microwavable rice for dinner every night, I needed something to do. Iris and Dotty even barred me from working more than forty hours a week.

Would it be inappropriate to reach out to my professors about next semester's work to get a head start? Probably. But solitude was driving me to consider it. Several times.

Sending that email on Christmas Eve would look rather depressing too.

"Jude Law, you're so beautiful, but that's somehow making me feel worse." I sighed and sunk into the couch further as Jude looked up drunkenly at Cameron Diaz on the TV. Then she tugged on his tie and Jude fell forward.

I used to love this scene. Melt at the way Jude melted.

Now all I pictured was Dorian putting his hand over mine when I adjusted his tie at the movie premiere.

Just because we have a deal doesn't mean I don't respect your boundaries.

That's what he had said, his gaze completely consuming me.

I needed to take a break. This was getting unhealthy.

Pausing Jude Law's beautiful face, I threw on my coat and boots, grabbed my purse where my telephone booth was hidden away, and braced for the snow.

I couldn't eat chicken and rice one more time, so I stepped into the sidewalk's slush and ventured out for food.

Breathing in chilled my throat, forcing out a dry cough. Twilight was starting to hit the sky, despite it only being five o'clock, triggering the streetlamps to switch on. A thin layer of snow topped of each lamp, while the windowsills jutting out of the buildings were catching the falling flakes. They resembled those ceramic Christmas village homes with the tiny bulbs in the windows.

Whereas my poor tree was sagging under the weight.

"Sorry bud." I patted its frozen bark before walking to the market two blocks down.

By the time I had a box of raw pasta in hand and was walking back, the sky was completely dark and the angelic swirling light designs that the city hung between each building over the streets sparkled at full force.

The warmth of the apartment complex hit me with a gust of wind as I entered the building. Slowly moving up the stairs, I unbuttoned my coat and pulled my keys out. The complex was quiet with so many traveling for the holiday. The sound of my boots hitting the stairs rung out. Unfortunately, our floor still had some neighbors home—

What the hell was he doing here?

At the end of the third floor where my apartment door resided, was Dorian.

"Adelaide, I know you're home. Mia said you were staying here during holiday, so please just open the door." Dorian braced the threshold as if he could reason with the door to open.

Even from behind him his presence made my heart hammer. His coat was tossed on the ground, so I was stuck staring at the muscles in his forearms where a black henley sweater was rolled up at the elbow.

I stood still trying to figure out if this was some hallucination. Maybe I had been eating bad chicken all week. Maybe Nancy Meyers put hallucinogens in her films.

But if I wasn't hallucinating, then how was I going to leave the building without him noticing and still make my pasta …

"She's not here, pretty boy!" My neighbor's sudden appearance jolted me—and the box of pasta.

"Maureen!" Dorian cheered.

Time to intervene. "I am so sorry, enjoy your Christmas Eve," I apologized, swept Dorian's coat up, grabbed his arm, and pushed him into the apartment.

Before I could shut the door, he was already speaking.

"Why haven't you answered my texts?" he asked.

I kicked my snowy boots off and quickly peeled the numerous layers from my body, dropping them on the coat rack in the foyer.

Five minutes ago, I couldn't feel my toes. Now my cheeks were splotchy like I was struck by rogue raspberries, and my hands wouldn't dry no matter how many times I wiped them on my jeans.

"Because I told you I'd be busy," I huffed, trying to avoid his eyes. I pulled my sweater over my head and then unzipped my jeans—

"Bloody hell, I'm not sober enough for this." He covered his eyes and turned away.

I rolled my eyes. "You can turn around. I have leggings on under these."

"Oh." He twisted and braced the threshold as I let my jeans puddle around my ankles before stepping out. He cleared his throat. "Why didn't you tell me you were spending Christmas alone?"

"I'm pretty sure my first answer also answers that." I walked past him and moved down the hall into the kitchen. A tinge of annoyance followed as he strode behind me. I had plans for tonight: pasta and Jude Law. The last thing I needed was *him* here. Missing my friends had begun to fill the space in my mind that was Dorian.

"It doesn't look like you're busy," he argued.

I opened the box of farfalle on the island. "I'd say cooking dinner makes me pretty busy."

"It's Christmas, Adelaide."

"Christmas Eve, actually. And I don't like celebrations anyway, you know that." Turning, I reached for the pot on the top shelf, my arm brushing against the Christmas garland.

Instantly, he was beside me, his arm sweeping past mine to grab the pot. It clanked against the countertop as he looked down at me.

"Why aren't you looking at me?" he asked.

"I'm looking at you right now." I hated it.

"You know what I mean."

"I'm in a rush, that's why," I exhaled, moving around him to fill the pot up in the sink.

"In a rush to do what? Spend the holiday alone like Maureen?"

"What's wrong with being like Maureen?"

The water stopped. His hand sat atop the faucet lever.

"She has a cat and lives alone," he responded.

"Sounds significantly better than being stuck with you."

"Significantly?" he scoffed. "Really?"

"*Relly*," I imitated his accent.

He narrowed his gaze. "Fine. Maybe I was wrong."

"Thank yo—"

"You're way too stubborn to be like Maureen," he finished.

I glared at him. "That's an admirable quality. Some would even say attractive."

"I think there are many things about you that people find attractive, Adelaide." A muscle moved in his forearm, his hand gripping the edge of the sink.

I pressed the side of my hip against the sink, needing the equivalent of a pinch to *wake up*. But it didn't diminish the drumming of dormant muscles in my chest that clung to my ribcage and urged to escape. They pattered at the pace of a piano being struck with *need*.

His head tilted down just a fraction of an inch, but it was still something. Something that brought the tips of our noses closer than they were before and interrupted the stream of the bulb's light above.

"Do you mean that?" I asked.

"No." A satisfied smirk slowly intruded his serious look.

Instinctively, I dunked my fingers in the pot and threw a handful of water at him.

His reaction was delayed. The result left his hair at the front of his head riddled with droplets. Lashes, skin, and sweater polka-dotted in it. He stared at me in disbelief before plunging his hand into the pot. Water was in my eyes before I could duck.

The volume of water that passed between us was vastly different. He was sprinkled in it, whereas my face was soaked.

I grabbed the half-full pot and catapulted it—

"*Shit!*" he ducked, but not fast enough. He stood back up with defeat. Hair was matted to his forehead, already curling.

"I think that makes us even now." I gave him a smug smile, empty pot in hand. Water was still swimming down the side of my jaw.

His tongue pushed against the inside of his cheek in comical disbelief. He swiped his hand across his forehead, sending water flying toward the cabinets.

"Alright, that's it. Let's go." He announced before shaking out his hair with his hand.

"Go where?"

"To complete your list. Now put your trousers back on."

33

Don't, Just Don't, Think About Kissing Her — Dorian

"Shouldn't you be wearing a hat or something? Maybe a mustache?" she asked as we stepped out of the cab and onto the Westminster Bridge.

"Why's that? Don't want to see my face?" I cocked a brow.

She pulled her knit hat over her head. It was cute. Really cute. And distracting. Definitely something a friend shouldn't be thinking.

Watching her leg bounce in the cab was painful enough. It'd graze my knee every few minutes and make me flinch. The longer there was contact, the more I wanted to lean into her.

"What if someone sees us?" She pulled the collar of her gray coat tighter around her exposed neck.

"It's the holidays, I'm not too worried about anyone taking our picture. And anyway, I'm usually in Italy with James by now, so that's where they'd be looking for me."

She glanced around, realizing I was right.

Christmas Eve, around the London tourist sites, was quiet. Few people passed us on the bridge. Not enough to barricade any of the wind shoving at our coats.

Big Ben winked at us from above with its warm yellow face. Lampposts peppered across the Bridge mirrored the same light.

I took my burgundy scarf off and threw it over her neck, tugging her forward to secure it in place. She let me pull her in. I couldn't tell if she was surprised by the action or simply alarmed that she was accepting it. Her black hair cupped her face, held down by the cashmere.

"Why aren't you in Italy with James right now?" she asked.

"Do you really need me to answer that question?"

"Maybe I wanted to hear you admit it."

"Admit that I wanted to be around you? I didn't think that was something I had to disclose." I adjusted her hat. It didn't need to be adjusted. But I was restless. She made me restless.

I was getting dangerously vulnerable. Maybe it was the four glasses of gin I had at the pub before walking to her flat. But realistically, it was the moment I saw her in the dim lighting of her kitchen that unraveled me. This harsh craving to hold her sparked. It hit me like a truck. Two weeks away from her was unsolicited torture. I should've been fine. Our deal was complete. She helped me pass the class. She didn't have to see me. She probably didn't want to see me.

For the first few days, I believed that. But the way her neck craned to meet my lips thirty minutes ago, I didn't believe it anymore. Especially when the small phone box keychain was hanging from the purse on her shoulder.

There was something between us. And I was going to tell her. Tonight. No excuses, no redirection, and no flirting that curbed the truth.

If she said Sabrina was the only problem, then I'd explain on Adelaide's behalf to her friend.

If she mentioned Victoria, then I'd tell her it was over. I'd explain how I stopped at Victoria's earlier (before dreadfully hitting the pub) to tell her I was done. That I loved someone else.

If Adelaide didn't feel the same way, then ... I guess I'd spend my holiday pretending that my heart wasn't slowly bleeding out.

Returning to campus would be another problem. One I couldn't withstand to imagine right now. Not when she was standing in front of me with the tip of her nose pink from the air.

"So what are we doing here?" she asked.

"You'll see. It's just a short walk." I took her gloved hand and slipped it into my coat pocket.

A cold, but quick stroll across the length of the bridge, and she was already trying to pull me in the opposite direction.

"You want me to get on *that?* No way." Despite the intimidating look of determination on her face, panic was evident in her voice.

"It's on the list! And you can't live in London and not go on the London Eye," I explained. The spinning structure sparkled above us like a perfect white snowflake. It did look quite large from this angle though.

"Dorian, no, really I can't do this." Her hand gripped mine with the power of a vise.

Despite losing feeling in my fingers, I squeezed her hand back, trying to give her a place to focus. "I'll be with you, don't worry. But I can't let you miss this, not with the snow coming down and the Christmas lights up on the bridge."

If she said no again, I was prepared to turn us around. I wanted to help her face a fear, not traumatize her.

With her hand cutting off the circulation in my palm, she stared up for a few moments before she finally gave in and continued to walk, allowing us to approach the entrance where one of the large glass globes was coming to a stop and opening.

An employee in a branded jacket nodded for us to go on.

"What's going to happen if I vomit? Because as of right now, that's incredibly possible."

The uneasiness of her legs was apparent as we stepped inside, the door closing behind us. I guided her to the long bench that sat against the back of the globe before her legs could give out from the sudden motion.

"No one will see you vomit"—because I paid an exuberant amount of money to have someone let us on despite its closing to the public three hours ago.

"What if I vomit on you?" Out of context, it sounded like a threat.

"I'll send you my dry-cleaning bill then." That earned me a laugh. *Finally.* My shoulders relaxed.

But once the ride kicked into gear and we began moving, her hand shot to my leg. I covered her knuckles with my palm, trying everything in my power not to flinch at the way her fingers splayed across my thigh.

"How high up are we? Actually, never mind, I don't want to know." She spoke in a rush, her eyes squeezed shut.

I peeled my gaze away from her to look at the skyline. The inside of the pod was dark, but the city lights exploded with color. We had a bird's eye view of all of London's most notable sites.

Tower Bridge was outlined in white bulbs while the London markets were illuminated by Christmas trees and hot chocolate stands. Snow fell in slow motion, melting into the Thames River below. There was so much to look at. So much light pulling the eye in different directions. I wasn't sure if John Constable, a painter known for his landscapes, would even know where to start.

I looked back and her eyes were still shut, leg bouncing away.

"Hey, look at me," I said softly.

I squeezed her hand. She didn't budge. Picking up my palm, I carried it to her face and paused instantly.

What am I doing?

I took in the features of her face in secret, absorbing the arch of her cheek bones and the length of her dark lashes. My heart pounded in unison with each part I memorized. Before I could get to her lips and torture myself more, I cupped her jaw.

Her eyes immediately opened. Surprise passed over her face before I opened my mouth.

"You're going to miss it," I told her.

"How pretty could it possibly be?"

"Very pretty," I assured. "Come on."

I stood and gave her my hand. She went a step further and held onto my arm as if I was courting her, nails digging into my bicep. Four steps and we were in front of the glass.

Her hold on my arm loosened slowly and then pivoted to the glass altogether as she admired the scene outside our personal snow globe.

"It's gorgeous," she exhaled. Her warm breath marked the glass.

"Was it worth it?" I asked.

"Worth being splashed with water and dragged out into the cold?"

I rolled my eyes. "Taking a chance. Being scared," I clarified.

"You sound like Sabrina." Fatigue sat in her voice.

"Why is that?"

"She tried to make the same argument with me before leaving

for Paris—that I don't take chances. That I let fear consume me."
Her finger tapped the glass where Big Ben stood.

"Why'd she say that?"

"Because she thinks I'm making myself unhappy by avoiding my love for James."

My heart sunk to the bottom of my stomach. Thunderous pumping blood pounded in my ears.

My love for James.

"Your love for James ..." I repeated.

She faced me, light bouncing off the right side of her face. "It's ridiculous, I know. She thinks we're in love with one another and that I'm trying to avoid it."

The pounding quieted.

She turned back to the view.

"What makes her think...that?" I asked. A bitter taste sat at the bottom of my throat. I couldn't fathom saying, *What makes her think the two of you are in love?*

Since the day James mentioned asking her out, we rarely spoke of her to maintain sanity. The need to question him on when he asked her, how he asked, and how she reacted, was insistent.

I assumed she must've said no since I never heard about a date. But Adelaide said no to many things, even to those she wanted. She was stubborn.

"She said I've been acting differently: isolating myself at these events, going out when her and Mia are busy. Drinking coffee. Maureen even mentioned the cute guy that walks me home."

Shit. So much for doing a good job at upholding my end of the deal.

"You hate coffee." It came out more like a question.

She ran her fingers over her brow. "I haven't been sleeping

well."

"Nightmares?"

"Something like that."

"I can understand." I nodded.

A pause.

"Do you like James?" I asked.

She turned in surprise. "Are you asking me if I like him *romantically?*"

I gave her a look that said, *What else would I mean?*

She waited for an answer.

"Do you enjoy torturing me?" I asked.

"I didn't know James's interests fell into the Torture category."

"Not James's. Yours."

"Would it bother you if I liked him?"

"Not in the way you're thinking."

"And what way is that?"

The way that I'd never be completely happy for my best friend without also constantly craving touching his girlfriend. "That's an answer you don't get to know right now. Now answer the original question."

"I don't. James is just my friend," she said softly.

The fluttering in my ears finally stopped.

"It was worth it, by the way," she continued. "Experiencing this." Her small smile was warm and thankful.

Before I could gather enough words to respond, we were back on the ground. I was clutching her hand so she wouldn't trip when stepping out. After passing the attendant a tip, we were walking back over the bridge. Snowflakes collected on her scarf and hat, even sticking to her dark hair.

I tucked her hand back into my pocket to keep it warm. It was torturous, doing this to myself. But a voice at the back of my head was telling me to absorb as much of this as I could before she possibly rejected me.

"Was that rain?" She held out her gloved hand as if to catch something.

"What?" I was more focused on her hand in mine rather than the weather.

"The rain—"

Her words were cut off by buckets of rain colliding with the bridge and river. The snow that had been falling was quickly replaced by a downpour of rain. She yelped and tugged on my hand, pulling us into a run.

"Let me guess, no umbrella!" she shouted over the raindrops pounding the cold asphalt. The scarf flew across her mouth against the wind.

"It's not like *you* thought to bring one!"

Once we were across the bridge, I searched for a place for us to stop while we waited for a car. But everything was closed. It was Christmas Eve. And it wasn't like Westminster Abbey offered much coverage with its sky-high spokes.

The only solution I could spot amongst the blur of the lights was the last spot I wanted to be stuck in. But Adelaide was shivering.

She didn't hesitate to follow me as we passed Big Ben and crossed the street. Jumping onto the sidewalk, I ushered her into the small box.

"A telephone booth?" she laughed as I shut the red door behind us.

"Not my first choice, believe me," I exhaled and shook out my hair. Dark strands of her own stuck to her face as she peeled her knit hat off.

I leaned against the side of the phone box, across from the actual telephone, to give us—her—space.

"I'll call a car now that we have somewhere to wait," I said. The weather drummed all around us as I called my driver, avoiding Adelaide as she peeled wet layers off herself and wiped shook them out.

"Yes, right by Westminster," I explained. "Thanks." Once I hung up and returned my gaze, she was already putting the scarf back on. "He'll be here in about twenty minutes."

She nodded, looking around the tight space. Looking anywhere but my face.

I should tell her. Right now. This was the time.

But watching the night sky cup her face in a series of shadows, and witnessing droplets trace the shape of her jaw as she admired the rain, my whole speech evaporated. I didn't want to lose her. I couldn't lose her.

What would I even say?

I tried, you know. To look at you as a friend. I really did. But every time you smiled. You laughed. You breathed. Your lips parted. All I could think about was kissing you. And you're not supposed to want to kiss your friends. You're not supposed to want to brush the straps of their tops off their shoulders and kiss down their neck and across their collarbones.

"Dorian?" Her voice was soft like silk. The embodiment of liquidized pearls.

My gaze dove to her.

Maybe if I didn't answer she'd say it again. But my mind worked too quickly, wanting to know what she needed, so I responded, "Yes?"

"Thank you, for tonight." She gave me a short smile. "I can't remember the last time I had that much fun around Christmas."

"I was hoping you'd enjoy it." I rubbed my hands together without the company of her gloved hands.

A moment of silence passed before my curiosity got the best of me. "Why can't you sleep?"

"What?"

"Earlier, you said you started drinking coffee—"

"Oh, I told you. Nightmares." She fiddled with the ring on her index finger. A ring I was pretty sure I had kissed that August night.

"No, those were my words that you went with. What is it really?"

"I'll answer your question if you answer mine."

I rolled my eyes. "Fine. What's your question?"

"You said you weren't sleeping either."

"That's not a question."

She continued, "You said you understood having nightmares. So what's keeping you up at night?"

"Why do you want to know?"

"Can't answer my question with another question," she rebutted.

"I imagine all the paintings in my home being stolen or lathered in peanut butter beyond repair."

"Are you ever serious?" She narrowed her eyes.

"Some would say damage to artwork is the most serious enigma of them all."

She exhaled in annoyance and turned for the door—

I caught her elbow and stopped her.

"Fine, fine." I took a breath. "You."

"Me?"

Liana Cincotti

"Yes, *you*."

She froze. "What about me?"

"I dream about you."

She stared at me in disbelief.

"You're really going to make me say it again?"

Her eyes darted across my face. She didn't believe me. But she wanted to. Or else her elbow wouldn't be in my hand still.

"Yes," she repeated.

With the slightest force, I tugged on her arm. She obliged, taking a step. Her eyelashes were still wet, pulled into sharp points like the tip of a detailed paintbrush.

I let my hand travel down the length of her arm before stopping at her fingertips, holding on.

"You keep me up every night. I dream about August. And I dream about the night before Halloween when we kissed. And I dream about seeing you kiss someone else. I dream about things that haven't even happened."

The tightness in my throat made it feel as if I just ran five miles. I was capturing air from the contained space to keep from saying anything else.

"Oh."

"Yeah." I rubbed at the skin on my forehead. *Way to look pathetic, Dorian. She's horrified now.* Part of me wanted to retreat, while the other half was grateful the words were finally out.

"Do you wish they had happened—the dreams?" she asked.

"That wasn't the question."

"It's a new question." She stepped forward.

"Adelaide," I warned. This was an opening to embarrass myself. An opportunity to divulge how suffocated I was by the dreams of her   of us. I felt like a mouse backing away from a cat.

She took another step closer, forcing me into the wall of the booth, nowhere to go. I was pinned. I looked to the right where the bridge stood stronger than I was now.

"Dorian," she responded. Then her fingers found my chin and pulled my gaze down. My throat bobbed. A pathetic apology for what I was so close to doing.

"I'm not answering that question," I said firmly. "You haven't even answered mine." I was beyond flustered. "If this is your way of torturing me, it's working. Because I lose all ability to lie when it comes to you—"

"Do you ever stop talking?" she exhaled before grabbing the sides of my coat and pulling me down, crashing her lips against mine.

The rain seemed to cheer behind us as my shoulders fell backward into the glass.

My inner conflict immediately collapsed. A fortress built block by block left in disarray, and all the rubble sat in Adelaide Adorno's hands. I shoved more of the debris into her grip by taking her jaw between my palms and kissing her back.

Her hands found my shoulders, my neck, my hair, my jaw. She was shaping me like a sculptor. My skin felt hotter than the surface of stove after a pot of boiling water. I tried to take it all in. Absorb it. But I couldn't stay still. With a hand on her hip and another at her neck, I switched our places, pressing her against the glass.

I didn't pull away as I peeled off my coat. She took the wrists of the fabric, tugging it off the rest of the way. I didn't waste time finding her again, my hands catching her waist and pulling her into my chest.

I couldn't get her close enough. I couldn't get enough of her.

How is this real? How is this real?

She parted my lips as if demanding admittance for something she'd been patient for. I'd let her do whatever she wanted.

"God, Adelaide," I groaned.

I absorbed the taste of the coconut lip gloss I stared at all night, sweeping my hands over her frame. I memorized her hips. I memorized her lower back. Her breathing, the back of her arms, the arch of her neck. Wet strands of hair even wrapped themselves around my rings.

I was suffocating and breathing the freshest air at the same time. I couldn't fathom how she was real. She was everything I never knew I needed. And now I couldn't let go.

Our hands moved along each other's bodies in conversation.

I love you, the hand cupping her jaw, said.

I love you, the hot breath I was gasping for, said.

I love you, the desperate kiss I pressed against her lips, said.

Silence rang out from her end. I couldn't read any of her movements.

And then, the sound of a car horn blared in the street.

We jumped away from each other. Grogginess swept my muscles.

She exhaled.

I inhaled.

I counted every inch that stood between our lips, my brain calculating the number of seconds it would take to reach her again. No different than any other time I was around her.

But as we caught our breath, all I could think about was how I was supposed to ignore my feelings now.

"Tell me to stay," I said.

"What?" she breathed.

"Tell," I exhaled. I couldn't catch ahold of my breath. She had it all. "Me. To. Stay. With. You."

"You're supposed to be in Italy with your family and James."

"They are the last thing I'm thinking about right now."

"Dorian …"

"Tell me something, Adelaide. Because I care for you so much that I'm losing sleep over it."

"I … I don't know."

I steeled myself. "When I come home, I'm going to come see you. And if your answer is still 'I don't know,' then I'll leave you alone."

I may have said those words, but I wasn't sure of how I was supposed to stick to them if her answer was anything but *I care for you too.*

34

Don't Spend Christmas Alone — Adelaide

Christmas morning, I woke to Kurt pawing at my balcony door, snow refilling the sidewalks, and the jarring realization that everything that had happened last night was not a dream. It was indeed real. Terribly real.

Finding Dorian at my apartment door. Letting him in. Going on the London Eye. Running back in the rain. Taking cover in a telephone booth. Touching him. Kissing him. Whispering his name. Feeling his hand leave mine as he dropped me at home, no lingering words. No declarations of lo—

Stop. Stop, stop, stop.

"Kurt, stop!" I shouted, the bell on his collar ringing through my brain.

I looked up and he was sitting politely, snow collecting on his white coat on the balcony. His pink nose tilted innocently as I noticed a tiny note tied to his collar.

"Ugh. Fine, I'm coming." I threw the duvet off and swung my legs over. Catching myself in the mirror, I remembered I had put Dorian's UK flag shirt on in my drowsy state last night.

Oh. My. God. I scrambled for a sweatshirt—one that'd mask

the smell of his cologne—before opening the balcony door. A cold breeze and a few snowflakes tumbled in, along with Kurt who squeezed through the crack. He meowed his thank you.

"Hello, Kurt," I sighed as if I was greeting the coworker who refused to save any donuts for the rest of the office.

He ran straight for my closet far away from the balcony to the pile of blankets folded on the floor. He nuzzled in until his tail twisted like a whip and curled around him.

"Now that you're sitting still …" I walked around my bed and crouched in front of the closet, untying the note from his collar.

It was short in sweeping cursive:

Happy Christmas from Maureen & Kurt.

I exhaled. Looked like we were both riding solo today.

Spend the holidays like Maureen? Dorian had said. There was nothing wrong with being alone. I thrived on being alone. But after spending the night with him … I wasn't alone now. Dorian Thoughts occupied every corner of my mind.

Iris and Dotty extended an invite, of course, but I felt intrusive, interrupting their conversations with their nieces and nephews and not having gifts to bring along.

Grabbing a pen from my nightstand, I scribble on the back of the note:

Tea? — Adelaide

I tied the message back onto Kurt and gripped the blanket he rested on, sliding it across the hardwood floor, down the hall, and out the front door.

"Go!" I cheered. He yelled at me in protest as I shut the door.

I raced to my room, threw on a semi-respectable sweater that made me look semi-responsible, switching the Christmas tree on before I was back at the door, answering the knock

"Oh, I'm sorry, did you have plans already?" I paused in the doorway, taking in Maureen's black dress pants, burgundy blouse, and matching cardigan, pearls dangling from her ears. The ends of her short white hair were flipped in like a blooming flower.

"No, I just like to dress up for the holidays," she responded curtly. She shoved a pile of envelopes into my hand before walking through the foyer with a tray of cookies covered in plastic wrap.

I closed the door before I realized the envelopes were my mail from downstairs.

Pretty sure it was illegal to collect someone else's mail, but I guess we were passed that since we had unwritten shared custody of Kurt. She fed him and I housed him. Now she got to deliver my mail.

"Where are you originally from?" I asked. I had never heard her talk long enough to realize she wasn't British.

"New York," she answered, finding her way into my kitchen without any help. I trotted in behind Kurt where she sat at our small circular table already unwrapping the plastic to reveal shortbread cookies sided in red and green sprinkles.

"Oh, I have a friend from New York! His name is Mart—"

"I haven't been to New York in thirty years so the chance of me knowing your friend is about as likely as Kurt being my mother reincarnated."

Alright then.

I sifted through mail: letters from Mia's siblings, shiny Christmas cards from Sabrina's extended family, retail coupons for me, junk mail.

"Can I make you some tea?" I asked.

"That is what I came for."

This may have been a mistake. "Earl gray, English breakfast, peppermint or green tea?"

"English breakfast. With honey. Please."

I set two small plates on the table and then filled the kettle with water, switching on the stove.

"Your roommates not here with you?" She gave a quick glance around the kitchen. The pearls on her ears danced back and forth.

"They're both with family," I said, dropping the mail on the table and sitting across from her.

"Do you dislike being around family?" she guessed.

"Something like that." I placed one of the cookies on my plate. "Thank you for these."

She waved her hand. "I'm surprised you're not with the boy. The pretty one."

"Oh, we're not really dating or anything."

Her brows rose. "Never said you were. Friends celebrate holidays together all the time. I just asked since I saw him drop you off last night."

"Oh, well, we're not close enough to be spending holidays together."

"I wasn't trying to make assumptions." She held her hands up, almond acrylic red nails pointed toward the ceiling. "But I tend to have a good read on men."

"Oh, do you date a lot?"

"Not men." She shook her head in distaste. *Can't blame her.* "But I know men." She pointed at me. "So what's wrong with him?"

"What?"

"The boy that walks you home every night. What's wrong with him if you're avoiding him? Because by the look on his face last night, he would've spent the whole month with you if you asked."

"I—" had no idea what she meant by that and I was slightly concerned by how much she watched us from her window. "No, nothing's wrong with him. He can be argumentative and frustrating—all the time actually. But he's also considerate and kind and witty."

"Ah, I see."

"See what?" I leaned forward as if she had some insight into my future.

"You love him."

The kettle shrieked behind me.

"I—what?" This was like the Sabrina conversation all over again.

"The water." She gestured to the pot.

Dumbfounded, I tended to the kettle, pouring the hot water into two mugs before dropping the tea bags and honey in.

"Be careful, it's hot." I handed her the mug.

"I wouldn't have guessed," she responded sarcastically, accepting it and blowing a flow of steam toward me.

I mimicked the motion before asking, "Do you dislike being around family too?"

"Something like that," she repeated.

"What do you usually do on Christmas?"

She blotted her red lipstick with a napkin before taking a sip from the mug, swallowing. "Nothing too different from most days.

The only exception is I go to midnight mass the night before and the cookies I make are green and red. If it's not too cold, sometimes Kurt and I will go down the street and sit in the park and await the snowfall. Watch families gather in doorways with gifts and casseroles. Children forced into matching garbs with pouts on their faces."

She looked down at the table, a sad smile on her face before clearing her throat. "A little too cold for that today though. Kurt and I will stick to the couch."

"I'm around all day. I wouldn't mind some company, especially since I've been watching the same Christmas movie on repeat for the past four weeks."

"Which movie?" she asked, lifting her mug to her lips.

"*The Holiday*."

She smiled. "The scene where he shows up drunk and she grabs his tie—*the best*."

"Yes!"

"Kurt and I watch it every year. Isn't that right?" she asked affectionately, leaning over to him on the floor to scratch his back. He purred in protest when she pulled away, leaning back to—

"Kurt, *no*," Maureen tsked as the cat jumped onto the table and sent the pile of mail across the floor, paper hitting the ground in a perpendicular fashion.

"It's alright," I assured, kneeling down to collect each envelope one-by-one, tossing it back onto the table as Kurt ran from the kitchen.

"You may dislike your family, but it doesn't seem like they dislike you," Maureen commented.

"Excuse me?"

Without answering, she handed me a white envelope under

Liana Cincotti

the table. Addressed to me. From 'Auntie Laila Adorno.'

I slumped on the floor. My mouth dried up. The moisture on my tongue fled and redirected to my eyes. My throat swelled with emotion.

She responded. She actually responded. I was angry at her for not responding, and she had.

Relief rolled off me as I slipped my thumb under the envelope and tugged. Inside was a card filled with her handwriting.

Dear Adelaide,

I'm so happy to hear from you. It's been so long. Thank you for the birthday wishes. Massachusetts misses you. And so do I. I talk about you all the time, especially to Benedict. He's my fiancé—we started dating two years and just got engaged last month. He knows all about how smart and driven you are. I even showed him all of the Beverly mood boards you made in high school that hang on your bedroom walls. I'm so happy they're hiring; it sounds meant to be.

I'd of course answer any questions you have. Why don't you give me a call when you get this?

P.S. I loved London. There's nothing better than the view of Big Ben at night. (Just stay away from the telephone booths—they're riddled with germs.)

Hopefully I can come visit you soon, if you'd like that.

— Auntie

I exhaled.

She had a fiancé now. She told him about me. She missed me. *Massachusetts misses you. And so do I.*

The part of my brain dedicated to family memories and nostalgia locked up like a vault respired just a bit, dense air releasing.

She responded. She wanted to visit.

A wet saltiness hit my lip.

"Gosh, I'm sorry," I laughed, wiping a tear and standing up, returning to my chair. "I don't even know why I'm crying, it's just a card."

"Nothing to apologize for." She shook her head. "Are you close with your aunt?"

"No," I responded with honesty for the first time in years without second guessing it. "We haven't spoken since I started university four years ago. I—uh—I moved in with her when my mother left. My aunt wasn't thrilled to be straddled with a kid."

"Is that what she told you?"

"She may as well have. We barely spoke when I lived with her."

"How old was she when you moved in?"

"Twenty-five."

"Wow, young." She tapped her nails against her mug. "Well, if I know anything in the seventy-nine years I've been around, it's that being in your twenties is arguably the most difficult time of your life. Everything you do in that decade forms what's to come. And it feels as if you're never doing the right thing or making the right decision. That's not to say how your aunt acted was right. I don't know her. But I wonder if that at all had to do with her silence. I know that I made more than enough mistakes at twenty-five."

I pressed at the corners of my eyes, trying to push down the puffiness. In three years, I'd be the same age my aunt was when she took me in. I couldn't imagine that burden. I took a big gulp of the bitter tea to halt my tear ducts.

She continued, "The mistakes I regret the most are the ones I didn't allow to happen. You have to make decisions with purpose, knowing that they may not be around forever. Whether that mistake could be not asking your aunt about the past or letting that handsome friend slip from your life."

Another tear escaped, running down the angle in my cheek. I inhaled.

I wanted to ask her about her mistakes, her regrets, but that seemed too soon, even if she was witnessing me having an unexpected breakdown over family trauma.

So instead, I asked, "Maureen, do you like to read? Or at least drink wine and eat cheese?"

35

Don't Wait Until You Regret It — Adelaide

As 8 p.m. appeared on the clock, Maureen (and Kurt) retired to their apartment with a promise to return for January's book club in two weeks.

Darkness and exhaustion swept me. I switched off the lamps peppering the flat before ending up back in my room.

I stopped at the door and looked at my bed with aversion. My pillows and duvet were rustled from how I left them this morning. Unmade and unkempt. But the dreams that rested between the dips in the mattress caused by restless turning were what stopped me.

Would it be ridiculous to sleep on the couch just to avoid another dream? Shake up the night routine and hopefully jumble the dreams?

"I'm going insane," I muttered.

My phone buzzed in my pajama pants pocket. I pulled it out and found James's name on the screen.

"Hi James," I smiled. "Merry Christmas."

"It's *Happy* Christmas. If you're going to live in London, you have to learn the lingo." I could hear the buttery-sweet smile in his voice too. "But Merry Christmas to you too."

"Apologies, *mate*," I responded. "How's Italy?" I kicked off my slippers, switched off my light, and slithered into my bed. The darkness through the balcony door dragged against the walls. I was sure it was still snowing, but I couldn't see it.

I rolled on my side and put the phone on speaker, watching the young family across the street move through their apartment window. It was painted a butterscotch yellow in the dark.

"Beautiful as always, and still warmer than London, that's for sure. I'll miss not having to pack on so many layers." There was a *clink* of wine glasses and a murmur of voices behind him.

"I know it's only been ten days since our final but I'm starting to miss you," I said

"Hop in a cab, I'll find you a flight to Rome this instant."

I laughed. "Sure, let me grab a cab with the pajamas on my back and the retainer in my mouth."

He paused. "You're kidding."

"Of course I am! I'm not impending on your vacation just because I'm alone. Mia will be home in a few days for New Year's Eve anyway."

"I guess we'll be back not too long after that."

We.

"Is Dorian with you?" I couldn't help but ask. I bit my tongue, praying I wasn't on speaker phone.

"Yeah, he's sitting with my mother right now—we're at dinner together. I needed a break from all the scheduling, so I left him to listen to plans about The January while I stand outside pretending that I got a call." He laughed. It sounded like he was turning his head to look.

"What's happening in January?"

"*The* January."

"Is that how we're talking now?"

"It's an annual ball. You haven't heard of it?"

"I have no idea what you're talking about."

"It's the only gala in London that happens in January, hence the name. It raises money for fashion museums throughout the UK. You really haven't heard of this?"

"No James," I laughed. "I'm not part of the underground exclusive cult this entire university is in. Continue. Explain on."

"Fine, fine. My mum and Mrs. Blackwood are both on the board of the Art and Fashion Legacy of London so they're in charge of planning it. It's the first Friday of January so every Christmas they're running around with their phones attached to their heads making phone calls."

"You sound thrilled about this."

"Ironically, I do enjoy it. It's hosted at an art museum so it's quite beautiful. But being dragged into calling the caterer and helping make the guest lists? Not my favorite pastime. Wait— you'll come right?"

"I'm only just hearing of it now! I'll think about it."

The idea of seeing Dorian for the first time in a public space after kissing him sounded … risky. I couldn't even think about him in solitude without my stomach twisting into complicated, unforgiving knots.

"I'm putting you on the guest list. Mia and Sabrina too."

"I'm so grateful that you're always looking out for my schedule."

"It's before the semester even starts so you won't have any impending work. And you owe me a dance from Halloween anyway."

"Fine, you caught me! I'm available, I'll come!"

"Thank god because I wouldn't survive an event without Adelaide Adorno."

"I'm sure I'll be so much help," I said sarcastically.

"Your company will be, trust me."

There was a comforting lull that passed between us. One that was soft enough to push my eyes closed.

"Alright, I have one more call before I fall asleep. Send me all the details and we can talk about it more when you get back," I said.

I hung up and searched for the number that sat at the bottom of my contact list but at the top of my mind. I pressed *Call* before I could second guess it and back out in the morning, knowing Maureen would be proud of me.

"Hi Laila. Do you have time for those questions?"

By the time our call finished, that vault tucked away in the back of my brain relaxed a bit more. It was awkward talking to her. Between fumbling over each other's words and trying to fill the silent gaps so that we stayed on the topic of cover letters, I was tired, filled with an anxious buzz. Especially when she asked if we could talk again next week. I agreed, thinking that if I said no, I'd regret it.

36

Don't Ever Trust Him — Adelaide

Even in the years I was close to my aunt, when my parents were together, and she came over for holidays, took on babysitting duties, and made me the victim of poor hairstyles before Saturday soccer practices, I never knew how … funny she could be.

When we lived together, she went to work, and I went to school. At night, she'd cook dinner (I assumed, I never saw) and leave it on the counter for me. Her portion would have already been picked off the serving plate.

I didn't know if she had friends at work or hobbies outside the office or if she preferred sour candy to chocolate. She wore a variation of the same trousers every day and answered emails like they had an expiration date. That was all I knew. She was the coworker that sat in the cubicle farthest away from me, in a way.

On our second scheduled call, I learned that she was recently promoted to manage a team—

"—of *interns*. Half of them think they know more than me and the other half really do know more than me." I received a series of questions on *How many emails is too many emails?* and *Are Friday meetings out now?* et cetera. "I need your insight. I want to be the cool manager."

I read her my Beverly cover letter four times before we finally decided it was perfect. Then I emailed Sylvie for that recommendation letter, and she responded within minutes, promising to send it to the HR department.

An hour into the phone call, I learned that she got a mini goldendoodle—apparently that was a dog—before the fiancé (Benedict) moved in. She said it was lonely without me.

We stopped there and pivoted back to the fiancé.

I didn't ask why we never had these types of conversations before when I really needed them because I was too fearful to mess up. To throw tacks out on the road that we were smoothly cruising along now.

"You need to talk to her at some point," Mia reminded me as we crossed the slushy street to the pub where it was filled with others who chose to spend New Year's Eve with friends and lovers rather than family. Lampposts were still decorated with green garland and artificial sparkly snowflakes, acting as a guide in the busy street. Based on the density in the city right now, London had to have made the top of every *Where To Celebrate New Year's Eve?* list.

"One conversation at a time." I clutched the scarf that Dorian had left me, trying to keep it from flying off. I resisted the urge to press it to my nose and smell his cologne.

Her head whipped around as our leather boots hit the sidewalk. "Does that mean you're going to be having the *other* conversation? With Brina?"

"I ... " I had to tell Sabrina.

Tell her what exactly? That I can't stop thinking about the man she's in love with?

I *couldn't* stop thinking about him. And knowing that he felt the same way …

Mia noted my silence and continued. "I told you my original stance on this: if you don't care for him, then it's not worth upsetting her. But if you do … Well, I get it. Especially after what you said happened on Christmas Eve. But you should tell her."

We reached the pub and she held the door open for me, letting a gust of hot air and the strong scent of bourbon funnel out before we stepped inside. Moving toward the bar, our shoulders bumped sequins and skin. My wool sleeve was snagged by the time we took a seat; televisions with the countdown to midnight hung above. I pulled my coat off as she ordered us drinks.

"Does this mean you're going to tell him how you feel?" Mia asked, her elbows on the bar.

How I feel? As in the stabbing fire poker to the gut I suffered from each time I saw him? That fountain pen drag across my heart as if the features of his face were being drawn into my blood? The absolute nausea I got any time I thought he was going to tell me he was in love with Victoria and didn't want to see me anymore?

I was sure those explanations would go *so well*. I'd throw myself into the freezing cold Thames before I even gave myself the chance to say, "fire poker."

"You look like you're over computing."

"I'm just …"

"Overwhelmed?" she guessed.

"Very," I sighed, accepting my drink from the bartender and taking a heavy swig.

Mia followed suit. "Have you talked to him since?"

"I haven't." I said it with a tinge of regret because he had given me an opening. In the form of a text the day after Christmas.

Heard you called James. How are you?

Lighthearted. Nothing serious. Yet, I still couldn't pull myself together to respond.

I itched to call him, ask how he was, nag him for pictures of his meals in Italy. I wanted to hear him say that he cared for me again in his soft, sultry British accent so I could confirm that I hadn't made it all up. So I could kiss him when he came home and not wonder if he'd pull away.

His hold on me had become plant overgrowth; a vine wrapped around every bone in my chest.

"So you're avoiding him?"

"My specialty, isn't it?" I raised my glass. "It was a horrible idea. And if I continue to avoid him, I'll still end up seeing him at this ball where he'll look atrociously more attractive than usual."

"Maybe the words will come out easier."

"Which words?"

"'I like you.'"

I pressed my fingertips into the corners of my eyes.

What Mia thought was some major revelation for me actually felt bland, because the past four months have felt much more tumultuous than *like*.

The mistakes I regret the most are the ones I didn't allow to happen.

I looked around the bar. Smiles painted the faces of everyone squished into the tight space. Glasses clanked, shoes stomped, giggles shrieked, and plastic noise makers sang. A cacophony of happiness that somehow unified for a symphony. But a peacefulness resonated between those who held hands beneath high top tables and splayed out fingers on partners' lower backs.

"I have to tell him," I decided.

"You do?" Mia's eyes blew up. (Not literally but in width they sure did.) Her iridescent pink eyeshadow elongated.

"I do. The moment he gets home. I have absolutely no clue what I'm going to say, and this may be the one thing I've never planned ahead for and I should. But if I start planning then I'll start overthinking and it'll never happen. Once I tell him, I'll explain everything to Brina."

"Wow, I can't believe this."

"I can't either."

She squeezed the hand that wasn't clutching my drink. "Whatever you need, I'll be here."

"Thank you." I leaned my head against her shoulder, staring up at the television casting some performer singing a New Year's-related tune. "In the meantime, I think I'll have a few more of these." I dropped my empty glass on the bar and asked for another.

And another ten minutes later.

And another ten minutes after that.

And maybe I only asked for half a glass after that because there was no way I drank that much already. The bartender only put the glass in my hand a few seconds ago.

"No. More. Drinks. Got it?" Mia said in a demanding tone. "I'd prefer if you were conscious for the walk home. Especially when midnight is in two minutes."

I waved my hand. It wasn't like I was *drunk*. I never got drunk. Especially not over a guy.

Before I could take another sip of what was left at the bottom of the crystal glass, my phone buzzed in my pocket. Grabbing the phone, the notification came up blurry, its bright screen blinding me in the dimness of the bar.

I rubbed my eyes and squinted in frustration, trying to get the words to focus as I opened the alert. But as the headline cleared up, I didn't have to read it more than once to understand what it said.

Any fogginess that was clouding my thoughts or making the music in here actually sound good, diminished, along with the air in my lungs.

Both faded at the sight of Dorian's lips against Victoria's.

Dorian Blackwood and Victoria Sutton Exclusive Again.

Bile rose in my throat.

I scrolled past the photos as quickly as possible looking for the context in the article.

"*Blackwood (photographed on the left) and Sutton (photographed on the right) were spotted together outside Sutton's apartment on Christmas Eve. Their relationship has been in question since their break-up last year, however with the couple being spotted on Christmas Eve, kissing, we can finally confirm that they are back to—*"

On Christmas Eve.

"What's wrong?" Mia's voice interrupted but it sounded far away.

I was trapped inside a snow globe, and she was knocking on the glass. I stared at. The words weren't forming. She gave up and then realization hit. She took my phone.

Her gasp was muffled. All I could see was Dorian's dark hair mixed with Victoria's blond.

"This can't be real," she said from a distance.

"It is." He was wearing the same clothes I ran my hands over that night.

There were even Christmas lights hanging above them at Victoria's apartment complex like a goddamn holiday card.

"Addy, are you okay?"

"I'm fine." It was fine, my heart wasn't being torn and pulled out of my chest like a garden tool scavenging for unrequited blood.

I guess there's no point in telling Sabrina now. There's nothing to tell. She'll need me anyway once she sees this. Someone will need to hold her while she shakes and cries. I need to get my own tears out of the way.

"I just—I need to leave."

"Let's go then." She collected her coat and put her glass down.

"No, stay here. I'll go."

"But—"

"Mia, I need to be alone."

She sat back down, agreeing, before jumping forward to give me a hug and releasing me.

I pulled on my coat and rushed out onto the sidewalk.

I couldn't muster up a walk in the snow, so I held out a shaky hand until a cab stopped. I got in and gave the driver the address before my voice could succumb to the emotion in my throat.

My body and mind were building up like a wall of bricks, fortifying our wall, just as they always had. A wall so thick that it had become numb. Overgrown in vines and moss. But right before the last brick could go in, all the tears slipped out.

It wasn't until I was back in my flat that I realized I had been clutching his scarf.

37

Don't Underestimate Your Public Relations
Degree — Adelaide

The photo of Dorian and Victoria spread like ink in water. And it had only been twenty-four hours.

Dorian Blackwood Off the Market.

There wasn't a celebrity news outlet that wasn't talking about it. Meaning I had been subjected to seeing the photos enough times to know the exact shade and brand of Victoria's lipstick.

I should be checking my email, waiting on Beverly's response. But the inside of my brain was frozen on a silent movie frame. Dorian and Victoria's name appeared in a static sparkle that wouldn't let me look away.

When I wasn't thinking about them, I was thinking about all the women he had been with and how I sized up to them. The ones with the wealthy families and built-in careers. Was I some charity case? An experiment?

It wasn't until I got into bed that night that I allowed myself to cry again.

I didn't even feel sad. I was infuriated. Tears just happened to slip out in between.

But the worst part of all, was that I missed him.

I hated him. But I missed him.

I missed the way he squeezed my palm in the rain. I missed the way the umbrella shook above our heads when I made him laugh. I missed the way his voice deepened when he said my name. The way he leaned into me when I spoke. The way he held me even when we were arguing. The way he openly told me about his life like it was a collection of buried diary entries no one else had read.

I missed the way he liked me.

A knock sounded at my bedroom door.

"Go away, Mia," I responded, my face shoved in my tear-stained pillow.

The door creaked open anyway.

"Hey," I said annoyed, sitting up quickly.

Swaddled in a blanket, she intruded anyway, slipping into bed beside me. She greeted me with a horror-stricken face.

My heart sank. "What is it?"

"You need to see this." She handed me her phone. I rubbed my wet eyelashes.

This couldn't be real. A trick of the eye. The lack of natural light in the room. It had to be.

"Please tell me we're both imagining this."

"It was published an hour ago," she responded.

What Mia *wasn't* saying was that it was published by one of the largest tabloids in London.

One of the largest tabloids in London just published a photo of Dorian *and me.*

Well, *I* knew it was me because I was there, in that telephone booth on Christmas Eve. Our only witnesses our shadows. And my guilt.

As for everyone else in the UK, they were seeing this photo for the first time. A photo of Dorian Blackwood kissing an unidentifiable girl.

Mia stared at me as if I was contemplating taking scissors to the front of my hair to give myself bangs.

"I'm not going to freak out."

"You're not?"

"I'm not because … because you can't tell that's me since my back is to the camera, so it's fine," I convinced myself.

"It is?"

I closed my eyes in a pathetic attempt to meditate the situation away. "It is."

"So you don't want to read the article?"

My eyes shot open, and I picked the phone back up.

"Dorian Blackwood is back to his old ways again, spotted with a new lover. However, her identity is unknown. He was seen on Christmas Eve kissing a brunette in London in a phone box. Blackwood is pictured clearly kissing a short brunette, her back to the camera.

This comes just hours after a photo was released of Dorian Blackwood and Victoria Sutton kissing the same night, the photos taken only four hours apart. We can confirm these were taken the same day in accordance with our source. We were already aware of Dorian Blackwood's dating habits, but what we really care about is finding out who the brunette is."

I had never seen so many pictures of the back of my head, but it looked like I needed to do a better job at straightening my hair.

I handed the phone back to Mia. "It's like Halloween all over again, and people forgot about that too. This will blow over. But right now, no one knows that's me, so I just need to stay away from him to avoid any possibility of people making a connection, and we'll be fine."

"You're being awfully calm."

"Would you rather I have a mental breakdown? Because I already did that."

She picked her phone up, looking at the pictures again. "At least I get a visual from the story now."

I took my pillow and whacked her.

She laughed, falling backward. I followed the motion, lying beside her.

"You never told me what happened after you guys kissed. Did he say anything?" she asked the ceiling.

I exhaled. "He told me he cared for me."

"Do you believe him?" The pillowcase rustled as she looked at me.

"I don't. Not anymore." The ceiling's closed mouth in the form of a white crack stared at me. It told me I was an idiot. Or at least that's how I felt.

"Do you want to know what I think?"

"I assume you're going to tell me whether or not I say yes."

"I believe him. And I think he's probably been meaning to say much more than that for a while."

I smooshed the side of my face into my duvet, looking at her. "Then why was he with Victoria on Christmas Eve, too?"

38

Don't Tell Her You Love Her — Dorian

There was a constant, unstoppable patter in my chest that refused to settle. If I was older than sixty, I'd question if I was having a mild heart attack or just really serious heartburn from all the pasta this month. But honestly, it started the moment I woke up this morning knowing I'd be getting on a flight to come home, where Adelaide was. Or hopefully was.

When I had called her before the flight took off, the call was short. She was busy working. Fortunately, that's all I wanted to confirm so I could stop at her flat without her knowing.

"I dropped the pocketbook off in her mailbox," I told Jasmine over the phone, practically jogging to the bookshop from the flat. Waiting on my driver or a cab would take too long. Even if it was tremendously colder here with the packed snow on the pavements being blown around by the wind.

"You did?" she gawked. It sounded like she was in the middle of eating. "You sure that's a good idea?"

"Jasmine, I took the damn bag all the way to Italy with me because I couldn't stop thinking about her. I should've given her the gift on her birthday like I wanted to rather than letting this friendship linger so long." I refrained from mentioning the baseball cap keychain I clutched every day like a pocket watch.

"Why don't you just give it to her in person?"

"As much as I'd love to see her reaction, I want it to be a surprise. She's at work right now anyway. I'm on my way to see her."

"Are you nervous at all?" her tone was soft.

"Exceptionally. It's pathetic."

"You shouldn't be. I bet she's missed you."

I missed her.

During holiday, I was drawing her profile on café napkins like I was selling silhouettes for spare change. I found her in the rain-fallen nights. In every keychain and cheesy postcard. It was the reason why I had several pushed into my back pocket, too indecisive to pick one. (One with Italy plastered across it like a tacky billboard, or a picturesque one with a painting of the Colosseum? I wasn't sure which, so I got both.) Luckily, finding a silver keychain was easy enough.

London was calling me home all week. But it was in the form of her heartbeat rather than the nostalgia of my childhood.

I sighed, avoiding the gaps in the pavements filled with recent rain. "I wish you were here. You're better at this stuff than me."

"*At dating?*" she questioned, abashed.

"Yeah right," I laughed. "I was referring to saying how you feel."

"I don't know. It sounded like you did just that before you left."

"What I told her is only a quarter of how I feel. I can't imagine if I tried to say anything more. I didn't hear from her at all while I was gone. And I know her phone was working because she talked to James."

"She talked to James?" Her arched brows were visible through the speaker. "Hm. Did she call him, or did he call her?"

"Does it matter?"

"Of course it matters!"

"He called her."

"That's a good sign then."

"It is?"

"It says that she wasn't reaching out to anyone."

"That doesn't make me feel better."

"Well, I didn't say it'd make you feel better, I just said it mattered! If she called James, then that'd be a different story."

"I guess."

"Wait—does James know you're going to see her?"

"Eh, no. He doesn't."

"Dorian." She always had a soft spot for James. We all did. *It was James.*

"The January is in a few days, Jasmine, and I want to bring her as my date if she says yes. You know that's always been James's thing. He loves this event and I'm not going to upset him right after our holiday."

"What's your plan? Show up to the ball with her and see how he reacts?"

"No, of course not. I'd tell him beforehand."

Her disagreement was palpable through the phone. "What are you going to say to her when you see her?"

"'How was your holiday?'"

"That's all you've got?"

"When I left, I opened the floor for her to tell me how she's feeling. If I say anything more, then I may as well throw myself into the Thames." No response. "Hello?" I checked.

"Did you know the last time the Thames froze over was in nineteen forty-seven?" she asked.

"You really thought now was the best time to look that up?"

"Gotta make sure you won't be hitting a river of ice on the way down."

I rolled my eyes. "I'm calling the lawyer and cutting you out of my will."

"Aw, I was in your will?" she cooed.

"Every time I call you, I regret it more than the time before."

"It got your mind off what you're going to say though, didn't it?"

Without realizing it, I was outside the bookshop. "I'm here," and filled with a mixture of dread and eagerness.

"Just be honest with her. Women really aren't all that complicated. We're just overthinkers."

"Thanks, Jasmine. I'll talk to you later. Love you."

"Love you," she responded before hanging up.

I smoothed out my navy sweater and straightened my cap before pushing the front open.

My heart was running at the speed of the transit system, whirling around in my chest with no track and a broken brake. I glanced around the bookshop as if it'd slow the speed.

Several people were shopping, wrapped in scarves and twill coats, noses bitten by the wind. Books smacked the shelves, shoes scuffed the floor, and conversations were quiet but blended, bringing a collective loud noise into the store.

Then it stopped.

And I found her on a short ladder at the back of the store with a box in her arms that she was pulling books from and sliding onto the top shelf. I watched her for a moment as she'd check her long sleeve top to make sure the box wasn't ruining the fabric.

She looked so beautiful. With a long skirt on and heeled boots, she was picturesque. Watching her push a strand of hair behind her ear felt like a missed opportunity for a painting.

I didn't even realize I had been holding my breath.

It felt like my heart was wilting and thriving all at the same time.

A century old fireplace sparked to life in my chest. One that had been dormant for what felt like my entire life. The flame flicked at the hearth as she searched the shelf. Her deep brown eyes read the spines. The same brown eyes that pulled every etched note out of my chest.

Nothing was just brown anymore. The purse that hung from her shoulder most days was no longer just a glove-tanned leather, but the same color as her hair under the darkness of the bookshop awning.

The tree that greeted us outside her flat at night was the same shade of her eyes before she leaned forward and kissed me. They were the color of the espresso I made every morning for the past five months. Most mornings I made it just to remind myself of the color without having to stare at her.

I love her. I love her so much.

She dropped a book and yelped as it struck the floor. No one seemed to notice though.

I jogged over and picked it up, handing it back.

"Hi," I said, looking up at her. It felt like a warm shot of espresso ran over my skin standing this close to her.

And then she looked at me like I was a ghost. Her eyes were wide with surprise. An unwanted surprise.

After accepting the book, her hand recoiled into her frame.

My heart sank. I was back on that sidewalk in the rain in October.

Don't waste your time because I'm not capable of loving you, she had said.

"What are you doing here?" she asked before stepping off the ladder. Her skirt swished around her ankles as she stepped down.

"I came straight from the airport. I wanted to see you." I scratched the back of my neck. All of the confidence I gained on the flight diminished.

The unexpected alertness in her eyes quickly shifted to reservation. She put the box of books down. "Really? You wanted to see me?"

"Of course I wanted to see you."

She brushed her hair out of her face before finally looking at me. "Did you stop and see Victoria too?"

"You saw the photos." I had completely forgotten. The news was a quick phone call between me and my publicist, but it wasn't anything new. Nothing anyone in my immediate life had paid attention to. I assumed by now that she'd realize none of it was fact.

But this only made her scowl deeper. A crease formed between her brows, not unlike how it appeared during our earlier arguments.

She lowered her voice, "Of course I saw the photos, they're *everywhere.*"

"It's not what you think," I urged, reaching for her.

She pulled away, crossing her arms. "It doesn't matter what *I think* because there's literal proof."

"Adelaide, I know how those photos look, but *she* tried to kiss *me.*"

"She didn't try—she *did* kiss you. And I hate that I even know that but I'm grateful because I don't think you would've ever mentioned it."

"That's not true," I shook my head.

"Really? Then why didn't you mention it once when you came and saw me after? Didn't think to mention it on the London Eye or in the telephone booth? It wasn't like we were low on time."

"I—" *Because I was going to tell you I loved you and that I left her.* But looking at her now, there was no way in hell she felt the same way. Not when she was so quick to believe that I'd cheat on her.

She laughed. She *laughed*. "Honestly Dorian, I'm thankful you don't have an excuse, because I don't want to hear it. If you had let me finish what I had tried to say over the phone, you would've saved yourself a trip because we need to stop talking indefinitely."

"You were going to tell me over the phone that you no longer want to speak to me, *and just expect me to abide?* And after what I said to you before I left?" *Tell me you care for me. Because I care for you.*

She was *unbelievable*.

Her cheekbones were matted maroon. "Do you understand how embarrassing it was to spend my holiday thinking about you constantly, only to find out that you were with someone else *hours before?*"

True, venomous guilt sank in as I realized that her anger wasn't powered by hatred, but by sadness. "Adelaide—"

She waved her hand, stopping me. "I don't care, and I don't want to know. I meant what I said about not forming relationships. I have no interest in entertaining this anymore." It felt like a serrated knife was being plunged into my chest. She was twisting it and pulling like a caught fishhook. "Our deal is over, so we don't need to see each other. You passed the class. You can be with Victoria, and I can stop hurting my best friend."

I opened my mouth to argue, but there was nothing left in me. I was on the verge of needing CPR.

She took that as an invitation to finish the conversation. "I'm trying to build a career here. A life." Her voice softened. "I'll never be taken seriously if my name is only ever attached to yours ... so no one can ever know about us. No one can ever see us together. You have to pretend that you never met me."

With that, she crouched down, picked up the box of books, and returned to her ladder.

I was numb.

I pressed my hand to my back pocket, feeling the impression of the souvenirs, before walking out of the store and leaving a trail of unspoken words behind me.

Suddenly, we were strangers again.

39

Once I was convinced he was nowhere near the store, I grabbed my coat, entered the cold, and cried.

I *wailed*.

I probably looked frantic to the tailor across the street. He could snap a picture and send it to his family group chat for all I cared. It didn't matter since my throat was swelling up with emotion and cowering screams. If I didn't take a breath soon, I was nervous it'd pop like a high-voltage light bulb.

Was this what people meant by heartbreak? Because it felt less like my heart was breaking and more like I wanted to drown in a cookie 'n' cream frappe while I curled into a ball and let all my stored tears feed the pipes in our apartment to save money on the water bill.

Maybe those were the same things.

(That was my humor covering up the reality of the situation.)

Honestly, it felt as if he had a hand around my heart and *squeezed*. He squeezed so hard that blood was trickling in slow motion through my gut and filling up my mouth. I pressed my glove against my lips to shallow my hysterical breathing.

He admitted to kissing her. He admitted to seeing her. *And he kept it from me the whole night.* He couldn't even fathom up an excuse. He had kissed me and told me he cared for me.

I care for you.

You keep me up every night.

I dream about things that haven't even happened.

Tell me to stay.

It had been so long since my heart felt like this that I almost forgot it had the capacity to break.

Don't be in love with him, my heart pleaded. *Please don't.*

With the lampposts as my consoler, I followed the dreaded path that Dorian and I usually took to my flat. Only, this time, I stopped at the café across the street and asked if they could make a milkshake. (They had ice cream on the chalkboard menu.) The barista either thought I was really affected by the windchill, or knew I had been crying, because she didn't say no.

"You're home!" Mia cheered as I walked through the doorway. Her smile fell as she noted the milkshake in my hand and the redness under my eyes. "How'd it go?"

"The equivalent of a car crash." I lifted the straw to my mouth.

"Are you alright?" Sabrina's voice shocked my system. I looked behind Mia and found her on the living room floor, her suitcase exploding with clothes and wrapped gifts. She had no earrings on but fresh lip gloss.

I sniffed quickly and pulled together a smile. "I dropped one of my keychains on the way over and it broke. I didn't mean to be so dramatic about it," I laughed, quickly pulling my layers off.

"I can fix it, if you'd like?" she offered, standing.

"No, no, it's fine. I want to hear all about Paris." I pulled her into a hug. "I missed you," I said into her floral-scented hair.

"I missed you too," she urged, squeezing me. Pulling away, she gasped. "Before Paris though, I have to tell you that your idea worked!"

"My idea?"

"About post-grad! I told my dads about how I planned on finding an interior design position."

"You weren't supposed to tell them that until you actually got the position," I reminded her.

"It's fine, it's fine. My dad apparently had this lab interview lined up in Edinburgh and he said if I took it and got the job, he'd get me a part-time design position with this huge home design studio to work on the side. And part-time positions usually lead to full-time positions, so I'm basically hired!"

"Andrew came up with this?" Mia asked in disbelief.

She nodded uncontrollably.

But that was the last thing I was thinking about.

"Edinburgh? As in Scotland?" I asked.

"Yeah ..." she said, realizing. "It's only for the summer. If the position goes well, they have an office here in London I could transfer to. I just have to deal with lab life for a few months."

"What are you doing after graduation?" I turned to Mia. It was only four months away but suddenly it was on our doorstep.

"If I can't get a full-time job, then I'll have to go back," *to Washington*. "The rent has been affordable thanks to Sabrina's dad, but I can't live off a part-time job forever. My parents already want me home and they're paying for my student loans so ..."

My heart dropped. I felt sick.

Sabrina's moving to Scotland, and Mia's moving back home.

I was trying to digest it, but it wasn't working. I knew distance would form between us at some point in life, but I didn't expect it to happen this quickly. Not right now.

"We still have a few more months together," Sabrina said.

"Yeah, there's still a ton of time for me to find a job," Mia smiled.

I nodded, trying to force my mouth to smile. But it wasn't working. If Sabrina had no use for this apartment, then there was no point in her dad renting it to us so affordably. I'd have to find my own place.

I was going to be alone again.

"We'll make the most of the semester. Take weekend trips. Get dinner more often. We already have something planned for this week!" Sabrina gushed.

"You planned something?" I asked.

"Gosh no. James texted Mia and I about The January last week! Let me go check the post. Invitations for The January are always sent the week of."

The front door closed, and Mia stared at me with concern, as if I was going to explode.

"What do you want me to do? I can send a fake email that says you have to re-do an exam on the same day? Or I can start injecting your water with something that'll make it look like you're sick?"

"Inject it *with what?*"

"I don't know, maybe food coloring or something? If we turn your tongue a weird color, I bet that'll scare Sabrina enough to let you stay home."

"It's fine, I want to go."

"*You do?*"

"You guys are leaving in May. I spent the entire fall semester buried in work and now I only have a few months of us living together to make up for all the outings I missed."

"Even if Dorian is there?"

"He won't be a problem."

The door swung open. Sabrina walked in with three envelopes, and two boxes, one the size of a sheet cake.

"You sure did quite a bit of shopping while we were gone," she gestured to me before placing the boxes on the coffee table.

"I didn't buy anything."

Her brow rose. "These are addressed to you."

We gathered around the table immediately as if we were preparing for an emergency séance. If a séance solely involved staring.

"Could it be from your aunt? You have started talking again," Brina guessed.

"Only recently though."

"Will you just open it!" Mia begged.

I tore open the package big enough to hold a sheet cake. They scooted closer on the rug as I flipped the top over.

"Wow," they exhaled. *Wow* was right.

It was a dusty lavender gown made from a thin organza fabric. With a plunging neckline down the center of the breastbone, it met at a thin bow that kept the chest together. It was fitted from the waist to the hip. While the bottom half was a drop waist skirt, composed of three individual tiered layers. Thin lilac and mauve beads peppered the chest and tiered layers.

It looked like a dress made for a fairy. Or the wife of a very wealthy pirate.

Under the thin straps was a note that said *Happy Christmas*.

Dorian. He must've dropped this off while I was at work.

"Oh my gosh, it must be from James!" Sabrina gasped.

Mia's eyes widened. Crap. I may have forgotten to fill her in on the whole Sabrina-thinks-James-and-I-are-in-love situation.

"Next one," Mia ordered, sliding the smaller box across the table.

I peeled off the tape and ripped open the side only to find a gift bag. Carefully sliding it out, the tissue paper ruffled as I found the contents.

A note: *I should've given you this on your birthday.*

And a Beverly crescent bag. An *original* Beverly from the *original the 90s collection.*

I lifted the crescent moon-shaped purse made of a pearlescent silk and almost screamed with joy. *James.*

"Remind me to ask James for gifting advice," Mia commented.

"Is that what I think it is?" Brina inhaled.

I nodded my head, refusing to look away, afraid it was going to evaporate into strands of thread.

"It matches the dress *perfectly*. Go try it on!" Sabrina urged.

My stomach lurched. "Oh, I can't, really. I can't accept something that … nice." *I can't wear a dress he picked out.*

I looked to Mia for help, but she was running her fingers over the beading still.

"Of course, you can!" Brina argued. "It's a gift, you should always accept a gift. I also doubt you remembered to buy a dress. Not like anything could top this anyway."

40

Don't Let Her Change Your Mind in that Dress — Dorian

Where the hell was James? It couldn't take him *that* long to get another drink. Unless he somehow ran into his mother. Or my mother. Or Gretchen. They most likely had a running list of people that needed to be greeted who hadn't been welcomed yet.

Hopefully he'd speed up the greetings because without him here, people thought I wanted to talk to them.

Little did they know, I wasn't much for talking right now. Not when every thought I had went back to *her*.

You have to pretend that you never met me.

She couldn't have cared less about letting me go. I walked into that bookshop, and she'd already made up her mind about us. It didn't matter what I said. She was done.

After my heart was ripped from my chest, she simply returned to work, unaffected.

One half of me prayed she wouldn't come tonight, for my sanity. While the other half had this *innate need* to see her.

In the meantime, I was trapped talking to this egotistical investor about his plans to "transform" my father's movie into the next box office hit because James abandoned me.

"Action movies these days never have enough pyrotechnics. So I told your father, the more pyrotechnics, the better," he said, pointing his overpriced pinky ring at me.

"Of course," I repeated for the fifth time. They were always so busy listening to themselves talk, they never noticed. I could probably start responding with the ingredients to a meat pie and he wouldn't notice.

I tried to tune his voice out with the ensemble of string music playing at the back of the room.

I watched velvet suits and glittering gowns enter from the grand marble staircase, down into the ballroom. I recognized many of the guests since they attended every year. Some were in the entertainment industry who worked directly with my parents, while others were from old money, politics, or friends of Mrs. Beverly's from the fashion industry.

I didn't see James by the stairs greeting anyone, but he could also be in the gardens right outside. It was too dark to tell, especially with the tall French doors at the side of the ballroom closed from the cold.

"Did you know it was my idea to keep that last scene in? Your father didn't like—" The man's mouth was moving, but I wasn't hearing the words.

I could feel her in the room before I saw her.

Standing at the top of the staircase somehow looking more gorgeous than the first day I met her.

It was her, my heart pounded. *She was here.*

It was like seeing your favorite painting for the first time. This strong urge to feel it, wrap yourself in it, cover every wall in it.

She was my favorite painting.

I could see the shape of her waist and the outward slope of her

Liana Cincotti

hips. Even her chest was accentuated by the deep neckline and thin straps. As she took a step forward, a slit that ran up her leg was revealed. My jaw went slack as she rushed to keep the fabric closed at the top of her thigh. The bottom of the pale purple dress shifted like a field of lavender taken by the wind around her heels.

"Bloody hell," I muttered, pulling at the tie gripping my throat.

Her gaze swept the room and suddenly ... it stopped on me.

Her lips parted while her eyes sparked, roaming my figure. The grasp on my glass tightened.

You have to pretend that you never met me.

She whipped her stare away and picked up her skirts, taking the stairs with haste.

I handed over my drink. "Can you excuse me?" I started my strides before he could answer.

It was the masquerade all over again. I couldn't control the instinct to find her before someone else did.

She was going to hate me. Probably more than she already did. But this could be the last time the two of us were ever in the same room.

No one can ever see us together.

Moving through the crowd, I adjusted arms, and shifted shoulders and skirts to get through. I lost sight of her the closer I got. But a few more dodges and I could see the bottom step, *just* as her heel hit it.

Before I could change my mind, I took her hand and pulled her into the center of the ballroom where everyone was dancing in unison.

"*What* are you doing?" she breathed.

I pulled her into my chest. With one hand on the middle of

her back and the other in her palm, I was breathing fresh air and suffocating all at the same time. The feeling of her exposed leg through the slit of the dress against my thigh was causing the latter.

"I'm dancing with you, what does it look like?" I replied, trying to steady my heartbeat.

The air coming out of her nose, hitting my shoulder, was hot.

"Did I hallucinate the last conversation we had? Or did you hit your head off someone's headboard and forget everything I said?" she asked impatiently.

"I try not to make a habit of hitting my skull off my headboard, thank you for caring though."

"Oh no, I was more worried for the status of Victoria's bedframe." She smiled.

"You have a lot to say for someone who got to do all the talking last time," I argued, but the chandelier light bouncing off her merlot-painted lips made it *much* more difficult to maintain my frustration.

"Not my fault we had a lot to catch up on. If I was prancing around London with other men, I'm sure you would've had more to say."

"Is Adelaide Adorno admitting jealousy?"

"I hate you," she seethed, squeezing my palm.

"I don't believe you."

"You're a pig," she scoffed.

"That'd probably be more believable if you weren't looking at me like you wanted to kiss me."

She looked away. "You're predictable."

"At least I'm not jealous."

"Better than being obsessed."

"Obsessed? You think I'm obsessed with you?"

"It wasn't a question." She looked up at me with a satisfied smile. "It's the reason you foolishly pulled us into the middle of the ballroom, completely ignoring everything we agreed on."

"*Agreed on?* Are we talking about the same conversation? Were you in the same bookshop?"

"So you admit to remembering the plan?" She searched my face.

"I heard the plan, yes. Didn't mean I had to do everything you said though."

She laughed. "That's rich coming from the man who was *begging* for *my say* on staying in London for holiday."

"*Begging?* Says that one who was begging for me to kiss her." That wiped the smirk right off her face.

"I was not begging."

"Fine—pleading."

She narrowed her eyes. "It's not like you hesitated."

"I wasn't implying that I had. I don't regret kissing you."

She focused her gaze on the gardens behind me. "Why are you doing this?"

"Because I can't just forget about you—"

"I meant the dancing, Dorian. People are going to put two and two together."

Now I was the one exhaling a hot breath. "It's just dancing. Let people think what they want."

The music continued at a brisk pace. As the woman beside us left her partner's hold to spin, I let go of Adelaide to do the same before pulling her back into my chest. Her head fit into the niche of my neck as we swayed, watching the next pair repeat the same steps together.

"You could've left," I whispered. The scent of vanilla in her hair was intoxicating to withstand. Usually, I could remedy the problem by stepping away or pressing my mouth to the side of her neck. But the former would result in a scandal. While the latter would also result in a scandal, but it'd be much more satisfying and accompanied by a kick in the shin.

"What?" she asked.

"You could've pulled your hand away. Not dance with me."

"It's not like you would've listened to me."

"Adelaide, we both know I hang on your every word. I couldn't ignore you if I tried. If you said no, then I would've let go." My heart reached my throat as her eyes shifted to my face. I wanted her. Every *fiber of my being* craved her. I swore it was written all over my face in permanent ink.

I love you. I love you. I love you.

"The purse would've matched the dress," I told her.

"Purse?" Her eyebrows shifted inward.

"Did you not get it?"

"You bought me the purse?"

"Is there someone else buying you gifts?" I tried to laugh but it died on my tongue.

"I—no. I just assumed it was James."

"*James?*"

"Well, it's an original piece from Beverly. And then the note mentioned my birthday, but I saw you that day. I would've thought the keychain was my gift—"

"You thought that's all I got you?"

"Apparently not seeing as you sent the dress too."

"Dress? *This dress?*" I dragged my eyes up and down her figure trying to confirm this wasn't some spur-of-the-moment purchase I made and sent while drunk. Despite loving to think about every curve of her body, I would've remembered buying this.

She nodded in confusion.

"Someone sent you this dress?" I asked.

Her mouth opened—

"Mind if I cut in?"

41

Don't Go to the Gardens — Adelaide

Without even looking, Dorian began, "Not right—"

"James, hi," I said, startled, finding him in an ash gray suit. I let go of Dorian immediately as if we were caught making out.

Everyone was beginning to change dance partners and shift around the ballroom for the next dance—my chance to get away from Dorian. "That would be great."

Accepting James's hand, I watched Dorian's wilt at his side, looking staggered as we stepped away. My view of him disappeared as other girls approached him like pinecones congregating on a branch. Other guests filled in my view of him.

James's hold on my frame was light once the music began again. I elongated my steps to keep up with the singing of the violins and the guests around us. Every few steps, his hand would slip off my back and I'd rush my footwork to keep it in place. His right foot forward, my left foot back, his hand on my back, and our elbows up. The room was a crowd of sparkles as dresses were spun and champagne was sipped.

"You and Dorian alright?" he asked.

"Of course," I reacted. He smiled but the corners of his lips barely pushed at his cheeks.

"I wasn't sure if I was interrupting something."

"Just the agony that is Dorian talking."

"Ah he does like to talk." He laughed lightly. It had an unsettled fizz to it. "Anyone else around here subject you to boring conversations?"

"Unless you count the guy at the coat check, no. I know approximately four people here and that includes you."

"That's not true. You've met my mother, and she's here. Dorian's parents are here too, have you met them yet?"

"That sounds about as terrifying as it was to meet your mother."

We turned together and now I was facing the glass garden doors. "She can come off that way at first, but that's only at events. She'd rather people she doesn't know to just leave her alone, especially if she's in the middle of having a drink." He raised his brows. "Mrs. Blackwood is the same way, but she doesn't show it on her face. She'd want to meet you though."

"I appreciate you saying that, but she looks like she'd ask me to lint roll her shoes if I approached her."

He laughed. "You're not the only one that thinks that— maybe the lint remover part since that's a tad specific—but Dorian's father said she was always had this look on her face that said, 'leave me alone.'"

"Her husband said that? Really?"

He shook his head. "Not in a cruel way, no. They attended university together—that's how they met. They were both in this film history course and she'd sit at the front. If she wasn't greeting someone she knew, then she'd be sat at her desk, pencil between her fingers, writing things down with a furrowed brow. Until she dropped it one day—or more so flung it—and it bounced right off Mr. Blackwood's head when he walked in. She apologized profusely. He said that's when he realized how kind she was. That the face was a façade. A way to get people to let her concentrate in peace."

"And he asked her out after that?"

"God no," he laughed. "He was too nervous to ask her on a date. She wanted to make it up to him, but he refused. Instead, they ended up trading class notes in the library after. It ended up getting so late that he offered to walk her home from campus. Every night after that, he'd walk her to her flat just to spend more time with her. That was until she took a liking to him too and asked him out herself."

The visualizations I had been creating of young Mr. and Mrs. Blackwood screeched to an echoing stop.

"What?" I stared at him.

"I know. He walked her home every night for like three months until she caught on that he liked her. The only reason I know all of this is because he tells it every year during our Italy trip. He swears that if he didn't walk her home all those nights, that she would've never gotten to know him."

I flexed my hand over his shoulder needing something to focus on that wasn't the film reel of Dorian walking me home every night for the past four months.

The music felt louder. It was plucking sharp chords through my eardrums and making my eyes water. Where was Dorian? I didn't see him. Was he dancing with Victoria now? Was she here? Had he walked her home too?

James's voice calmed the noise. "You know, Adelaide, I've been meaning to tell you something—ask you something really,

298   *Liana Cincotti*

but this is much harder now that I'm standing in front of you ..."

I curled and uncurled my hand. My nail beds were even clammy. "Yes?"

He opened and then closed his mouth. When he started again, it was so quick I almost missed it. "The dress looks perfect on you, I'm happy it fits."

My feet stuck to the floor, bringing us to an abrupt stop in the crowd. "You sent me the dress?"

"I—uh—let's talk outside." He stumbled over the words, but his hand was firm in mine as he guided us out of the dance, through one of the many glass doors, and into the snow-dusted gardens. I held onto my skirts tightly as we fled into one of the few lit areas where the back of the museum was covered in dead vines and lights.

His palm was my heat source. The January air was biting down my arms and chest. I rubbed my skin to make the goosebumps disappear and the thoughts wipe away.

Of course, Dorian didn't buy you the dress you fool, you're no different than the rest of them.

"Please, have this," James said, taking off his coat jacket.

"Oh, no that's alright—"

"Adelaide, just let me give you the jacket. You're cold and I'm the one that dragged you out here," he said desperately.

I nodded. Draping the jacket over my shoulders, it ended at the middle of my thigh.

Taking a step back, he started, "You really had no idea that I sent the dress?"

"Why would I?" I asked, just as confused. This entire development didn't make any sense. Dorian bought me the purse that I had spent years looking for, for my birthday, and gave it to me *after* he saw Victoria. And James bought me a dress to wear tonight.

"Gods," he sighed, brushing a hand over his face in frustration, pacing.

I stepped forward, holding onto his suit jacket. "I didn't mean to make you upset or offend you. We've never exchanged gifts before. If I had known I would've gotten you something."

He waved his hand. The intricate lighting strung through the vines bounced off his jaw. "That's not the point," he exhaled. "I didn't expect anything in return. It wasn't supposed to be just some Christmas gift. I just—I—I don't know."

"Was I not supposed to wear it tonight?"

"No, no," he shook his head. "I was hoping you would."

I stepped forward again. Close enough to brush his arm. "James, just tell me what's wrong."

I touched his hand. It was surprisingly warm. But he pulled away, dropping it at his side.

"Because I love you, Adelaide," he said weakly.

My heart dropped to the grass like a stone.

"You what?"

"I love you. I bought you the dress, hoping you'd wear it knowing it was from me, and that'd mean, that maybe, some part of you would feel something too because I couldn't find the confidence to tell you how I was feeling face to face. But here we are," his laugh dripped with sadness.

The words on my tongue dried up. I didn't know what to say. I was nauseous; my heart outside my body and the air trapped between us. He was supposed to understand. To understand how my brain and my heart worked. That this never worked for me. He wasn't supposed to get this close because I couldn't give him that.

And now he'd leave me to protect himself.

"Please say something," he pleaded.

I was replacing the cold gusts with the hot air in my chest. In and out. In and out. *He's going to leave you. Your friend is going to leave you, just like Sabrina and Mia. He's going to leave and find someone else who can make him happy and give him a family with twins. And you'll be alone for the rest of your life, holding onto trinkets and the scent of sawdust at the bottom of drawers.*

I shook my head. "You know I don't do this."

"I know, I remember what you had said. I've thought about it every day since. But you don't just *choose* not to love. You can't control that. And if even some part of you cared for me, I had to know."

"I do care for you, *of course* I care for you. You're one of my best friends. But I ... I'm not ... I don't fall in love."

He dragged the corner of his lip under his teeth in thought. His cheeks were so flushed. I wanted to press my hands to the sides of his face to warm his skin and beg for his forgiveness.

"Who did you think bought you the dress?" he asked. His voice was solid, unwavering.

"What?" I pulled my arms around my chest.

"When you got the dress, who did you think sent it?"

"Does it matter?"

He rubbed the back of his neck and sighed. "It was Dorian, wasn't it." It was an answer, rather than a question.

"Well, yes, but—"

He scoffed. "I should've known."

Turning away, he strode through the garden back toward the ballroom with his hands stuffed in his pockets. The layers of my dress kicked up as I rushed to catch up to him.

"Known what?" I shouted from behind him.

The snow-soaked grass brushed the tops of my feet as I passed walls of dead hedges.

"James please, just talk to me. I promise this has nothing to do with Dorian."

He halted. The stairs leading back into the ballroom were only a few steps away. He turned and his face was a perfect painting of sadness: disheveled air, red-rimmed eyes, pink cheeks.

"This has everything to do with Dorian," he exhaled. "Because you're in love with him, aren't you?"

"Of course, not—"

"I wish I believed you. But the look on your face says it all. The worst part is that I get it, because I've known him my entire life."

I was stuck. I didn't know what else to say. How to convince him otherwise.

He continued, "I know that you think you can't fall in love, but you don't get to make that decision. You can choose not to date and to keep yourself at arm's length from others who love you, but you can't choose not to fall." He sounded tired. Crestfallen.

"James, I don't love him."

"Stop lying to yourself," he said with the light nod of his head. "Stop lying to me and giving me hope."

I clutched my chest as he walked away, taking the steps two at a time and re-entering the ballroom, leaving me with his jacket.

I sank into the stairs. I wrapped my arms around myself, clutching my skin like a blanket and letting his jacket fall behind me.

302   *Liana Cincotti*

The edges of the gardens blurred. A soaked postcard. Tears filled my eyes. Goosebumps puckered around my ankles and the side of my thigh where the dress parted.

What's wrong with me?

I stared up at the moon as if she'd have the answer, but her lingering stare and crown of constellations that reminded me of Mom only made me feel worse.

One of the doors behind me let noise from the ballroom escape. Footsteps tapped the stone and then hit the stairs. Suddenly, Dorian was in front of me.

"Finally, I found you. We need to go— Adelaide, what's wrong?"

I sniffed and wiped the wetness from under my eyes. "Nothing, I'm fine."

I hated that every time I looked at him, I saw the boy in the telephone booth, before I saw the man who preferred Victoria.

"Love, look at me," he said, and I shivered. He stood on a step below, leaning down. I sat rigid, trying not to give in as his hands consuming my jaw with concern. His entire being overwhelmed me. "Are you hurt? Tell me what's wrong," he urged.

I brushed his hands away, rubbing the last of the blur from my eyes. "I'm fine, really." He gave me space as I picked up James's coat and stood, fixing my skirts. "I was just about to leave actually—"

"You can't go out that way." His hand on my elbow stopped me from ascending the stairs.

"And why is that?"

"Because we have a problem."

42

Don't Read the Article — Adelaide

The frigid, solid grass was crunching beneath my heels, trying to trap me in the soil as we ran further into the maze of snow-dusted hedges, trees, and stone walls.

I would complain about it aloud again if it weren't for Dorian's threat to carry me himself if I didn't keep up. Clutching onto his hand to not fall behind was painful enough.

"You're positive that's what the article said?" I asked.

"I think I know how to read, Adelaide," he argued.

"But how would they know it's me in the photo?"

"*I don't know!* I heard one person mention it at the bar, I saw the article over their shoulder, and the next minute, I realized every photographer in the room was walking toward me and then searching for you. I didn't exactly take the time to do an in-depth read. I'll make sure to ask next time," he breathed. "Let's stop here."

We squeezed between a wide marble statue and what must've been the row of hedges closest to the street. Car lights popped through the branches every few seconds. I couldn't pop my head over the bushes to find out without a pair of stilts.

Shoulders pressed together, we watched our breath leave our lips as strings of photographers jogged by.

"Whose jacket is that?" he asked in a hush tone.

"You think *this* is the time to be having a conversation?" I whispered, pulling the jacket off in a rush despite the freezing temperature. He gaped as if he had forgotten what I was wearing.

He cleared his throat. "It's James's, isn't it?"

He pulled his jacket off his shoulders and rested it on mine.

"You two are relentless." I rolled my eyes. "Give me your phone." He stared at me. "Now." Begrudgingly, he handed it over. I typed in his name and clicked the first article I found. My stomach plummeted.

"Who Is Dorian Blackwood's New Love Interest, Adelaide Adorno?"

I skimmed the article, rushing.

… met in late August…together at least once a week … close with Blackwood's friend James Breyer … raised in Boston by her parents … father Francesco Adorno … absent for the past ten years … her mother, Angela Adorno, was removed from guardianship a few years after … unable to provide confirmation on Blackwood and Adorno's current relationship status … can confirm that was her in the photo of Christmas Eve, the same night Blackwood was seen with notable ex, Victoria Sutton.

I should be furious. Overwhelmed. Scared that everyone knew. But I couldn't stop returning to their names. Francesco and Angela.

I was a hollow body trying to register next steps. Make a plan. Crisis management at its finest. But I hadn't planned for *them* to be in there too. It felt like there was a hot spotlight pointed at my head and the crowd was booing me off stage as I clutched my blanket and called for Mom and Dad.

"Adelaide …"

I wiped my eyes. "I want to go home."

My feet ached as I made it to the third floor. I craved a moment to not think about Dorian or James or Victoria. To be alone. To shower and strip off this dress and never look at it again.

But as soon as I opened the front door, Mia was holding Sabrina on the couch. Sabrina who was visibly shaking and wore the gloomy sky on her face in the shape of murky mascara running down her cheeks.

I froze in the doorway.

"Why—why didn't you tell me?" she croaked.

I forgot.

Amongst everything that happened tonight, I had forgotten about Sabrina.

"I—I didn't want to hurt you," I explained. My voice shuddered as I entered the living room and crouched on the rug in front of them. "I had no idea who Dorian was until the day after I met him. You know I would never have gone near him otherwise."

She began shaking her head. "I must have looked like a fool this entire time to the both of you—in love with this man who had absolutely no interest in me because he was kissing *you.*" Another wave of tears coming down her cheeks.

I wasn't sure if the "both of you" was referring to me and Mia or me and Dorian but I still flinched.

"She had no idea, Brina," Mia reassured.

"I can't believe you knew too." She looked at her with horror.

"Mia only knew because she was there when we met," I urged.

"But you both knew and said *nothing*. Like … like I was someone you had to keep secrets from because I'm some horribly misunderstanding human. I can't believe you were seeing him *every week* and neither of you ever thought to say something."

"I thought about telling you all the time, but I was so scared of hurting you. The only reason I was seeing him so much was because I was tutoring him," I explained desperately. "He would have told everyone what happened between us if I didn't."

"The last time I checked, Adelaide," she bit, "no one can make you do anything."

I shut my mouth. She was right. It was a pathetic excuse I had been leaning on all semester in hopes of protecting her.

She sniffed and pulled away from Mia. "It doesn't matter, none of it matters." She bit her quivering lip. "The photos say it all. He's obviously interested in you, and you obviously care for him. I was so dumb to think I had a chance anyway." She sniffed again, but tears clumped her eyelashes together. She built up a sad smile. "I wish you had told me. We were supposed to be friends."

"*We are.*"

"I … I just need some time. Give me some time."

I nodded, backing away and hiding with my guilt in my room.

"I saw everything online … I thought I'd call," Laila hesitated over the phone.

"Oh god, it's reached the other side of the pond?" I threw my face into my pillow the next night, only popping out of my room throughout the day for food when I heard Sabrina leave, trying to give her space.

"Only because I'm constantly on Adelaide Radar. One of the interns is apparently a huge Dorian Blackwood fan and noticed the last name. She sent it to me as a joke. Little did she know that the girl in the photos was actually my niece."

"You saw the photo?" I ran my hand over Kurt's fur as he rubbed up against the side of my bed.

"Photos."

"Agh." Kurt jumped and ran out of the room as the mattress squeaked under my weight.

"I can't believe you're seeing someone and didn't say anything! I made you listen to my mother-in-law rant for forty minutes the other day."

"I love how *that's* what stuns you of all things."

"How are you doing?"

"Not great. I feel like my entire future just went up in flames."

"Hey, that's not true. It's just one article."

"Hundreds of articles now. They're all the same story just expanded. Beverly's never going to hire me, and I'll make no money, and I'll have nowhere to live once I graduate."

"You can always come home." An awkward silence filled the speaker.

"I … I could never do that to you. You have a fiancé now."

"And he'd love to meet you. Space in our home will never be a problem. It's always open."

I picked at the seam on my duvet, trying to figure out to start this conversation. A thread fell between my fingertips as I responded. "Thank you, by the way, for everything when I was younger. I can't imagine how much of a burden I was when you were only twenty-five."

"Adelaide, you were *never* a burden. Why would you think that?"

"You weren't really around so we never spoke. I honestly thought I was in the way."

"That had *nothing* to do with you. Honestly ... I thought *I* was in *your* way. I was so scared of messing up that I didn't know how to be around you. If I was a friend, then I was being irresponsible. If I was strict, then I'd look like I was trying to replace your parents by enforcing some lifestyle on you. I had only just graduated college and could barely figure out how to find a good plumber and do my own taxes, let alone how to care for my niece whose parents failed her. I was at the most confusing time of my life, even if you hadn't been living with me. I thought giving you space was the right decision. You were already so grown up for fifteen—you didn't need me.

"But as I've watched you grow from afar, I know how much I've failed you too. Which is ironic, because my biggest fear was to be as distant as my brother." She exhaled. "Did you know that I was the one that signed you up for soccer when you were a kid? I took you every weekend to get you out of the house so you weren't around when they fought. I wanted to sign you up for all these sports and activities, but I was still in school. To this day I feel like I failed you by not doing just that—not acting soon enough. I never wanted you to think I wasn't here for you. I'm *always* here for you."

My throat was tight. "I never realized ..."

"It's my fault for not saying something sooner and reaching out first. This home will always be just as much yours as it is mine. So if you want to come home now, or after graduation, I'll be here waiting for you."

43

Don't Be In Love — Adelaide

A week until the start of the spring semester, when I'd be surrounded by even more wandering eyes and questions than I already was, and these women were absolutely *no help*.

Cheese and wine, they said. *It'll be fun*, they said. I wanted to remain curled up in my personal hobbit hole, but I couldn't miss book club if I wanted to. Not when I had invited Maureen.

In yoga pants and a sweater, I buried myself into the cushion of the loveseat beside Mia, hiding from the circle of women.

"One second, everyone in the ballroom is dancing. Then the next, phones start pinging and all the photographers flee the museum for the gardens. I had no idea they were looking for Addy and Dorian until I saw the article on Brina's phone," Mia recited.

Dotty and Iris already heard this story, but they gasped with everyone else anyway.

"Did you escape?" Cora questioned.

"This wasn't some spy mission guys." I shook my head.

"No one got any—additional—photos of them thankfully," Mia answered.

"How did Sabrina take it?"

I brought my legs to my chest and rested my chin on my knee. "She was upset. Really upset," I exhaled. "Rightfully so. I've been a terrible friend. I expected her to say that she hated me, but she only asked for space, so I've been giving her that. We talked this morning though, and it went really well."

This morning, Sabrina had shuffled into my room with her pink fluffy slippers wanting to talk. She crawled into my bed and shooed my laptop out of my hands.

I twisted my gold rings off and on my fingers. She picked her nails. Thick silence radiated between us.

Her glossy lips parted. "I can't believe you had to tutor him," she thought aloud.

I twisted, finding a small smile curling upward. It made me burst with a giggle. Her smile heightened until a laugh sparked from her.

"And for free," I added, laughing again.

"You didn't charge him?"

"Talking to him was painful enough in the beginning!"

We collectively exhaled.

"You really didn't know it was him that night?" She turned to me.

"I had no idea, *I promise.*"

She nodded. "So ... is he a good kisser?"

"Brina!" I shrieked, covering my face.

"Fine, fine, too soon!" Her cheeks slowly deflated from their blush pink joy. My hand tingled with warmth as she pressed her palm over mine. "I'm sorry about the article ... I should've said something sooner. I can't imagine what it was like to read about your ... past, and not have your friends by your side."

My throat swelled. "It's alright. I deserved it."

"You didn't deserve any of it. And you should've told me about Dorian the second you realized it rather than keeping it from me like I'm some terrible friend who would resent you for who you love."

"No, no, I don't love him. I want nothing to do with him. For all I know, he leaked those photos."

"You really think so?"

"He was the only other person who knew where we were——"

"No not that. You really think you don't love him?"

"I——" I lost my breath. "I don't."

"Of course you love him. Oh my gosh, don't tell me you're doing this because of me?" She threw her hand to her chest. "I would never take that away from you. You love him and he loves you. What's more magical than that?" Her eyes darted across my face with optimism. "You *must* talk to him."

"I'll think about it."

She rolled her eyes as if she had expected that. "Alright, now," she exhaled, "the crescent purse?"

"From him." I winced.

"The time you said I couldn't come to the bookshop?"

"Him." I winced again.

"The Christmas tree you brought back that had a squirrel in it?"

"That was not my fault! How was I supposed to know the tree was hosting animals?"

She laughed so hard that she swung her head back and hit the bed frame, causing me to snort. I attempted to soothe the back of her head, but I was laughing too hard.

And in that happy moment, I let herself think about what it would be like to be with Dorian.

But sitting in the bookstore hours later, surrounded by women who have loved and lost, I was terrified.

"That's amazing! What did Dorian say?" Evelyn asked.

"What do you mean?"

"What did you say when you told him Sabrina was alright with everything?" she explained.

"Nothing because I didn't tell him. I haven't spoken to him since the ball six days ago," I said.

"So … you two aren't talking … at all?" Jane asked.

I shook my head.

"Do you plan on it?" Lottie questioned.

I shook my head again.

"Do you want to?" she followed up.

"No."

"That was an awfully quick answer," Beatrice muttered.

"There's no point since I think I'm moving back to Boston after graduation."

"You're what?" Mia almost shot out of her seat.

"There's nothing keeping me here. You're most likely moving back home, Sabrina is going to Scotland, and I'll never hear back from these jobs now. Not like I had a chance anyway, no one wants a new grad. I've either been ghosted by these companies or sent vague rejections."

"But you can't leave. There's so much for you here. Dorian's here," Mia rushed.

"I can't stay in London for a guy."

"You wouldn't be staying in London *for him*. I think he'd go anywhere for you if you left. But you came to London *for you*," Iris explained.

"I don't think I can."

No corner of London would be safe. I'd spend every second outside anxious to run into him on the train or the pub down the street.

No train ride or walk home or rainstorm would be ordinary. They'd all be glued to his singular presence. His figure leaning over me or his hand in mine or his wet hair dripping down onto my cheek and his head tilted back as he watched me from my balcony.

I prefer you in every room.

I think there are many things about you that people find attractive, Adelaide.

Tell me to stay.

Then tell me you care for me. Because I care for you.

I'd be trapped in *what ifs.*

My throat was constricting more, and the skin under my eyes was taut with tears.

"But why?" Iris asked.

"Because I think I love him." My throat burned as I got out the words, clogged emotions escaping in one thin river down my nose.

The room hushed as I wiped the tear.

Evelyn spoke up. "Oh hun, that's something worth smiling about, not to cry over."

"I can't love him." I shook my head.

"You're mourning something you haven't even lost," Iris stated.

"I *have* lost, because I can't have him. He's not mine to have."

"I think he would heavily disagree," she replied.

"I feel like I've been climbing this tree for my entire life, toeing the edge of happiness. But branches keep breaking underneath my

Liana Cincotti

feet and now I'm scared to sit on a stump, let alone approach an entire spruce," I rambled, more tears falling.

The women looked at me with turned down brows, slumped forward in their seats. Wine glasses were pushed onto the coffee table like a messy game of chess.

"But what would life be without the satisfaction of succeeding after a fall?" Maureen asked.

44

Don't Let Him Go — Adelaide

Thunder roared outside my balcony the next night. Kurt curled up on my slippers under my desk as I clicked out of my empty inbox and finished scrolling through positions in Boston.

My door creaked open, and Sabrina poked her head in.

"There's someone downstairs for you." She smiled.

My heart plummeted.

"Who?"

"You know who." She closed the door behind her. Kurt leapt from my slippers, letting out a disgruntled meow, as I jumped from my seat. I threw on actual shoes, smoothed out my sweatshirt and brushed a hand down my hair before running down the stairwell to the lobby.

I froze on the bottom step. Dorian was in a soaked black T-shirt and barn jacket under the awning outside.

Reluctantly, I took the last step and stepped outside, jolting him. "What are you doing here?" I asked, folding my arms deep into the crevices of my sweatshirt to avoid brushing the wet strands of black hair sticking to his forehead.

"Ya know, just enjoying the rain." He shrugged.

"Did you walk all the way here?"

"No, I took a cab. But I arrived ten minutes ago and have been pacing ever since."

"Why are you here?" I asked.

"I need to talk to you."

"Do you really think that's a good idea?" I checked around the street for anyone watching.

"Why do you think I've been out here for the past ten minutes?"

I sighed. "Someone's going to see us, you should come inside—"

He shook his head. "I just came here for one thing."

"Alright, what is it?"

"Christmas Eve, I asked—"

"The last thing I want to hear about is Christmas Eve, Dorian." I turned and pushed the door—

He grabbed the handle, caging me in.

"Let me finish," he said. I turned around, my back to the door, but he didn't move. I could see every crinkle that lined his lips. Each crinkle that I loved. Every feature he had offered up to Victoria.

All I could picture was him kissing her. Or her perfectly manicured nails running through his hair as she kissed him. I wondered if that's how he looked when *we* kissed. And if he ever thought about me while kissing her.

My dinner rolled in my stomach.

Now, his face was a mosaic of emotion while mine was numb, incapable of forming any expression that wasn't dismal.

"Christmas Eve," he restarted, "I went to her place to tell her it was over."

"You did what?"

"She wasn't happy about what I had to say. She told me you'd never want me and that you'd leave me before I even had a chance to tell you how I felt." I felt *ill*. I had done exactly what she said. "I've been trying to have this conversation with her for years, and she thought she could convince me otherwise by trying to kiss me but realistically, we've been through for a long time. I pulled away the second she was on me."

I stared at him in shock. I should believe him. But *what if?* What if he was lying? What if he went straight up to her apartment after?

The images of them from this semester wouldn't shift. I couldn't picture him pushing someone so beautiful off him. Someone that made sense for him on a tax bracket level.

"Why are you telling me this?" I asked.

"Because I want you to know that everything I've said to you is true. I want to be with you."

"Dorian, I'm leaving, after graduation. I'm moving back to Boston."

His face fell. "You're what?"

"I'm going back home at the end of the semester. There's nothing for me here."

"I'm here," he said.

"That doesn't change that you still love *her*," I pressed.

45

My heart clung to my ribcage. *This* was what she's been upset about? *This* was why she wouldn't answer my calls or look at me? She thought I was in love with *someone else?*

There was rain in my shoes and rain in my pockets and rain coating my hair and skin, but I'd stand out here all night explaining what happened if it meant she'd understand.

The words began tumbling out of my mouth without a second thought. "I don't love her, I love *you*, and if you had stopped making up your mind before I had a second to finish explaining myself, you would've realized that this entire time I've been trying to give you the space you wanted. I've tried to get over you each time you told me you weren't interested so I could hopefully salvage some shred of my dignity, but all I could think about was *you*. All I ever think about is *you*. You're all I paint for God's sake."

Exhale. Inhale. "The problem was never that I loved *her*, because I didn't. It was always that I loved *you*."

She stared at me with cheeks completely flushed. Rain filled our silence.

I wanted her. I wanted her. I wanted her. I had never wanted someone so strongly before and it terrified me.

"You can't just make me fall in love with you and take it all back," I whispered. "Say something. Please."

Her eyes were dewy. "Are you sure?"

"What?" I asked dumbfounded.

"Are you sure that you love me? Because if you take it back in a few months or a few years, I don't know if I'll survive it when being in love with you has already been this treacherous."

"Did you just say you were in love with me?"

"Treacherously so, yes." Her eyes darted across my face. "So tell me Dorian Blackwood, *are you sure?*"

"I was sure the first night I walked you home," I exhaled.

A smile finally kicked up on her face. At last, I let myself touch her, my hands going to the sides of her jaw. "I adore you, Adelaide Adorno. I love absolutely everything about you."

She pulled her bottom lip between her teeth. "I love you too."

I groaned. "This may be hotter than the time you buttoned up my dress shirt."

"Kiss me," she breathed.

"Finally." I leaned down and pulled her in the rest of the way.

The second her lips hit mine, all the tension in my body diminished. Her gasp between our lips was swallowed as I refamiliarized myself with the divot in her collarbone and the muscle in her arms and the dip in her waist. I took note of it all as if I was rushing to collect evidence that'd wash away soon. Two steps forward and she was moving with me, her back against the building, and out of the awning.

She giggled as the rain hit us, but she didn't break away, only dug her fingers into my hair deeper.

I could do this for a lifetime.

Hold her. Kiss her. Paint her. Listen to her breathe.

"*Dorian,*" she murmured.

"*Hm,*" I mumbled against her lips.

She pulled away, hands still at the back of my neck. Rain licked at her eyelashes and glazed her hair. My lips hovered between her brows. I close my eyes, trying to catch my breath as if I submerged from a lake.

"I can't stay. This can't be my reason to stay," she whispered.

I didn't have to ask why. It'd take time for me to earn her trust. I understood. I wanted more for her than myself.

I asked, "Do you love London?"

"Of course. But I don't have a job lined up or—"

"Are you happy here?"

"I am." She didn't hesitate.

"Then you have to just trust that the rest will figure itself out."

"But what if—"

"Just give it a try. If you're unhappy after a month or two months or two years, then we'll pivot. You lead and I'll follow."

46

Don't Forget to Enjoy Life — Adelaide

Holy shit. Holy shit I got the job. I got the job on the day I was graduating—or, to be precise, five minutes before I was graduating. (The owner of Grace & Gears in Edinburgh said it would've been sooner if the email of my marketing plan from semester one hadn't ended up in her junk folder.)

But after two interviews in the past two weeks, I got it.

"Why are you shaking like a soda bottle?" Mia asked behind me.

"I got the job!" I attempted to whisper as the line in front of us moved forward. Students stepped on stage to get their diplomas.

"You did? That's incredible!" She jumped (while attempting to whisper).

"What is it? Why are you guys jumping?" Sabrina asked from behind Mia, popping her head out.

"She got the job!" Mia shrieked. Fortunately, the applause drowned out her volume.

"You got the job?" Sabrina joined our jumping circle. "We're going to Scotland together!"

"Just for the summer!" I clarified. "The position ends in

September, but they said if everything goes well, I can move to their London office once it's up and running!"

"Did you tell Dorian?" Mia asked, stopping our hopping.

"He texted me that he knew I'd get it. Now he's in the process of writing down every art museum in Scotland for us to visit."

"Oh gosh, I'm going to be a third wheel," Brina feigned illness.

"He's not moving in, he'd just visit." I whacked her with my sash. "Who would've thought a project would get me a job?"

"Me. That's why I told you to send it in," Mia pointed out.

"I can't believe that out of all the jobs you applied to, the one in Scotland said yes! This is fate! We were meant to live together!" Sabrina shrieked.

"What about me! I'm just going to be alone in our apartment," Mia complained.

"You'll have James," I reminded her, since they'd be working for the same media company, the one she had begged him to get her an interview at.

"That's true." She shrugged.

"I can't believe you got it." Brina smiled again.

"One job offer out of how many positions I applied to this semester? Three hundred?"

"It probably would've been two if Sylvie had actually sent that recommendation letter."

"You don't know that she hadn't."

"If her and her daughter were leaking information about you and Dorian the whole time to the press, then I doubt she wrote you a reference."

"I still can't believe Victoria's her daughter." Brina shivered. "So weird."

"I'm more stunned that she had been lying about the Board caring about scholarship students' personal business. I thought they were going to pull my tuition and instead they apologized for her behavior and fired her."

"*Tenure Professor Fired* definitely gave the students something else to focus on all year."

"Adelaide Adorno," one of the men on stage called.

"Go, go, go," they urged, pushing me forward.

I attempted not to wobble in my heels as I took the steps onto the stage. I accepted the diploma, shook a hand, and then posed like everyone else did, facing the crowd.

Dorian's blushful smile and wink in the second row made me beam.

I'm proud of you, it said.

Beside him was James, whistling for me.

I was filled with gratitude that our friendship survived after the night of the ball. With all our secrets laid out, we became a tightknit group that spent the spring semester studying together, barhopping, and creating way too many blackmail-worthy embarrassing memories.

I resisted blinking as a camera flash snapped and I was directed off the other side of the stage, back down the stairs. I was faced with a sea of smiling faces anchored by blouses and flowers and cards. My chest began to tighten. Small, thin papercuts dove for my heart as I looked at all the mothers and fathers and siblings.

I spotted Sabrina's dad in the balcony to the left, in front of the windows. While Mia's mom and dad and sisters and brothers sat just a few rows to the right of them.

"Adelaide!" The shout swiveled my focus to the right, where in the first row of the balcony stood a group of women flailing their arms with excitement.

Iris, Dotty, Cora, Evelyn, Jane, Beatrice, Lottie, Maureen.

And Auntie Laila.

They were holding cards. For me.

She came all the way here, *for me.*

My entire nervous system bubbled with unexpected, unfathomable, joy. I couldn't contain the tears springing to my eyes as they applauded and blew me kisses.

I raised my hand and waved. I could only imagine how I looked: a smile that made my cheeks puffy, and watery eyes that made it look like I was holding in a sneeze.

They waved their arms, pointing to the chair, making me realize I should probably sit down.

As I turned into my row and sat, I couldn't help but watch them for the entire ceremony, trying to confirm it wasn't a hallucination or a trick of the light.

Watching them, I realized exactly what it must've felt like to have a scrapbook made for you. Because I was looking at one in motion.

Maybe life wasn't all about protecting yourself and trying to push away pain.

Maybe forgetting was all about forwardness. To remain steady on the path forward while trying to pick up as many stones filled with gratitude and joy and hope so that the resentment that fueled the lack of forgiveness didn't overwhelm the present.

There was something beautiful about falling in love with the uncertainty of life.

Marty's Bagel Shop
2 Ivy Lane, New York, NY 10014
Marty Matthews

Hi Marty,

I didn't forget to write you, I promise! However, it is very likely you've forgotten all about me by now, seeing as you gave me your list back in October … What can I say? I don't like to send an update until I'm happy with the result.

I can confirm that I completed everything on your list: went on the London Eye (begrudgingly), sent a postcard back home (reluctantly), tried something new (painting!), got a shirt with a UK flag on it (hand-me-down), used a telephone booth (that's a story for a different time), and kissed a Brit!

Ironically, the Brit part turned into a boyfriend! You'd like him a lot. Maybe he could draw you a new logo! Not that you need a new one …

To be honest, I thought I'd never finish the list. But looking back on it now, I have so much more to do here. Just last week I accepted a job offer in Edinburgh for the summer and I'm over the moon about it. *Finally*, all those late nights spent studying that you got stuck hearing about paid off. I've already started planning some weekends to take the train back to London to see everyone. Even my book club is going to visit in July and then my aunt in August.

I simply cannot wait. There's so much to look forward to.

Currently, I'm sitting at my desk, writing you this letter, while 1. the sun comes through my balcony, warming my face, 2. the half-packed suitcase at my feet taunts me, and 3. my boyfriend sits on the balcony painting, looking up every few minutes.

The two of us are going to visit his sister Jasmine in France for a few days before I start my new job. I'm beyond excited, and I'll definitely be making a new list.

Apologies again for the long awaited follow-up!

Love,
Adelaide

The First Night in France

I sat on the windowsill of the fire escape and let the moonlight soak my face. The colorful buildings outside our window (many which we explored with Jasmine today) were no longer eccentric pastels, but instead, grays and blues under the dark sky. Every few minutes, a car would whiz by on the street below and interrupt the chatter of friends clinking their wine glasses in the restaurants' waterfront seating.

"It's beautiful here," I hummed, closing my eyes.

"It is. France looks good on you," Dorian said, in the middle of undressing.

"You're just saying that so I'll give you the last bite of my croque monsieur." I waved the European equivalent to a grilled ham and cheese.

"How dare you accuse me of such things," he countered.

"*Accuse you?* I don't think it's an accusation if you've asked for a bite more than five times!"

"Come on, love, just give your boyfriend a bite," he teased, bracing the windowsill and leaning over me. His linen shirt was unbuttoned, falling open. I hated letting him win, but I gave in and let my eyes dip below his face, taking in the muscles and smooth skin of his chest.

"Something on your mind?" he asked in *that* tone. The tone where his voice lowered an octave, making all the muscles in my body feel like a deflating chocolate cake pulled straight from the oven.

"Nothing at all," I lied.

"Tu mens très mal, ma chérie."

I swallowed. A blush crawled up my neck. "What does that mean?"

"You're a terrible liar." He leaned in closer, his lips hovering above mine. I could smell the mint on his breath from the ice cream we shared earlier. I wanted to be consumed by it. So I let my lips part and I—

"Dorian!" I shrieked as the sandwich in my hand was replaced by salty ocean air, finding it in his conniving cheeky mouth instead. *"You're evil!"*

He ran away from me with sharp laughter and a mouth full of bread and cheese.

But there wasn't much space to run in Jasmine's guest bedroom, so we ended up in circles, the bed becoming an obstacle to jump on.

"Dorian Blackwood let me attack you!" I hissed, trying to keep my voice low before jumping on the bed again.

"Fine." He stopped abruptly, letting me bump into him, the sandwich already gone. In one turn, he pulled me over his shoulder and threw my back onto the mattress, his fingers running up and down my torso, tickling me.

Laughter bubbled up and down my throat. I tried swatting him away but then he'd pepper my neck with kisses.

"Despite the fact that you wouldn't share your sandwich with me, I want you to know that I do still love you," he said. "Très,

très bien."

"You're going to wake up Jasmine down the hall!" I exhaled, trying not to laugh so hard.

Based on the death-grip hug she gave me off the flight this morning, I doubted it'd upset her too much. But I wasn't going to be her reason for losing sleep.

"Fine, fine." He let go but pressed one more solid kiss to my mouth.

I sat up and his eyes grazed my figure. I could only imagine what I looked like. Probably a portrait of stray hairs sticking upright on my head like a field of wheat.

But he had that soft look on his face. The same look he had the night I told him I loved him. And the night of my birthday when he stood under my balcony.

It felt like a wood-burning fire keeping my hands warm.

I leaned in slowly and pressed my lips to his. A thousand kisses later and I still couldn't shake the feeling of giddiness and *need* that he sparked in me. His hands found my jaw and I leaned in closer—if one could even get any closer than this. It felt like every touch and movement was another version of him saying *I love you.* His lips were soft and demanding.

And he tasted like butter.

I slowly pulled away, not wanting to miss the dazed look he always had after. Getting up from the bed, I rummaged through his disheveled suitcase.

"What are you doing?" he asked.

Once I found what I was looking for, I tossed the garment— a Red Sox cap keychain still attached—at his chest and grabbed my crescent purse. "Put your trousers back on, we're getting another sandwich. *Then* we can kiss."

Acknowledgements

I originally began writing this story in 2021. I was in the midst of my junior year of college, balancing a double major, two jobs, and a commitment to be a positive, social human despite wanting to curl up in a ball anytime something didn't go exactly as planned (as it was in my mental five-year plan or Google Calendar).

This is all to say that the desire to write a book during this burnt-out fueled time wasn't out of boredom, but an idea for a novel that wouldn't leave me alone.

I wrote, designed the cover, and published it within six months simply for fun.

But three years and three—two and a half? (secret book three has a draft!)—books later, I knew I could improve it.

When my second book, *Picking Daisies on Sundays*, found so many of you, a newfound desire for *Don't Be In Love* grew. Therefore, I wanted to rewrite *Don't Be In Love* so that it fit my experience and unique writing style as a twenty-four-year-old compared to my twenty-one-year-old self.

This overly detailed explanation is to acknowledge you, the reader, as the reason that this entirely new version exists. My life has changed in so many ways since then. I never imagined myself being able to get here. The heartfelt emails, direct messages, videos, and comments mean more than I could *ever* explain. I save and read every single one. They keep me going.

I may write for myself, but I finish the stories for you.

So thank you for having so much faith in me. I would send a Boston Red Sox keychain and postcard to every single one of you if my cramped hands could physically manage it.

Thank you to the incredible early readers, Zilan Polat, Merjan Abuzahrieh, Bethany Carino, Claire Santacroce, Mónica, Author Holly Jukes, and Aiyla Khan, who helped form the final story. You are the reason for some of my favorite scenes existing now.

As for the people who are stuck seeing me on a daily basis...

To my writing club—all of which is filled with non-romance readers—thank you for your constant enthusiasm and support. Having peers in your passion provide you with motivating feedback and hilarious reactions is so important.

Thank you to my family for celebrating every milestone that I downplayed. I didn't realize I needed someone to share all my achievements with.

And thank you to my best friends and my boyfriend, who have had to listen to every chapter idea, book cover design, and rant over whether or not I should just quit. I'm thankful that I never did.

Liana Cincotti creates characters and stories about romance, self-discovery, and travel for both teens and adults. She has a Bachelor of Science in Marketing and Accounting at Merrimack College, and now works in Marketing and Communications.

On her best days, you can find her sharing tubs of cookie dough ice cream with her friends, meeting with her writing club on Wednesdays, or curling up in the corners of bookstores reading the newest romance.

Befriend her online @LianaCincotti or on her blog, www.WithLiana.com

Made in the USA
Middletown, DE
20 February 2025

71582760R00199